Norse Jewel

Gina Conkle

This is a work of fiction. Names, characters, places, and incidents are either products of the writer's imagination or are used fictitiously and are not to be construed as real. Any resemblance to actual events, locales, organizations, or persons, living or dead, is entirely coincidental.

Norse Jewel
Copyright © 2013 by Gina Conkle
ISBN-13: 978-1542533140
ISBN-10: 1542533147

NYLA Publishing
350 7th Avenue, Suite 2003, NY 10001, New York.
http://www.nyliterary.com

1

Land of the Franks
AD 1022

*S*moke and mist parted, luring gawkers and traders alike.
"Come, see the goods," a voice beckoned from the crowd.

Canny merchants in billowing robes examined exotic wares: fragrant spices, cloth spilling rivers of color, and barrels of rich Frankish wine. Morning air filled with foreign words and the clink of foreign coins. Bretons. Castilians. Saxons. All mixed with the Danes, those giant men who fingered giant hammers with relish. A gaggle of freewomen gossiped while gutting slippery fish. Scores of seagulls squawked, diving at fish heads the chattering women tossed aside. Helena watched these curious sights, so different from her humble village. All would be well, except she was a stolen woman, taken in a raid on her village. Human chattel to the Danes.

She scanned the heavens and curled her fists.

I will return home.

A cool, mocking laugh intruded. "Praying again?"

Sestra, a buxom, flame-haired woman, swigged water from the drinking pouch they shared. Like Helena, her wrists were tethered by long leather bindings to a stake in the ground.

"Good morning." Helena reached for the proffered pouch.

"We'll see soon enough," Sestra groused. "Prayers don't work, you know. Find a good protector. Work will be light then." She finger-combed her tangled hair for maximum effect and purred, "Find the *right* protector, and you won't have to lift a finger."

Helena bristled at the suggestion. "I *will* have my freedom again." She winced at the sight of loud warriors sharpening their axes around a smoky fire. "First, I need to get away from here."

"Give it up. Accept your lot in life. We are captives. Slaves. Thralls. The language doesn't matter, the master you serve does." Sestra scanned the horizon, assessing a Flemish merchant fussing with his robes.

Both women were Frankish and of similar age but worlds apart in experience. Helena wanted to argue her point, but Sestra held up bound hands.

"Let me give you some advice...advice that's saved my hide. Forget about home, and don't fight. Those who fight don't live long." Sestra tapped her own smooth cheek and gave Helena a knowing look. "Look at what happened to you."

Helena tested her cheek, touching skin scabbed and smooth. Outer wounds heal, but wounds to the soul cut deeper and lingered long. Aye, some things were worth a fight. Her hands slid to the leather pouch that hung from her neck. 'Twas tucked between her breasts inside her dress, the contents safe—for now.

"The wound stopped the Danes. What's done is done..." She squeezed her eyes shut, banishing images of that day, "...but I will not accept this as my lot in life."

A stench of fish assaulted Helena. When she opened her eyes, the freewoman who brought their provisions approached and her gap-toothed smile held no cheer.

"Won't have that for long," the hag sneered, pointing at the lump under Helena's bodice. "Should've let him take yer puny purse."

The old woman dropped bread to the ground and planted work-rough hands at her hips as she loomed over them. Chills swept Helena's limbs, owing nothing to morning's dampness. She folded her legs tight to her body. Her bindings chafed tender flesh. The brutal Gudrud's attack broke like sharp-tipped fragments in her mind as the grizzled woman cackled.

"He returns. Soon," she crooned. "Dung for brains has he. Felled by a Frankish maid in front of the other men. Yer kick hurt more than his man parts. Ye damaged mannish pride." She waggled a finger at Helena and sang a gleeful warning. "Get sold today or sleep with one eye open. Night's when he'll get revenge."

"Leave her be," Sestra hissed. "Isn't it enough you torment us daily?"

"I can forget to bring food for the likes of ye," the old woman jeered.

"Be gone. We don't need you."

Two pairs of stunned eyes turned to Helena, who sat tall with her chin tipped high.

"Want me gone, do ye? I can forget yer food. See how those haughty words taste when yer belly aches from hunger." The fishwife's rheumy eyes narrowed on the small bulge under Helena's bodice. "Hope whatevers ye got was worth it."

The freewoman sauntered away, jibing about less thralls to feed. Helena clenched the pouch, the stone within hard to her fingers. After she had been wounded, the other Danes belittled Gudrud for losing a tussle with a mere woman. Magnuson, their leader, let her keep the well-worn pouch, deeming it worthless upon quick inspection.

"Well, she did serve a purpose. I, for one, like to eat," Sestra said, eyeing the bread.

"I couldn't abide her taunts anymore." Helena's shoulders slumped as she dusted off the loaf and tore it in two. She passed the larger portion to Sestra. "And now my outburst cost us both. Who knows when she'll bring food again."

Sestra inspected the bread's soft innards and scooped a handful. "Forget it. Eating is the least of your worries. The hag had one thing right. Gudrud will return and you *cannot* be here."

Helena tucked her bread portion into her lap.

"I could try running away."

Sestra choked on her bread. "Remember the Basque woman?"

Helena hugged her legs still folded tightly to her body as visions of that day returned: A twilight trip to answer nature's call in the forest, and she had seen the black-haired Basque woman slip from sight. The fishwife screeched an alarm. Men yelled. Hooves thundered. Tree bark had bitten into Helena's skin as she sunk into it to avoid the blur of men atop horses. Then, somewhere in the dense forest, the Basque woman's blood-curdling screams carried through the air. None had heard or seen her again.

Helena eyed that dark tree line. "A bad plan."

Sestra snapped her fingers twice. "Look. Buyers come. Heed the old woman," she chided. "Hide your wound. And smile. Men like a woman who smiles... a *friendly* woman."

Aye, survival first.

Her breath quickened as she whispered a short prayer, but heaven stayed silent. Gulls squawked and dove in the salty sea air, like her, seeking survival. Helena tugged at her braid, covering her wounded cheek with loose strands, and prepared for the loathsome ordeal—one human selling another. Beside her, Sestra's voice touched a seductive note.

"For these men, I can smile *very* nicely."

"You say that about every man."

Sestra snorted and nodded at the horizon. "Judge for yourself."

Two long-limbed, thickly muscled warriors walked through the morning mist. Hard Danes and wiry merchants alike paused mid-conversation to dip their heads in greeting to these two. One was dark and amiable, yet large as a bear. The other, wary like a wolf, was fierce and blonde. He wore his sword strapped across his back and listened quietly to his friend, but his ice-blue eyes measured the camp. Sestra, ever the fount of knowledge, tipped her head toward the blonde man.

"See that? His leather belt," she said with calculating awe. "A sign of authority. Kings served. Battles won. *Many battles.* A Norse chieftain, by the look."

Bronze and copper squares were stamped into his wide belt. Each token bore a unique design that caught the eye. But, he did not need the belt to command respect. The air around him crackled with authority. He moved like one belonging to an honored warrior class. Helena suddenly realized that her home village of Aubergon, her whole life, had been sheltered and small.

Beside her, Sestra poked her arm. "You speak Norse. What are they saying?"

"I understand some." But, her gaze wandered to the sinister horizon where the Basque woman had disappeared.

Her heart beat faster. A copper tinge filled her mouth at the sight of the dense forest, dark even in the morn. Aye, get sold this day—a far better fate than risking escape or facing the cruel Gudrud when he returned.

Sestra prodded her again. "Helena. Aren't you listening? What is he—"

"Shhh," Helena set a finger to her lips and canted her head to listen.

"...a *farmer*?" The bear man spoke the word as if he tasted brine. "I don't see it. Hakan the Tall, a chieftain of Svea becomes Hakan...the farmer." His booming voice flattened. "Why?"

"I tire of this life."

"Do we not gain gold aplenty from fat foreign kings?" The bear man jingled a bag at his waist and grinned.

"This isn't about gold."

Yet, the wolf-eyed chieftain loosed a bulging bag from his belt. 'Twas obvious he didn't waste coin on fine attire: his scuffed leather jerkin and faded blue trousers, tucked into fur boots, had seen much wear. No sweeping capes or brash torque hung about his neck, such as usually graced the necks of high-ranking Norsemen. What manner of chieftain would dress so simply?

"What are they saying?" Sestra whispered.

"That you need to be quiet so I can eavesdrop better."

Sestra paused midst cleaning her teeth with her sleeve. "Oh, very funny."

Helena smiled and faced the men, but their voices were too low, all the better to sate her curiosity for the one called Hakan. He crossed his arms and stood like a warrior-king, but of course that was harebrained. What did she know of kings? Whatever his rank, he lured her. She couldn't help but follow the knit of the Norseman's muscles under burnished skin. What would it feel like to touch him there?

Amidst her fascination, Magnuson, leader of the Danes, approached. At the sight of him, an ugly shiver traced her back.

"Hakan." The Dane clapped a heavy hand on the chieftain's shoulder. "I hear you seek a woman to teach you Frankish words."

"An *old* Frankish woman. To keep my farm, help with my wine trade."

"Old? Young? What does it matter?" Magnuson grunted and splayed his fingers her way. "Frankish women here. Three of them. The rest...Sarmatians, Flemish, many from Eyre."

"And not one of them long in years."

Hakan rubbed his jaw as his gaze swept the row of women. Wide silver bands etched with intricate swirls wrapped around his strong arms. Helena frowned as Sestra brazenly thrust her curves at the men. Is that what it took to escape this place?

The bear man laughed and pointed at the blatant display. "This one could teach you much."

The chieftain scowled. "And cause trouble."

Sestra's come-hither smile melted to a sulk under his harsh glower. Her disappointment didn't last long as more men ambled on the horizon. The maid's face lit up when she spied a lavishly dressed merchant drawing near.

Magnuson rubbed his hairy cheeks. "Old women give fewer years of service."

Helena wrapped her skirt close about her legs. Listening to their rapid Norse took all her concentration.

"What happened to that one?" Hakan asked about her.

A flush of warmth poured through Helena, alert to *his* attention. She stiffened and couldn't look higher than the chieftain's silver armbands, where a blood-eyed beast carved in silver winked at her, a trick of the morning light's reflection.

"An unfortunate mishap." Magnuson shrugged a massive shoulder under his bearskin pelt. "One of my men...she fought him, his knife slipped, caught her jaw..." The Dane slid his finger from jaw to ear, mimicking her wound. "...but, if 'tis old you want, come this way."

The chieftain turned his back on her.

Helena dropped her forehead to her knees. If she met him as a freewoman, would he have lingered? Or asked her name? The unbidden questions faded as the overbearing Magnuson spoke, and the men moved away. She scolded herself for her lack of courage in failing to meet the Norseman's stare. Was her cheek truly awful? Her fingers gingerly tested the scab.

"Stop," she whispered and lowered her hands.

Beside her, Sestra greeted a be-ringed Castilian merchant, whose rich robes boasted silken tassels. Near the

Dane's camp, rough warriors emerged from a tavern. Their crude jests abraded her ears.

Greater is the need to flee this place than feel sorry for myself.

Her stomach growled and Helena checked the bread nestled in her lap; best she ration the fare. Her fingers pulled a bite-sized morsel from the loaf, as Magnuson's rumbling voice played in the background.

"Older, quiet...women who know their place..." He extolled the virtues of the poor woman whose name he didn't know. "...give you a good day's work."

Half listening to his merchant's pitch, she rolled her eyes. So disgusted was she, Helena almost missed a rarity. But she didn't. Her hand stopped mid-way to her mouth.

Unbelievable.

The chieftain, the one called Hakan, spoke *gently* to the older captive woman.

The slave, huddled and silent on the ground, failed to respond.

He knelt in the dirt and touched the woman's shoulder with care—an odd thing for a warrior. The captive had been too far away for Helena to render aid when the Danes first brought her to camp. Yet, she was close enough to see that she stayed curled in a tight ball, sometimes rocking and moaning.

Drawn to the scene before her, Helena's gaze followed the Norseman's large hands as he cradled the silent woman's head. She leaned forward, straining against her tether for a better look. He could have been holding a newborn babe, so tender was he. Then, his thumb cautiously brushed open the corner of the thrall's mouth.

"No tongue?" His hard look shot accusation at Magnuson. "You're trying to sell a woman who cannot talk."

"Not always a bad thing." The Dane shrugged at his weak jest.

"Not when I need her to speak Frankish."

8

"She *is* the oldest here." Magnuson waved his hands over the array of women.

The chieftain stood up and silenced Magnuson with a thunderous glare. He did not draw his sword as other affronted warriors might have done. Instead, he opened his coin pouch and counted a few gold pieces.

"For the goats and sheep already on my ship."

The Dane closed thick fingers around the coins dropped in his hand and joined the Bear Man and the Castilian, both charmed by Sestra. The whole camp, a blend of voices and laughter, played background noise to the interest threading from Helena to the chieftain. All faded to a hum. Her bread slid to the ground, forgotten. She sat up taller, studying the Norseman as his long fingers retied his coin pouch.

Embers of attraction flared for the unusual warrior. He moved with fluid ease for one so large. Or was it simply his care with the older woman that made him appealing? One could even call him kind. Hope of finding strength and kindness in one man poured a balm on her soul, and left her curious for more.

Her guarded survey inched upward to his broad shoulders, the sort that promised safety and protection. 'Twas an odd notion about a man who came solely to purchase a woman for labor. Helena's lips twitched at such foolishness, and her gaze drifted higher to a square jaw and firm lips, then higher still.

Ice-blue eyes stared back.

Helena froze.

A strange enchantment mesmerized her. She had once crossed paths with a lone wolf in the forest near home. Such a beast would devour the weak. To her relief, that wolf had turned and disappeared. Though dangerous, she willed this two-legged wolf closer. The price was tension coiling inside her.

Like a predator measuring prey, the Norseman's hard stare traced her frame, lingering at the curve of her hips. Peculiar warmth poured through her as she stared back. He

9

did not leer as other men had, but Helena recognized male interest.

Sunlight broke through mist, bouncing off the sword strapped across his back. A large, red stone glimmered from the hilt. Something of a smile crossed her face. This chieftain's clothes were faded and well-used, but his armbands and sword were finely crafted with matching designs and matching red stones.

The chieftain scowled and crossed his arms.

Her smile wilted. Was she over-bold? Her manner was nothing like Sestra's. Helena swallowed hard and licked her lips, working to put her smattering of Norse words to work.

"Smiles...you do not like," she said in soft, faltering Norse.

"A woman's false smiles, no." His voice was deep and smooth to her ears. "You speak Norse."

"Some, but I smile...friendliness only." She cleared her throat and dared to say, "I seek freedom...nothing more."

The chieftain's head tipped with interest. "Strange words for a thrall."

"I wasn't born to this." She held her head high, ignoring that she sat in dirt at his feet.

A light flashed behind the Norseman's eyes. He loosened his stance, and Helena knew she had penetrated some unseen shield, drawing him closer.

"Status of birth matters little. How you live each day...that's your true measure."

A breeze blew thick blonde hair that fell past his shoulders. The stoic chieftain stood like a rock, staring at her with unnerving intensity. A kernel of interest sprouted betwixt them, but she needed to nurse this cagey conversation. Her hair blew across her face, a momentary mask.

"A warrior who speaks like a..." She paused, searching for the right word. "...a wise man...'tis rare."

"Fools don't live long."

Helena motioned to his belt. "Marks of a warrior?"

"I have...been places."

10

"I have not." Her bound hands tapped her chest. "But, you need one who speaks—"

Suddenly, wild bellows cut her short. The chieftain pivoted, alert and ready, facing the clamor. Danes emerged from red-striped tents, cheering and pointing at a dark rider who came from the forest. Iron battle rings clanked across the horse's chest, a nerve-chilling noise to raise the dead. The rider's bulky frame and bald head were familiar. Helena's heart pounded hard and fast long before Magnuson raised his fist and roared her worst fear.

"Gudrud returns!"

Cold flushes gripped her as the old woman's singsong words played in her head.

Night's when he'll get revenge.

Staring at the menacing warrior, Helena's hands squeezed together as a worried supplicant. She would beg this Norseman, this one called Hakan, to take her. He was her only hope.

When she turned around, the chieftain was gone.

2

Hakan's boots slammed hard-packed earth, taking him closer to his ship and farther from a fool's deed. The dark-haired thrall snared his interest, and that irked him. Bring her home? Impossible. He needed the steady hand of an older woman to keep his farm, not a woman with full curves and long legs to tempt him from his purpose.

She had stared at his coin pouch. A woman out for gold? Nay, she lacked the self-serving gleam of other grasping women. Mayhap, she hid her greed well. He shook his head, determined to leave.

Men tipped their heads respectfully as he passed. *Solace*, his thus named sword, pressed across his back, an ever-present burden. Many a warrior fought his whole life for renown. Not Hakan. He had status, but not what he wanted, the one thing that eluded him: a peaceful farmer's life. He wanted to return home and stay on his long-neglected farm...to die of old age, his hands covered with dirt, not blood. Many would scoff, but he was ready to replace *Solace* with a scythe.

Then, behind him, a woman's voice called, "Hakan."

He stopped. *She* called him, the dark-haired thrall. He already knew her voice above the din.

"Hakan!"

He set his hands at his hips. Noticing one woman was nothing more than inborn awareness, the kind that kept him alive. That same awareness told him ten paces ahead, a fat Flemish merchant and his round wife bickered. No threat there. Five paces to his right, a lone, feral-eyed Dane slid a whetstone down his sword. The seasoned warrior leaned over his weapon and nodded slowly at Hakan. A true threat. Magnuson and a cohort of men welcomed a rider more than fifty paces from the camp. A threat in numbers, not skill...most were ale-soaked and unsteady on their feet from last night's revelry. Hakan glanced at the shoreline. Three of his men lingered there. One battle cry and they'd be ready.

Straight ahead, his ship beckoned. Twenty paces behind, *her* voice, a desperate cry, reached him yet again.

"Hakan!"

He turned. The thrall rose high on her knees. Her long, mussed braid dangled like a dark brown rope. She strained against her tether, and even from this distance, he saw the leather bindings pinch her skin white. Hakan drew in a deep, rib-expanding breath.

The tides waited for no man.

Yet, his long strides stretched one in front of the other, returning him to her. The closer he came, the Frankish thrall inched back, her long legs folding underneath her until he towered over her.

"I'm here," he said in Norse. *Convince me.*

The thrall rubbed color back into her wrists. She blinked rapidly. His presence could be like a wall, or so his sister always chided him. Thus, he crouched low to meet her eye to eye. She brushed away dark hair, and her deep blue stare penetrated him.

"Hakan...Svealander?" She said.

Her voice flowed nicely to his ears, the kind of voice a man could listen to in the dark on a cold winter's night.

13

"Aye, Svealander." He draped his arm over his thigh and willed the picture of her wrapped naked in fur from his mind.

Silence.

Hakan dipped his head a fraction, searching her face. This close, he couldn't miss the wound: one side of her face was smooth except for a thin, curving scab which curled toward her ear. She would scar. Dirt smudged her slender nose and the soft, uncut cheek. He angled his head, trying for more from the quiet maid.

"Frankish?" He gestured to his mouth but spoke Norse. "You are Frankish?"

After Magnuson's attempt at deception, Hakan had to be sure. Her gaze darted to the tents. The thrall took a deep breath and spoke in Norse.

"Aye, Frankish." She stuck her tongue out at him. "And I'm not mute."

Hakan jerked at the unexpected display. She blushed and dipped her head. Faint freckles sprinkled her nose, and his hand clenched his thigh, tamping down the urge to explore them. He came to the camp to transact business only, not flirt.

"You know why I didn't purchase the other woman," Hakan said, and the beginnings of a smile spread.

She smiled back, displaying fine teeth. He liked her courage.

"How did you come to be here?"

A presence loomed and the Frankish woman flinched.

"She's Frankish," Magnuson returned. "But I just sold the red-haired thrall to Sven."

Hakan cocked his head side to side, examining her jawline. "Not interested in her. This one...mayhap...but her wound hasn't been tended." He noted wryly, "She speaks well."

Magnuson unsheathed his knife and began to clean his fingernails with the sharp tip. "She's not bad...a fair maid despite the wound."

14

'Twas not her fair face and form that troubled him, but the unwelcome yearning to touch her.

Hakan shook his head, reasoning the matter. "I cannot buy a thrall to have her die of fever. Infection could still set."

When he said this, the thrall licked her lips and sat up straighter.

"Namo Helena." She switched to speaking Frankish, pointing bound hands to herself and then to him. "Namo Hakan."

"Aye." *What game does she play, changing from Norse to Frankish?*

"You are from the northlands...Svea," she said slowly in Norse and tipped her head toward him. The thrall opened her mouth as if she wanted to form words, but couldn't. Her brows pressed together, she then spoke rapid Frankish, *"Hakan Norseman. Unsaron Frankia vint a Svealand."*

"She knows you are from Svea and want to trade Frankish wine." Magnuson translated her desperate-sounding Frankish, wiping his blade on his pelt. "Speaks some Norse. Helpful for you, eh?"

Hakan ignored Magnuson and let the urge to explore her win. He brushed back hair that fell over her face. Her breath came in a rush and her blue gaze darted from him to the Dane's tents. The woman was desperate and fearful. She needed protecting.

"So, you're quick-witted. You heard me talking." Hakan lowered his voice for her ears only. "What else did you hear?"

Dark-fringed eyes widened, but she said nothing.

Hakan locked his stare on hers and spoke louder to Magnuson. "Her price? The standard twenty gold pieces?"

"Ah, now in this we have a problem." Magnuson tipped his knife toward a red and white tent. "One of my men offered twenty-five gold pieces for her."

The thrall gasped and looked wild-eyed at Magnuson.

"Why didn't you say she was sold?" Hakan glared at Magnuson.

15

"Sold?" The Dane's thick lips stretched wide within his bushy beard. "Not...if you are more interested..."

"You seek a higher price."

Hakan stood up and Magnuson wisely sheathed his knife and raised a placating hand.

"Because of her wound, she'll be harder to sell. My man, Gudrud, knew this. He agreed to pay me for the trouble. He's a good warrior...served me well these years. I gave him the time he was gone to see if she sold, otherwise he will have to part with—" Magnuson shrugged dramatically, "—*twenty-five* gold pieces."

Hakan had never liked the Dane and liked less the lout getting the better of him. Pride made him want to gut the oaf. Magnuson had a reputation for double-dealing...selling goods and then raising the price when the time to collect came. Was this a fight he wanted? He ought to walk away.

Then, two hands touched his boot.

Hakan looked down at a dirt-smudged face. The Frankish maid nearly begged him, yet her shoulders squared proudly. A certain strength...

"What will he do if he has her?"

Magnuson's shrewd eyes slanted back and forth from thrall to chieftain. His voice brought to mind a slow, slithering snake.

"Gudrud can do whatever he likes."

The thrall's hands pressed harder. Ten pressure points dug into his leg through wolfskin fur. Seeds of protectiveness for this unknown woman surged within him. That feeling had lain dormant too long, yet now stretched like some unwanted curling vine. Her direct gaze snared him. Hakan unloosed his coin pouch and scooped out gold.

"I'll pay thirty-five gold pieces. Let there be no doubt she is mine."

The thrall's jaw dropped when he named her price.

"Done." Magnuson stretched both greedy paws to receive the gold. "I bid you safe journey, Hakan."

The Dane left, whistling his glee. Hakan knelt by the woman he owned body and soul. Best he keep her price to himself. The men would surely question why he paid more for a Frankish thrall—a damaged one at that. A feathery touch grazed his leg. 'Twas the tip of her braid brushing his knee, a dark curl against blue wool. That feminine hair taunted him as he pulled a long iron blade from his boot.

He sawed the thick leather strips that bound her. "May you prove quick-witted. You'll need be to survive." Hakan sheathed his knife when the leather snapped and towered over her. "Follow me."

Ahead, the dragon-headed lady summoned him. His ship, long lines and curved, polished wood, swayed hypnotically in the bay. She had never deserted him. He trusted her as surely as he trusted *Solace*. Few women were as faithful. Hakan scoffed so loud at this truth that seagulls scattered as he walked across the black pebbled shore.

Seawater sprayed his boots. He crossed his arms with certain satisfaction: the provisions loaded on his ship were fairly purchased for those he loved at home. Home. Svea. The words played on his mind, when Nels, one of his warriors, hailed him from waist-deep water.

"Hakan...Sven has urgent news for you on the ship. Something about trouble ahead."

Hakan waved his acknowledgment and scooped the Frankish maid roughly to his chest, levering one arm under her knees and another across her back. She yelped and curled her arms around his neck. That trusting response grabbed him at his core.

He sloshed through frothing water, welcoming the cold slapping his legs. That momentary softness with this thrall in the Dane's camp would not happen again. Frigid blue water swirled about him, a stinging reminder to leave well-enough alone. He lifted the maid higher against his chest to keep her dry, but the way she clung to him invited something more. At the ship, a grinning Sven leaned hairy arms on the rail.

"Last minute purchase, Hakan?"

Hakan grit his teeth and passed the thrall to Sven. To erase her enticing warmth, he dunked in the icy sea. Twice. Sven laughed, jostling the thrall like a sack of grain, as Hakan hauled himself up, swinging one leg after the other over the rail. Water splashed the deck, gushing from his drenched boots.

"Well?" Sven nudged the feminine armful at Hakan. "Where shall I put her?"

Hakan didn't like Sven's suggestive grin, but he had to think of her comfort. The hold? Narrow, cramped, and dark. The center mast? Animals clustered there. Hakan shook his head, vexed at having to give the matter any thought. She'd get no special treatment—better she and everyone else knew that.

"Put her with the other thrall," he said, gruffness edging his voice.

"Whatever you say, Hakan. Whatever you say." Sven chuckled but didn't move.

The maid's gaze flit like a nervous bird over the comings and goings on board. Her first time on a ship?

One of his men, Emund, tossed him a dry cloth, and he wiped his face. Hakan brushed aside an inkling of concern. The journey was long. She would have much time to adjust.

"Nels said you have urgent news." He balled the rag and tossed it back to Emund.

"Aye." Sven's face darkened. "Gorm's back. In Svea."

"Out of what hole did that viper crawl? Who told you?"

"Vladamir, the Rus merchant of Talinn. You know his word is solid."

The mention of his enemy punched Hakan's gut. The deck moved, unsteady under his feet, a problem that owed nothing to churning waters. Hakan turned and gripped the oiled rail with both hands, staring into the sea.

"Double shifts at the oars. We sail day and night and don't stop until we're home."

Sven, the thrall still in his arms, moved closer. "How much trouble can he cause now? The men—"

"Will do as ordered," he growled. "I'll double their portion. Gorm's up to something. To come back after all these years."

Sven hesitated but nodded. "As you wish."

Hakan's seafarer's mind ticked with plans for a speedy journey to Svea. As his friend walked away, Hakan released the rail and his gaze collided with the dark blue eyes of the Frankish woman. She peered at him over Sven's shoulder. A gentle mix of compassion and wondering shined from her.

Her lips moved silently as she mouthed words to him before his second-in-command settled her on a wooden chest. An icy shield rose against the desire to coddle her. Hakan turned away and heaved a sack of grain to his chest. She was a slave. He would soften to no woman. Softness weakened a man.

"Ingvar," he yelled, as he balanced the sack over his shoulder.

"Aye?" Ingvar wiped his palms on his thighs. His tunic was lowered at his waist, sweat dripping down his thin chest.

"Give food to the thralls. They're too skinny for my liking."

Hakan spent himself in labor, hauling sacks of grain to the hold. His body bore the loose-limbed feel that came only from exertion. In the midst of his toils, the befuddling puzzle solved itself. His thrall had mouthed *thank you*.

...

Helena broke bread into small pieces, eating and viewing the bustle on deck. Men shouted, rolling barrels and moving chests. Two young Norsemen walked down both sides of the vessel, ramming long, oak oars into place. The chieftain, wearing his iron helmet, paced the ship, barking orders and hauling large sacks. He stopped to calm a giant black steed tied to the center mast; giant hooves the size of bowls clomped the planks. Settling against a chest, Helena breathed the tangy air. She was safe—for now.

"I see we'll be together for the journey."

19

Sestra.

Her friend approached and her arms overflowed with two large fur sacks. She dropped onto a chest beside Helena and handed over one of the burdensome furs.

"A hudfat. You'll be glad for it when we're on open sea."

"And I am glad to see you." Helena smiled at her friend and held up weighty furs sewn together into a single, giant sack. "What do I do with it?"

"Sleep in it. The old, skin-and-bones Norseman took me below to get these." Sestra folded her hudfat and set it behind her as a cushion. "You haven't seen much beyond your village, have you?"

She rubbed the fur, some coarse, some soft. "I never ventured from Aubergon."

"You're bound to see much of the world now." Sestra grimaced at the harried, shouting men. "And very soon, by the way these men are moving. Something's afoot."

"They speak too fast for me to understand." Helena's fingers skimmed the inner stitching. "A clever idea, this hudfat. Good to remember for when I return home."

Sestra frowned. "You know you can't run away. What's your plan? Earn your freedom?" One cinnamon-colored eyebrow rose. "That only happens for highly skilled laborers like blacksmiths."

Helena smoothed the fur into a cushion and settled against a chest. "I will return home someday...'tis only a matter of time."

"Time's not against you, foolish maid, more like yon chieftain—" She cocked her head at the end of the ship. "—*Lord Hakan* to you and me. Better have something worthy to offer him."

What could she offer the chieftain?

Her body warmed to the answer her mind refused to accept. Aye, there had been that flare of attraction in the Dane's camp, but Helena would not lay with him. Not by choice. And something in his words told her that he was not ruled by a woman's charms.

At the far end of the ship, the large Norseman, fierce and distant, stood by the dragon's head prow. He shouted to the men, and a vast red and white striped sail whipped open, fluttering, stretching, curving. Men grabbed an oar and began pulling in round, powerful strokes. Beneath her, the whole vessel creaked and strained. Water drummed and slapped the ship's outer planks.

White sprays shot skyward, scenting the air. Everyone swayed with the vessel's hypnotic rhythm. Sven, the bear man and second-in-command, threw back his head and bellowed a Norse chant:

LIFT UP YOUR SHIELD AND AX
LIFT UP YOUR VESSEL'S OAR
HERE WE GO A VIKING
OFF TO FIGHT A DISTANT SHORE

COURAGE AND HONOR
SHIELD AND BLADE
ALL SERVE OUR CHIEFTAIN'S YORE
FOR WE ARE THE NOR'MEN
VALHALLA'S GLORY WE FIGHT FOR

Hard-faced Norsemen rowed to his deep cadence, answering with verses of their own.

Her homeland slipped further away, until the sliver of land disappeared. Helena pulled the hudfat around her shoulders and truth sunk into her bones: she was on a ship bound for a distant land, surrounded by pagan Norsemen.

Did she trade the Dane's cruelty for hardship from another Norseman?

A sharp pain pricked her eyes. She swiped at wetness dripping down her cheeks. Tears were a waste. She'd return someday. Touching the pouch hidden under her worn dress, she drew strength from that reminder of home.

Her gaze wandered to the warrior chieftain standing by the dragon's head.

He's going home. Why doesn't he smile?

3

*A*fter many days at sea...

A "Keep that up and you'll comb him bald." Sven's hearty slap on Agnar's rump barely moved the massive horse.

Hakan stopped combing and ran a finger under his leather arm brace. The ship was quiet, too quiet, save for the steady thread of oars swishing through dead seas. Fair winds failed them, leaving the sail limp and useless. The men bore splinters and blisters from so much rowing. Seal oil dowsed on wooden handles failed to blot suffering from their practiced hands. And now, the way Sven avoided looking him in the eye, trouble camped anew.

Hakan took a long draught of water from a bladder. "Say it."

Sven spat on the deck before grumbling, "We've been many days at sea. You drive the men too hard."

"And we've doubled the distance since leaving Frankish shores despite no winds." He dropped the empty bladder atop a bucket.

"Because the men row day and night." Now Sven looked him in the eye.

23

"We've made good time." Hakan dragged the curry comb across Agnar's flank. "I take my turn at the oars."

"Aye. You need rest as much as them." Grim-faced, Sven nodded at Hakan's sweat-stained arm braces. "Maybe more."

"The men are fine," Hakan said, doubt shading his words. "We push for Uppsala."

"They row with the dullness of old men." Sven's voice shot up in volume as he set both hands on Agnar's back, ready to clash. "Gorm could be gone."

"Or burning more farms." Hakan's voice dropped with bitterness. "Killing innocent people. Would you have me ignore the danger?"

"Would you ignore your men?" Sven spat on the deck again. "You aren't a Barbary pirate driving galley slaves. These men choose to follow you."

Agnar snorted as his hooves danced.

"Shhh..." Hakan stroked the steed's neck and failed to meet Sven's flint-eyed stare. "The men want to be home as much as I."

"We all want to be home...." Sven threw up his hands and muttered something about a stone wall.

Hakan dropped the comb in a bucket and fed his steed a broken carrot. Agnar's muzzle gently scraped his palm, accepting the tasty gift. Sven took a slow breath and squinted at open sea.

"Hakan, you've always been the better leader...clear-headed. But in this—" Sven shook his head and his deep voice rumbled. "—you push too hard."

"There is too much sea between here and home." Yet, as he said the words, control, or the desire for it, slipped.

His men, stoop-shouldered and vacant-eyed from the unrelenting pace, jabbed at his conscience. Even the best warrior needed rest. He examined a distant, blade-thin line that rose above the sea—Jutland's shore. They had followed it a few days, keeping the hint of land off the right side of the ship. He sucked in a deep breath of salty air and nodded.

"Tell the men we stop at Dunhad. They have until sunrise tomorrow."

Sven regained his loose-limbed stance, his face split in a jovial grin. "And you? *You*, most of all, need rest. Mayhap the diverting company of Jutland's wenches?"

"Someone needs to keep watch. Better I stay, then all the men can take their leave."

"Ah, the watch." Sven nodded sagely and cocked his head at the two women huddled by chests and barrels. "That thrall watches you daily...like a hawk."

No need to say which thrall. The heat of her stare often pricked his skin. On the hard push to Uppsala, her face had changed from curious to annoyed. She was well-fed, slept in a hudfat at night, and lifted not one finger to labor. What else did a woman need?

Sven persisted. "She might be a fine . . ."

"I've other things on my mind, as well you know. Nor do I mix with thralls." The words were spoken with iron hardness. "'Tis trouble."

"You sound like the king and his Christ-following teachings." Sven spat on the deck once more. "Words of weak men."

"Yet, Olof is king. Kept Svea's peace for many years. I honor him." He fed the rest of the broken carrot to Agnar and a thought born of Loki, the god of mischief, came to mind. "When we arrive in Uppsala, the widow Frosunda might be a fine—"

"Stop." Sven glowered. But he quickly regained his mirth and raised a chiding finger. "All the same, Hakan, no harm in looking back."

Sven whistled as he walked away, cuffing an oarsman's shoulder. Hakan watched his friend take hold of the rudder and guide the dragonhead toward Dunhad. When Sven bellowed they were going ashore for the night, the answering roar was deafening.

Weary, grateful smiles and nods from his men nudged his gut. They served him well, never questioning. Their reward?

Days and nights of rowing, with little rest to reach an enemy—*his enemy*—who might be gone. He flexed his shoulders against nagging tension and tapped a tired oarsman.

"Go rest." Hakan sat on the bench and let his body take over, moving the oar with mighty circles.

Wind began to stir and mild waves slapped the ship. In Hakan's sight line, long of limb and inviting curves, she dozed. Her braid was long undone and dark hair spilled past her shoulders. The thrall was fair of face under smudged dirt and that wound. Aye, many a time she had studied him like a hawk, but one more likely to bear talons and attack. The corner of his mouth kicked up. He really needed to know her name.

Suddenly, the ship erupted with shouts and laughter.

"Dunhad!"

...

Helena jerked awake from so much noise. The hudfat, soft and warm, made a large inviting pillow for late-day naps. She wiped her eyes and rose to her knees on the chest that was her perch. Her fingers curled over the wet rail. Torches illuminated the shoreline and a smattering of buildings. People milled about like small, black shapes in twilight. The only vessels were small fisherman's boats lining the shore in a single, neat row.

"A minor sea port," Sestra mused while plaiting her hair.

"I'm grateful for land—any land." Helena stretched like a cat, elated at the news. "Ahhh...and a bath." She fairly sung the words.

"Wouldn't get my hopes up." Sestra tossed back her braid and pointed at darkened skies. "Tis' nighttime, goosebrain. The men are going ashore, not us."

"What?" Helena shot to her feet.

In the background, Sven barked an order to the youngest warrior on the ship. "Emund, settle the thralls."

Sestra tipped her head at the shoreline and a trio in skirts, who laughed and waved at the men on the ship. Her

26

voice extolled worldly wisdom. "The men have been at sea overlong."

Helena glanced across the ship's deck. The vessel was alive with anxious preparations to head ashore; the warriors fairly knocked each other over in their haste.

"Food for you." The carrot-haired Emund spoke in a rush as he set bread and cheese atop a barrel. "Would you like to take it below deck? Better to sleep there. The hold's a tight fit, but dry." He squinted at swirling, moody skies. "Might rain."

"We aren't going ashore?" Helena set her hands at her hips.

"I'm sorry." The young Norseman shrugged his apology.

Denial of that simple pleasure to feel land under her feet? No bath? Her voice shook as she pointed at the animals.

"We're no better than sheep and goats." She glared at the small cluster of animals in the center of the ship. "I cannot believe this...this horrible treatment." Helena tugged at her stained skirt. "The deck is cleaner than me."

Sestra jammed her hudfat at the young Norseman and faced Helena. "Mind your tongue. These men are better than the Danes. Would you rather be with them?"

Helena turned back to the forbidden shore. She looked, but did not see, as blood thrummed her veins. She couldn't bear the truth of Sestra's words.

Hadn't she practically begged the Norseman to take her from the Dane's camp because she'd thought him *gentle*?

Sestra stood like a regal queen and addressed Emund. "My churlish friend may choose to sleep outside, but I prefer to stay warm and dry. Take me below."

"Are you sure?" Emund asked Helena as he folded Sestra's hudfat.

"Not if rain's the only chance to bathe." She gripped the rail with both hands.

"I have to tether you."

The Norseman's quiet edict delivered a new blow. Her hands rubbed her wrists where the pinkened skin mended

27

from the Dane's brutal knots. Emund winced at her fretting hands.

"I promise, the bindings won't be tight," he offered gently.

Air seemed scarce after he said *bindings*. Small points of sweat pricked her forehead. These Norsemen would tie her up because they expected her to run away. A woman alone? She'd never make it home alive—not this far. Helena laughed, a harsh, bitter sound. The young warrior flinched.

He motioned to the bread and cheese as consolation. "Please. Eat."

Food was the last thing on her mind as he led Sestra to the hold. Two men heaved a massive stone attached to a rope over the rail. Water splashed to the heavens. The vessel lurched to a halt, groaning and creaking. Sheep and goats skittered nervously from the jolt, their hooves clicking the deck.

Men jumped into the water, frolicking like children. A few stood in a circle by the chieftain and Sven. Their voices rumbled low...something about the watch. The warrior, Nels, lit two torches and set them high on both sides of the ship, then he dove into the cold sea water. Helena turned her back on everyone and leaned her hip against a barrel, staring into the disappearing horizon.

A chill breeze rustled her skirt, brushing wool against her skin. Her eyes rolled heavenward. Prayers seemed grudging and ineffective. Behind her, footsteps approached. Emund cleared his throat.

"Tis time."

Leather ties dangled from his hand.

...

Even the promise of rain failed her. Hours later, stars and clouds battled for space in the dry, black sky. She had dozed but awoke again, restless. Helena tugged at the loose leather wrapped around her wrists. The chieftain was responsible for this. He lacked even a splinter of kindness.

"*How* could I have thought him gentle?" she groused aloud, her fists curling into her skirt.

Behind her a male voice grunted. Startled, Helena jerked upright. She wasn't alone. Lord Hakan leaned a shoulder against the far dragon's head prow, his profile evident as he half-turned her way.

He stares east while I stare west.

Something made him drive the ship hard to the pagan northlands. Her lips curved in a smile. The mighty chieftain wanted to be as far from this Jutland port as she. With that came a snit of childish satisfaction: neither thrall nor master would have their wish granted this night.

But, there was one. Pale light caught smudges of dirt spotting her hands.

"I *want* a bath," she demanded.

The chieftain turned fully around and cocked his head as if mystified. Torches burned in the darkness, flickering shadows and light between them. Lord Hakan rested a hand on the dragonhead prow and didn't move. Was his brain fogged with distant thought?

Then she remembered: he doesn't know Frankish.

"Lord Hakan...a bath...some water...*please*," she yelled in Norse across the deck, gritting her teeth on *please*.

He surprised her and dipped a bucket in the fresh water barrel and, with his long-limbed stride, crossed the ship. Without saying a word, he plunked the bucket atop the barrel beside her and turned to leave. Not even a word of greeting? The view of his back irked her.

"But, my lord...*freedom*...for a lowly thrall?" She raised her wrists as he turned to face her.

His eyebrows rose. She was overly bold, letting waspish sarcasm slip from her lips.

"The bindings are foolish. Where would I go?" she finished testily, trying to tamp down her ire.

His stoic face was hard to read. Helena stood on perilous ground, and despite her daring, her heart banged a rapid warning. Lord Hakan moved closer, pulling a long blade from his boot. His advance was silent, and his mere size alone made her shrink against a barrel.

"What are you going to do?" Her Norse came whispery fast.

"Cut you free." Amusement sparked his eyes.

"You could have told me," she huffed as tension eased from her shoulders.

"I just did." One corner of his mouth kicked up in a half smile as he shook his head. "Rest easy. I do not harm women."

His words startled her. *Aren't all pagans raiders and despoilers of women?* She bit her lip and held that to herself.

The chieftain focused on the blade cutting leather. Unlike his sword and armbands, the bone-handled knife was plain, lacking intricate carvings or his favored red stone. His free hand, large and warm, closed over her wrists. When he spoke, his deep, smooth voice startled her.

"Can you swim?"

An odd question. She searched his face, but the Norseman focused on his knife strokes.

Her throat felt thick with him standing close. "I swim."

The man was a broad-shouldered giant, but not with the bull's heaviness of Magnuson. This chieftain was sleeker: he would outride, outswim, outfight the Danes.

The leather snapped. His fingers gripped hard, a warm vise to her wrist. The chieftain's eyes narrowed with stern command.

"Tonight, no swimming."

She stared at him as if he grew a second head. Was he a lack wit?

"You think I will try to escape?" She motioned to ink-black water. "That I'd jump into that?"

He sheathed the knife and settled in the shadows. "I'll wait here...in case you fall into the sea." He bared a tolerant smile and stretched his legs, one ankle crossed over the other.

Helena clutched the water bucket, wanting sorely to toss it at him. "Doesn't even a thrall get privacy?"

"Keep your garment on...you have privacy." The chieftain tipped his head against the barrel as if the whole exchange bored him.

Are all Norse barbaric? Can't I have a moment to myself? At least my thoughts are my own.

She craved setting this brute in his place. Barbs and insults would do. That was when a wayward smile crept to her lips—a small sense of power—as the barest seed of an idea grew.

He doesn't know Frankish.

Dipping her head, Helena smiled. Better to let him think she'd bow and scrape her gratitude for this morsel of kindness, allowing her to bathe. She moved behind a larger barrel and began to speak Frankish in soft, honeyed tones.

"You. Are. A. Lout." She whispered the insult as her fingernails dug crescents into the bucket's soggy wood. "Many days I suffer from neglect, but heaven forbid one hair's out of place on your horse. You whip that comb out in the blink of an eye. How I'd like to smash it over your head."

He sat in that closed, impassive way that defined him, studying the shoreline.

"You give more care to your four-legged chattel. I cannot understand you Norse. You pagans are beasts...worse than beasts."

Helena took a deep, calming breath and rolled up her torn sleeves. She dunked her hands, reveling in the luxury of washing, then splashed water on her face and neck. The cool trickle was heavenly.

"You're no better than the Danes." Helena exhaled her anger through each refreshing splash and worked to regain her composure. Self-control was not a luxury. She could not let her ire slip any more than it already had.

She lifted her skirt mid-thigh and scooped water onto her legs. Glistening droplets slid down her limbs. She huffed and vigorously rubbed her skin.

"I can't imagine you have a wife. You lack all tenderness." Her eyes focused on the cleaning. She leaned her hip against the barrel, pulling the skirt higher.

Her tattered hem clung high on her thighs as she splashed more water down her legs. She exposed too much flesh and edged behind the barrel. One skittish glance at the chieftain, and she worried for naught: his head tipped back with eyes closed. At least he spoke the truth about not bothering thralls.

"Not even a sliver of soap to clean my hair." She groaned and lowered tangled tresses into the bucket, finger combing the mess and wincing at the tug on her scalp. "I once thought you different than the Danes...I even thought you *gentle*." She rolled her eyes behind the curtain of hair. "How wrong I was. You heathens are all alike."

Sea water rippled softly around the ship, and her defiance kept building.

"You want to learn Frankish? *Aye,* I'll teach you Frankish," she said, her tone sly. She planted a hand at her waist. "But not so well, I think. I'll make sure you have need of me for a future voyage."

A door opened on the shoreline; noises of revelry spilled from that open portal, a slight diversion. Lord Hakan stirred, pulling small green leaves from a pouch. He chewed them as he watched the merrymakers stumble across the sand. Helena dipped fingertips into the bucket and touched her jaw.

"I'll bide my time. Earn your trust. Someday...someday you'll return to my homeland and need my help. Then, I'll flee. Aye, I'll run away."

The bucket nearly empty, she unrolled her sleeves.

"You are more endowed with brawn than brains. I doubt you'll even be able to grasp the Frankish language." Her voice was sweet and lightly mocking. "You're as thick-headed as those brutish Danes. When I think of how *I've* learned so many Norse words in so short a time." Bitterness and pride tinged her voice as she brushed back wet hair.

"'Twill take years to teach you." She shrugged her indifference. "Time will tell."

The bucket was empty. Helena walked to the impassive chieftain and presented her hands to him for the dreaded tether, a submissive gesture that failed to match her defiant heart.

"My Lord," she said in Norse.

He stood up and covered calloused hands over hers. His size, his warmth and nearness, made her uneasy as he led her to the chest that was her perch. When he knelt down, the curling hairs of his arms grazed her damp skin. He smelled of sea and leather and curiously a fresh scent...*mint*. Those leaves he chewed.

That pleasant surprise was lost when leather bindings swung from his hand—the same ties from which he had freed her for her bath. Lord Hakan crouched close, and his knuckles caressed her chin as though entranced by her. Little shivers danced along her spine from the feather-soft touch. Her body sung a traitor's tune, and she grit her teeth, trying not to like his nearness, his smell. Torchlight splashed the chieftain's face, revealing a smile that failed to reach his eyes.

"I do not have to bind you. But I will."

She shrunk in horror.

He spoke stilted Frankish.

"Some have said I have a quick mind. As you say, 'Time will tell.'" He shifted and his face was in the shadows, but the white flecks of his wolfish eyes glowed. "Do not think to escape. I'm a fair man but care not for deceptive maids."

His massive size closed in, blocking all light. Wedged between a barrel and the ship's side, sturdy wood imprisoned her. His skin grazed hers as he wrapped the leather around her wrists. She glanced down at the detestable strap, and a burst of rebellion flowered.

"Why the tether? What harm can one woman do?"

His eyes widened at her show of courage, or so she guessed from the way he tipped his head in acknowledgment.

"Aye, one woman." His mouth made a grim line and bitterness threaded his voice. "I have seen the destruction one woman can do." He knotted the leather. "The bindings stay."

Helena licked her lips, choosing silence. The chieftain's nostrils flared like some predatory beast scenting prey. Was this anger barely restrained? Or something else?

He touched the wet rope of hair that hung over her shoulder, letting his fingers slip between tangled strands. His thumb and forefinger found a single lock and stroked the hair down to the curling tip. Goose bumps skittered across her flesh from the intimate touch.

"What is your name, thrall?" He asked in the gentlest voice.

"Helena," she whispered.

"Helena." He repeated her name softly. The corner of his mouth twitched. He seemed pleased to know her name, but the pleasure was fleeting, replaced by fierceness. "I care not about trust, but I require obedience."

Helena swallowed the hard lump in her throat.

"Serve me, as well as Agnar—" His teeth gleamed wolf-like in the darkness. "—and you'll be rewarded." Rising, he towered over her. "Fail in your purpose, and you will suffer the consequences."

The chieftain stalked away and, true to his word, he did not harm her. 'Twas as if she did not exist for the way he ignored her. The Norseman kept his distance as one day slid into another, and the dragon ship carried her farther from home. Each day left her stewing over a baffling riddle:

If neither deception nor fleeing would get her home, what else could she do?

4

The chieftain plucked a glossy raven by its yellow claws from a loose-weave basket and released the bird. Everyone halted mid-task, gawking at the feathered creature circling the ship once, then twice, until it disappeared from sight. A kindly breeze slapped water against the vessel, moving the ship along like a chiding mother swatting her dawdling child. To the women, the men's stillness was unnerving.

"What was that about?" Sestra whispered, shading her eyes from afternoon skies.

"Some pagan rite." Disdain seeped from Helena's voice across the quiet ship.

Warriors glanced at her through iron-ringed helmets before pulling at the oars and the steady swish of churning water sounded again. She winced, intending no rudeness to them...only Lord Hakan, who stood at the prow—not that he noticed with his back to her. Really, she should be glad that he ignored her. He faced the east, which had become commonplace. His stance boasted authority: hands at his waist, one boot planted atop a sea chest, as if by force of will he'd make the ship sail faster.

A few days past she had learned what drove him, but she hadn't shared that knowledge with Sestra. 'Twas something to puzzle over and consider, a tidbit that drew her eyes to him often.

Her Norse had vastly improved from intense eavesdropping, a necessity for a woman in her circumstances. Since that night off Jutland's coast, she had shed most of her ire. Most of it. After Dunhad, the chieftain found plenty to keep her busy. Helena sat down on a chest and began mending a pair of his faded blue trousers. She stretched the garment across her lap and fingered the natural wear at the knees. She was supposed to mend a small tear in the seam.

Serve him well.

His words nettled. Her fingers skimmed the worn fabric as an idea formed. Why not sew the trouser legs shut at the knee? That would serve him well. Helena smiled, playing the image of Lord Hakan putting on the trousers and his foot jamming into a seam mid-leg. Her elk bone needle hovered temptingly over the wrong place.

"Helena..." Sestra hissed a warning.

She laughed softly. "I won't...not that he doesn't deserve it..." Her voice trailed as she followed the approach of familiar wolf-skin boots until her gaze met his face.

Ice-blue eyes surrounded by iron spied the needle then flicked to look her in the eye. Lord Hakan removed his basinet helmet and set it under his arm. His eyebrows rose a fraction as if he dared her. Could he know the lay of her thoughts? Helena matched his stare, but the lump she swallowed gave her away. With a sigh, she poked the needle into the correct seam and sat up taller at her perch on the sea chest.

"Again, you are quick to judge." His eyes bored into her as he spoke stiff-sounding Frankish. "May the raven not return. If it does, we're bound to more days at sea. If not, I led the ship well—" The corners of his mouth turned up. "—and you're free to serve me on land soon."

The taut thread nearly snapped as she drove the needle through fabric, bunching cloth.

He glanced at the trousers she mended. "A woman shouldn't have too much time to sit and think."

After the chieftain shared that morsel of wisdom, he gave her his back to survey ship and sea. Needle and thread jerked through fabric as she watched him move slowly across the deck, noticing his bare arms were as brown as his leather jerkin. He was defenseless today, wearing no sword, though his armbands shined. Of course they would. She had polished them to new brightness. A woman, she was learning, had to pick her battles wisely.

Lord Hakan raised his fist and roared, "To Uppsala!"

"To Uppsala!" The men thundered their response and rowed with renewed vigor.

Sestra's mouth rounded in a perfect O. "What was that about?"

Helena blew slowly at bothersome wisps of hair that fell across her face.

"In Jutland, while you slept in the hold, I insulted him. I tried to play him falsely—" She paused to concentrate on making tiny rips where her sewing went askew. "—but as you heard, he speaks some Frankish after all."

Sestra groaned. "Have you learned nothing?"

Helena held up her handiwork—a jagged line at best— and judged the last inch to be repaired. The chieftain would not get her best work. She flashed a smile behind the draped garment, ready to share a secret.

"I'm glad to have cloth in my hands again. I've missed it." She tipped her head toward the prow and dropped her voice. "What he thinks is punishment, I find a pleasure."

Sestra glanced at a pile of folded clothes stacked between them. "You're fairly skilled. Mended many garments to my two, but you cannot fight your place in this world."

"My place?" Helena snipped the thread with iron scissors and shook her head. "We've looked at this all wrong."

Sestra's brows knit together like two cinnamon caterpillars. "What do you mean?"

But at that moment, the air thickened with whispers: *Uppsala.*

Every man was on his feet and pointing east. Excited, rapid Norse followed, and then all sat down and drove hard at the oars, churning the sea with new-found purpose. The mending was folded hastily in the basket. Fair winds raced with the vessel as she skimmed gray-blue waters. The dragon ship veered to the left around a tree-covered finger of land.

Helena and Sestra stretched their necks to view what lay ahead: the wet horizon expanded to land...land with shapes that grew into massive, sun-bleached wooden structures bearing intricate carvings. Helena stood guard by chests and barrels, but unease coiled inside her as they slid into the harbor. This Uppsala, brimmed with people, threatened to swallow her whole. Amidst the noises, another whisper caught her.

"Be strong...courageous. Do not be terrified. Do not be discouraged..."

Helena whipped around, sure that someone spoke behind her, but nothing more than empty space and a comforting breeze curled around her. The whisper reminded her of a story she had heard often as a child...a story of slaves like her, slaves who conquered a foreign land in ancient times. Comforted, Helena faced Uppsala.

The churning in her belly eased a little and she smiled. She had been looking at matters all wrong. She glanced at azure skies and laughed, a joyous, mellow sound that turned heads.

"What's got you laughing?" Sestra's voice was jittery, lacking all her usual confidence.

Helena linked arms with her friend. "We are going to set this Uppsala on end."

The dragon ship jolted, shaking both thralls, but the men flew into action. Sven and other hearty Norsemen balanced on the rails with ropes in their hands, then jumped onto the landing beside the ship. Ravens scattered, cawing against the invasion of the dragon vessel roosting on Svea's shore.

Sestra's befuddled, hazel stare turned back to Helena. "I thought you were set on returning home."

Helena took a deep breath of tangy harbor air. "I am, but first we must vanquish Uppsala."

"A *slave* girl? Vanquish that?" Sestra snorted as she pointed at the bustle on land.

"There's more than one kind of victory."

Sestra groaned and dipped her head. "Have you learned nothing since your blunder in Jutland? Don't expect the chieftain to show you any more patience."

Both cast cautious glances at Lord Hakan shouting rapid orders. Silver fire glinted from his helmet's eye rings, a trick of the sunlight as he moved. Large planks emerged, one after the other, from the hold. Piece by piece, men created a wide ramp from the ship to the landing.

"These past days haven't been about patience." Helena folded her arms and watched the chieftain give clipped orders to his men. "More like a hard drive to see his son, Eric."

"He has a son?" Sestra canted her head at this news. Her eyes widened then narrowed with a calculating gleam. "Then he has a wife."

Helena shook her head. "I am certain he does *not* have a wife. My Norse has improved enough to catch that."

"Hmmm..." Sestra hummed a vague sound. "You are certain of this?"

Helena nudged her nosy friend. "I'm certain 'tis time you learned Norse."

Emund approached. "Please. Time to leave the ship. Nels will lead you across the planks and I will follow."

"Will you bind us?" Helena asked.

His chest puffed out as he waved them forward. "Lord Hakan has no need to bind you here. You will see."

They were a noisy caravan led by the chieftain mounted on Agnar. Sheep, goats, the unloading of chattel was a boisterous swell of noise and disorder. Helena snatched the mending basket, and they followed Nels, the black-haired, half-Gaelic warrior. The road ahead cleared, and Helena saw why.

Sheep and goats scattered, braying nervous cries as a frantic Ingvar chased them. Emund joined the effort but without success. A Norsewoman, her eyes rounding at the sight, snatched up her giggling child from the road and scurried back the way she came. One goat bumped the shins of a man loading an oxcart across the road, causing him to drop his buckets. His angry fist struck air. Ingvar, panting hard, leaned on his knees.

"These beasts...they are bad-tempered." His chest heaved as he yelled to Lord Hakan.

The chieftain scowled at the unruly scene. Atop Agnar, he circled the road, but the small herd would not obey. Lord Hakan groused under his breath when two bleating sheep darted toward the dock. Helena leaned toward Sestra and chuckled as his frown deepened.

"Appears the mighty Norseman can't command all with the bark of an order."

"From the look of things, we'll reach home late." Sestra's shoulders sagged. "Wherever home is this night."

"And he looks ready to draw his sword." Her eyes were on Lord Hakan, who blocked part of the road.

Yet, a weight—niggling guilt, really—pressed her conscience. Sestra touched the right chord. All of them were travel weary and in want of home, wherever that may be. Helena set the basket down to pick up a long stick from the side of the road for a make-shift shepherd's crook. With clucking and gentle taps, she brought the small herd of sheep and goats skittering close to her in a tight circle. Lord Hakan's ice-blue stare followed her as he circled the area slowly. His large warhorse came around to the west side of the road where he stopped. Horse and master cast a long shadow, blocking the sun as he issued another command.

"Nels. Emund. See to the cart."

The men began to load the oxcart Sven had left for them. Helena stayed with the herd in the cool cover of man and horse towering over her. Was he in some small way showing a kindness? Or a display of authority over her?

The pink nose of a tiny lamb nudged her leg. She knelt down and gathered the gentle creature in her arms, stroking his velvet ear. She peeked at Lord Hakan, who watched the herd, solid and forbidding.

"They're not vicious attack goats, my lord. Your harsh glares have no effect. They don't know you're chieftain here." She grinned up at him and released the animal. "Mayhap, they only understand Frankish."

The second after the brazen words left her lips, Helena clapped a hand over her mouth. Sestra and Ingvar gasped, gawking owl-eyed from Helena to Lord Hakan.

Lord Hakan was silent, unreadable with his iron helmet on his head.

She lowered her hand from her mouth. "I....I didn't mean to be so bold."

A rough, deep sound came from him—'twas laughter.

"I think you did." He removed his helmet, and his ice-blue eyes crinkled nicely in the corners. "But, you may be right about the Frankish. I bought them in your homeland."

Helena stood up and exhaled slowly, blowing a wayward wisp of hair from her forehead. Her face stung with heat despite the shade.

The corner of his mouth quirked as he replaced the cone-shaped helmet. "My thanks for your help."

"I...please forgive my wayward tongue...I..." Helena dusted off her shabby dress and grabbed the mending basket from the ground. She held the burden as a shield against the rapid thumping in her chest.

"Give the basket to Ingvar and come here."

Helena clutched the mending basket, but Ingvar pried it from her fingers and gave her a slight push. With heavy feet she moved across the hard-packed earthen road to stand an arm's length from the chieftain.

"Look to the flock." He bent close and spoke in a quiet, teasing voice for her alone. "Since you're better suited to calming beasts and the like."

Helena's head snapped with attention. She had called him a beast on the ship. Gone like a wisp of smoke was the humor, replaced by the impassive leader who surveyed the group's readiness. Agnar's tail twitched and one great hoof stamped the ground.

Lord Hakan rose high in the saddle and pointed. "We take this road out of Uppsala."

The business of moving thralls, animals, and goods commanded his attention. Sestra's eyes beetled from Helena to the chieftain, but she settled silently in the cart, and Helena, with Ingvar's help, herded the goats and sheep.

People stepped aside. Emund and Nels hailed friends, boisterous in their promises to meet later. Helena stole glances at the chieftain's broad back. A cool breeze caught the ends of his thick blonde hair as he nodded the occasional greeting. His sword hilt's red stone blinked in the swollen sun's light. The golden orb still hung in the sky, yet the day felt over long. She drank up the visual picture that was Uppsala: strange, long buildings with intricately carved portals, most painted bright red, blue, and yellow.

She *wanted* to learn more about this Uppsala and the fathomless man who called it home.

The notion pricked her skin with a pleasant flush. Then her gaze slid to the right of the road. A small green field with an ancient gnarled tree sat beside three large statues guarding the entrance of a massive stone building. One statue was made of bronze, bearing an exaggerated helmet.

"What is that?" Aghast, she pointed out the statue to Ingvar. "Never have I seen so much bronze."

"Tis Frey, god of fertility and marriage." Lord Hakan spoke over his shoulder to her. "Frey gives a long marriage and fertile home."

"And you think this heathen custom works?" she asked, not guarding her words.

He waved a hand at the crowds milling in the market place. "Heathen or not...judge for yourself."

"And what of you, my lord?"

"Frey failed me." His voice was iron hard. "I have no wife."

Helena itched to know more, but conversing with a man's back was a futile effort. Nels and Emund engaged Sestra in a lively description of mid-summer celebrations. Helena touched the pouch dangling from her neck inside her tunic, recalling her life before the Danes had stormed her village.

"I was to be married," she said, not expecting to be heard above the din.

"What did you say?" Lord Hakan tugged the reins, glancing over his shoulder at her.

The chieftain's attention startled her, but she answered him.

"I was to be married, but the Danes raided my village, burning and stealing." Her hand gripped the pouch under her bodice. The stone bride's gift was still hers.

Ahead, the earthen ribbon tapered off into trees and open fields. Lord Hakan angled his black steed around to walk slowly beside her. Her shoulders tensed. The chieftain had never bothered to ask the contents of her pouch, which pressed against her bodice. Would he demand to know now?

The Norseman tilted his head toward her and gentled his voice.

"The man you were to marry...he died?"

5

Her lips parted and she had to look ahead into the distance as much from the shock of a gentle Norseman as the raw picture his question brought to mind.

"Last I saw, Guerin had run to the safety of his family's tower. 'Tis made of stone. The Danes couldn't burn it." Her throat went thick as she admitted, "I'm sure he's still alive."

Awaiting my return.

"He hid like a coward while men carried away his betrothed?" Ice-blue eyes widened within the iron rings as he stared down at her.

"He's not a coward." She shot the words at the chieftain, forgetting her place. "The village...everyone ran from the Danes. Guerin's gentle and learned, not a brute like..."

She faced the road and clamped her mouth shut, swallowing her words.

"Like me," he finished.

Her whole body vibrated with a jumble of emotions as fractured pieces of that day splashed through her mind. Thundering hooves. Iron rings clanking. Screams of terror. Wild-eyed men brandishing heavy iron hammers flashed in fragments, then blessed blackness. Her free hand rubbed her throat, and the road before her turned into a haze. She walked, but knew not where she moved. Her breath was thick in her chest. Beside her, the chieftain's deep voice poured a soothing balm on her soul.

"Helena."

Drawn to his voice, she raised her head and faced him as they walked. Late-day sunlight skimmed his shoulders. The air was calm and clear, as if they were the only two.

He spoke in a way that lulled her. "'Tis a hardship, the way you've come to my keeping." Then his voice turned harsh, cutting like a blade. "But your man was a coward. I defend my own."

"I know the sort...live by the sword."

Her lips trembled. The chieftain's judgment held a sliver of truth that poked at a deeper heart wound: Guerin had failed to fight for her that day. Why? She ignored that painful truth, locked it away, and defended him.

"There are other pursuits. Guerin can read," she said, tipping her head high. "He was going to teach me."

The chieftain grunted at the mention of that talent, and his eyes within the forbidding rings pitied her before trotting ahead.

Helena gave her attention to the tender lamb beside her. She nursed her aching soul as she stroked the soft creature, regretting that she had revealed much to the Norseman. To what end? She gained nothing that could balance the scales in favor of freedom, but he learned of her.

She jammed her staff into the road, splintering the tip. When Helena tossed the broken piece aside, Uppsala was long gone. Tall trees with white bark flanked the road, sometimes giving way to grassy fields and farms. Ahead, the road forked, and the procession followed the dark horse and rider to the right toward a vast, open farm. A strange flat stone, a serpent carved in the flatness with stick-like slashes, leaned at the entrance.

Lord Hakan wheeled his great black steed around to address them. "Skardsbok Gard, farmstead to my sister, Mardred, and her husband, Halsten. Serve them as well as you would serve me."

"Hakan! Welcome home," a statuesque woman shouted as she ran toward them. She clutched her pleated skirts to her knees as her bare feet pumped the ground. Two others followed her, shrieking and waving as they made their way toward the gate.

Lord Hakan dismounted amid the flurry of colliding women. He removed his helmet and let a young girl tug at him. He swung her up in the air. The other two hugged and chattered so fast, Helena couldn't understand their Norse. They pulled him toward a longhouse and everyone followed. Helena drank in the sights of this vast, prosperous farm.

Three cauldrons rumbled and steamed over fires outside a large longhouse. Strips of salted fish flesh dried on wooden racks, the tangy scent strong. Men paused from their field labor to wave. Sheep and goats dotted the meadows, with dark green trees and a wide, tranquil river framing the land.

"Hakan. Welcome home." A brown-haired man emerged from an outbuilding, walking with a limp. He clasped Hakan's arm. "You are well?"

"Aye, Halsten, and I come bearing gifts." He waved to oxcart. "What I have is worth the wait...spices, threads, candles, oil, with more to come."

"Ah," Halsten crowed his pleasure.

Helena noticed his left sleeve was empty below the elbow.

Lord Hakan pointed to Sestra. "This thrall belongs to Sven. He will come for her tomorrow."

All eyes went to Helena. Under their measuring stares, her hands plucked frayed threads on her stained dress.

"This one will come with me." A corner of his mouth curved upward. "She has an able hand with beasts." Turning to Mardred, he asked, "But, I hope you and the girls will help her. She will take charge of my home."

"You would give a *thrall* your keys?" Mardred's lips pursed. "'Tis a shameful thing."

He shrugged away the condemning words. "When the time is right, she will wear the keys."

Helena studied the two. His sister shared the same strong jaw and lips as her brother, and she dared voice her thoughts against his forbidding presence. Mardred clucked her tongue and folded her arms under her bosom.

"There are many fine Norsewomen to marry. Just because Astrid broke her vows doesn't mean all women are spiteful. You plan on staying home with Erik?" Mardred tapped a finger against her arm. "Then, you should marry. Your *wife* will oversee your home, not me, my hands are full, and certainly not a foreign thrall who does not know our ways."

"I tried a wife once." Lord Hakan grabbed Agnar's reins, and he tipped his with a coaxing request. "I ask you to teach her our ways."

Mardred rolled her eyes, but her voice softened. "With all my spare time?"

Helena decided she liked the tall blonde woman who loved her guarded, warrior brother. Lord Hakan was about to mount his horse when Halsten touched his shoulder.

"Hakan, you've only just arrived. Have some ale—" Halsten lowered his voice. "—I must speak to you of urgent matters."

"A quick horn of ale." He untied his hudfat from the saddle and passed the reins to a man who led Agnar to a water trough.

Nels and Emund began to unload the cart. Insects buzzed and floated through twilight air. Helena bent to scratch a ewe's ears before Ingvar led the herd to a gated meadow. Unsure of her place, she stood awkwardly in the center yard. Lord Hakan stopped at the brightly painted doorway, a stark contrast of chipped red, yellow, and blue against the weathered longhouse, and beckoned the tall, older maid.

"Katla, please help the dark-haired maid with her bath. See that she gets a clean garment and bathes away from others...has privacy."

Katla glanced at Helena. "We are of the same height. She can have one of my tunics."

Mardred whispered something to the younger girl, who darted inside and returned with cloth bundled in her arms. Hakan rummaged through his hudfat under the curious eyes of his family.

"Give this to her to use as she likes."

'Twas a thick block of soap, followed by a flash of silver.

"Katla, Aud, go now." Mardred shooed her daughters away and her eyes narrowed with speculation. "Softening, Hakan? Or saving the thrall for something else?"

Helena's cheeks flushed and she averted her gaze to the younger girl, Aud. The little Norse maid was missing her front teeth, but she smiled and giggled, hopping from one foot to the other. Katla laid a gentle hand on Helena's shoulder.

"Come."

...

Hakan stood in the lintel, tracking Helena's progress to the river. Before she disappeared behind a copse of trees, Mardred sighed behind him. He was not without some understanding of the moods of women. Best face his sister and have done with it.

"Something you wish to say?"

"A fair maid, she is. I'd better get a Raven woman to look at that wound. A nasty cut." Arms still folded, Mardred's gaze narrowed on him. "And how did she come by this wound?"

His sister's prying ways were the same now as in years past. Their bond of love was so strong, he tolerated these faults; the weaker sex was limited.

"The wound is the work of the Danes, and rest your busy mind, Mardred. You know I don't mix with thralls."

Hakan ignored Mardred's *harrumphing* sounds and moved inside to the table, where Halsten offered him a horn of ale. Swallowing the cool liquid, Hakan took in the longhouse. Little had changed, save a new stone hearth built into the east wall. The familiar sights and smells comforted him.

The wood-hewn walls were not lined with warrior's tools. Halsten kept only a few iron-tipped spears. A lone Norse hammer hung by a leather thong near the door; rust tinted the weapon's edges.

A small black pot suspended by three iron rods simmered over a ringed pit. He breathed the aroma of mouth-watering stew and baking bread. Mardred was many things, among them an excellent cook. Hakan planted a foot on the bench and rested a forearm on his thigh.

"What are the urgent matters you speak of?" He glanced at Halsten. "I need to see Erik."

Halsten frowned. "There's been unrest since you were last home. Mysterious slaughters in the shielings of late. Men, animals. Farmers are staying close to their homes. No one takes their herds to the upper pastures this spring. People blame the king...the changes he brings."

"Oh, Hakan!" Mardred's hands folded into her apron, her voice rising. "These killings are causing terror. People say Olof's conversion to this one God has stirred up the wrath of Odin." She moved to the cooking fire and gave him a pointed look. "I say evil settles over our land."

Hakan took another swallow of his ale, impatient with these superstitions.

"The king converted years ago. Why does this matter now?"

"Because he plans to do away with the ninth-year sacrifice. He claims 'tis barbaric. The king has been to Gotland to meet with a holy man. But, so far, this holy man has not set foot in Uppsala." Halsten stared into his drinking horn. "And Gorm is back...most outspoken about the king's ways."

Hakan stiffened at the name. His grip tightened on his drinking horn.

"I heard." Hakan looked out the door at the waning light.

Halsten fingered the silver trim on his drinking horn. "He does not break our laws but works in the shadows, speaking ill of the king...claims Olof's beliefs anger our gods and cause these strange deaths."

"The superstitious Norse are ready to believe anything."

Halsten, a Danelander with a Saxon mother, shrugged, accepting this truth.

"Well," Mardred scoffed as she set warm bread on the table. "You must admit 'tis all strange. With the king's talk of a God in the air and not so much as a statue to look at."

Hakan grinned tolerantly at her.

"Mardred, there are many who believe the same as our king and that we are strange heathens." He swallowed the last of his ale and remembered Helena's rant near Dunhad.

Mardred's forehead wrinkled. "Then how do you account for the success you and others have when you go a-viking?"

"How do you account for the many ships lost at sea? Norsemen who fall under the sword? 'Tis our way of life. We live by the same risks that kill us. Don't worry about the rumblings of a few. Gorm will disappear same as he did years ago...unless someone kills him first." Harshness threaded his voice—he itched to be the one to send Gorm from this earth. "Perhaps our king grows soft with age. The man changed once to appease his wife." Hakan waved off his indifference. "Who knows? Mayhap he'll change again?"

"You always spoke so well of the king." Halsten leaned back, sounding surprised.

"*Because* the friendship is honest, I can say these things." Hakan downplayed the bond between him and the king. "I don't care about Norse gods or Olof's."

"Don't sound so cold, Hakan." Mardred's eyes sparkled with affection as she cuffed his shoulder. "You love the old king as you did our father."

Mardred moved to check the stew. A brother's inborn love to protect his sister rose like a shield. They had been through much together.

"These mysterious deaths sound more the work of a power-hungry chieftain with Berserkers...one such as Gorm." He cocked an eyebrow at Mardred. "Not Odin's wrath on Svea."

Hakan tapped the empty horn against his leg. Halsten and Mardred glanced uneasily at each other, as if willing the other to speak. Enough of this. The need for his son overruled.

"I tire of this idle gossip. I need to see Erik."

Mardred's forehead furrowed as she pointed her wooden spoon at Halsten. "*Tell* him..."

"There's more, Hakan." Halsten grimaced. "Gorm has been spending much time with Astrid and Erik. *Much time.*"

The ale horn cracked in his hand before he ran out the door.

...

The slow-moving river shrouded her like a wet blanket. She existed in the safe, watery world, chattel to no one, but when she passed the soap to Aud, the little girl laughed.

"Please come out." The little girl pointed at Helena's water-wrinkled fingertips.

The white blonde Katla raised a large linen for privacy. "Here. You must be cold."

The sisters wrapped Helena in kindness and warmth, treating her like a new friend. Katla's white blondeness contrasted with sun-kissed skin, and Helena noticed they were similar in age. The maid held up a soft white tunic embroidered with vivid reds and blues around the neckline.

"This is one of mine. I want you to have it."

Helena's Frankish dress, torn and frayed, crumpled in a soiled heap at the river's edge. She had labored long hours over that garment, stitching seams that hugged her waist. Now, a foreign undergarment, soft linen, slipped over her head. She looked up again, and a white woolen tunic shrouded her vision and flowed loosely down her body. Helena quickly stuffed her ancient pouch inside the bodice.

"Yours to keep," Aud chirped as she tied bright ribbons to the short sleeves high on the shoulders.

Helena rubbed her bare arms, staring at the pale, exposed skin.

"Aud, go find those pretty rocks you like." Then, Katla pointed to a log with a wide-tooth bone comb. "Please, sit, so I can comb your hair."

"I don't expect anyone to comb my hair." Helena didn't move. She hugged herself, not liking the air kissing her naked arms.

Katla patted the log. "Please."

The way her voice firmed, 'twas a command, not a request. Helena's fingertips dug sharp points into her arms, but she planted herself on the fallen log and watched Aud gather small stones along the river's edge. Katla's free hand gently separated Helena's thick locks.

"We treat our thralls well." The comb slid through hair, catching on a tangle. "But, my uncle honors you."

The painful twinge was momentary as the Norsewoman worked the knot to smoothness. Insects sung their night songs while the sun almost disappeared from sight in permanent twilight, though her body told her it was much later. The air hung heavy and expectant around Helena.

"And you want to know why?"

The comb caught on a snarl. "'Tis not my place to question," Katla snipped.

"But you want to."

Katla removed the comb. "My uncle does not mix with thralls, if that is something you fear. He won't harm you." She leaned close to Helena's ear. "Nor should a thrall have ideas about my uncle."

Helena's neck stiffened at the warning. That brute didn't need defending, but her retort went unsaid when Aud skipped near and spilled a pile of rocky treasures from her apron. The little girl hiked her skirt to her knees and trotted back to the river's edge, and the comb slid over Helena's tresses with ease once the warning was given.

"I do not fear him in that way, but he has power over me." Helena's hands clenched in her lap. "'Tis not to my liking."

"What happened to your cheek?"

Helena touched her face. "The Danes did this."

"Aud, bring the salve." The comb worked faster. "I would not complain if I were you. He'll grant you many freedoms."

"But not the one I want...to return home."

Helena bristled. This Norse maid admonished her as if she were an ungrateful child. What did she know about the loss of freedom? Katla slept with the knowledge that those she loved were safe. Helena opened her mouth to say as much when Aud presented a small clay jar of slippery yellow salve. She dipped one finger in the jar and traced slick, odorless balm up Helena's cheek.

"You are pretty."

The simple, child-like announcement warmed her. How long had it been since someone had told her that? She smiled widely at the girl.

"My thanks, little one."

Katla gathered Helena's hair at the nape and wrapped a leather thong around the thick locks. Aud set down the jar and picked up something shiny: cupped in her hands was a wide silver armband. She slipped the manacle up Helena's arm and secured it with a squeeze.

"Hakan's," chirped the girl. She pointed from the bracelet to Helena and back again.

Katla's chin tipped with pride and her vibrant blue eyes flared wide. "You wear the mark of Hakan the Tall."

Helena raised her arm high. Carved in silver, a clawed elk beast twined with a fierce-eyed wolf. Their battle curved around her arm possessively.

6

Hakan's head pounded. Crow's talons could be dragged inside his skull, so harsh was the pain. He opened the door of Olof Skotkonung's receiving hall, escaping the over bright morning sun. He leaned against the thick oak and let the cool, dim hall ease his ache. If Svea was in turmoil, he saw no sign of it here.

Rhineland glass vessels, threaded with blue trail and yellow reticella, sat on snowy white linen. Well-dressed attendants moved about the large room. Wood and iron shields lined the walls scarred from battles past. Silver-tipped spears straddled shields. High above an ornately carved chair, two Norse hammers crossed at the handles: the sign of a jarl in days of old...now the sign of his king.

"Hakan? Is it really you?" Olof rose from that chair.

Hakan approached the king who reigned over Svea's chieftains. A large fire blazed at an open hearth. The fire and long-sleeved, heavy woolen tunic told Hakan the years had taken their toll. Most Norsemen would relish the crisp spring air in sleeveless jerkins. But in the harsh north, the burdens of leadership had exacted their price on his elder friend. New lines carved Olof's face.

"I am pleased to see you, my king." Hakan bowed to the adopted father of his youth.

"Please, 'tis Olof and Hakan between us."

The ruler snapped his fingers at waiting attendants. "Bring mead and fine fare, my friend has come home."

Hakan winced and rubbed his temple and called out, "Watered down ale for me."

"Ah, those head ailments again. You've seen Astrid." The king's forehead wrinkled as he settled back into his chair. "Have you seen Erik?"

Hakan sat in a chair, smaller, but no less ornate than the king's.

"Astrid but not Erik. She keeps the boy from me and increases her demands." The words tasted bitter. "All the wealth of Byzantium will not satisfy her."

Hakan's hands curled into fists on white linen, but he knew anger and force would not work. Astrid was the weaker sex, and even more, the mother of his son. Nothing could sever that tie.

Hakan was certain Olof read the lay of his thoughts. Such was their bond. Silence pervaded, save for the servants setting a feast of sliced pork, cheeses, and the softest breads. Timid footsteps, slight whispers, and a boy set wide-mouthed silver chalices before them. Curling his fingers around a chalice, the king dismissed the servants.

"I have seen many changes come over Astrid. She hardens her heart in this hunger of hers, this hunger for *more*. Will she respect the divorce custom and let Erik live with you?"

Hakan sipped the watery brew. "Nay."

Olof's hoary brows rose a fraction. "You will settle this matter at the Althing?"

"I would prefer settling with her than the whole of Uppsala. I'll try again. Taking this dispute to the Althing is my final measure." Hakan tore off a hunk of bread.

55

Had matters between him and Astrid come to this? The Althing? The body of men to hear and pass judgment on disputes? Aye, chieftains had their authority, but times were changing. The Althing gave influence and power to all freemen. That assembly came with mixed blessings: power to the common man, but a painful, public spectacle.

"The sword cannot solve every problem. I hope this will be settled between you both. Surely, she will accept tradition. A boy needs his father." Olof leaned closer. "And you must know the love of a good woman. Not all women are cut from the same cloth."

"You speak like Mardred," Hakan said before sinking his teeth into more bread.

"Give Erik many fine brothers. And, they will grow to manhood in an Uppsala of peace and prosperity." Olof raised his chalice in salute.

Hakan speared some meat and grinned at his overlord.

"Out with it, Olof. I'm not some distant chieftain needing silver-tongued persuasion. What do you want?"

"You know me too well." Olof's eyes wrinkled from a sad smile. "I carved out this unity over Svealand, Gotland, and Aland with the might of my youth and have kept it with what I hope is the wisdom of an older man," he said with a raspy chuckle. "Of late, problems arise, challenges, to my rule." Olof's grey eyes resembled hard silver coins. "I need the sword of a young man to keep that unity."

Phantom weight settled on Hakan's shoulders as he studied the white tablecloth. He hadn't seen his son yet or his neglected farm. Olof leaned closer and stretched his hand across the table.

"You've seen other kingdoms flourish and fail." The king's voice deepened as he curled his hand into a fist, pointing a finger to the ceiling. "We are one...one rebellion away from being less than nothing. The changes I bring are best for our people. The Althing is good. But, our siddur that calls for *human* sacrifice every ninth year? That *blot* custom must end."

56

Hakan set the small eating knife on the platter and shut his eyes. His head pounded from meeting Astrid last eve. His son was hidden from him and his king, the man who had taken him in as an orphan...to whom he owed much, was about to make a request—the kind that came with a heavy cost. Hakan opened his eyes. Olof's passion needed tempering.

"Queen Estrid brought great changes years ago, and with her passing—" Hakan paused, searching the tablecloth. "—you clung to these beliefs even more. When I buried my father and mother, I buried my hope in gods. I care not about the afterlife." His voice hit a gravel-hard note. "Life here is hard enough."

Olof grasped Hakan's arm. "I know, my friend. You were not yet a man when I took the baptism. I thank Estrid for helping me see the truth of our ways and hope the same for our people, especially those I care for most." He affectionately slapped Hakan's arm. "Still, I must rule as I see fit...a careful path I trod. As your ruler, I bid you go to Aland and quell the rebellion there."

"Aland?"

"I've not received spring tribute from the overlord, Den Gamle. He ignores my summons." King Olof stared into open space as his fingers drummed the table. "Problems arise in Svea as well...mayhap small rebellions to an old man who holds new beliefs, or..."

"Knut of the Angles expanding his kingdom?"

The king snorted. "Nay. But, I need someone I trust to separate truth from tale." Olof's silver-grey eyes pinned him. "I need you. Get the tribute and let it be known: there will be rule of law in Svea." Olof rubbed his chin. "Keep half for yourself. The eiderdown and mink ought to convince Astrid to give you Erik."

Unclasping a gold armband, the old man placed it in Hakan's right hand. The scratched gold bore Olof's mark: dotted lines formed a triangle with a simple plant sprouting from it, the influence of Frankish artisans. A small cross, etched in metal, showed the lay of Olof's heart. The metal band carried a weighty price: time away from home, and Erik with *Solace* at his back.

Hakan inclined his head, tightening the gold on his wrist. Much ran deep between them.

Olof squinted shrewd eyes at him. "What's this I hear about laying down your sword to become a farmer?"

...

"Ahk," Mardred screwed her nose from the acrid aroma of burnt meat. "You must remove the stew when *almost* done."

Helena inspected the wide cooking pan. Black flecks rose to the surface as Mardred scraped a wooden spoon through the stew. Helena had left the pot too long on the fire *again*.

Turning a patient eye, Mardred asked slowly, "Have you never used soapstone?"

Helena, almost one month now in the Norse household, was a quick study. She blinked at Mardred, who attempted yet another cooking lesson for Helena.

Mardred tapped the large, grayish bowl, repeating, "Soapstone?"

Helena shook her head.

Sighing, Mardred continued. "Soapstone holds heat long after it's removed from the fire. Always take the dish off *before* fully cooked." Mardred chuckled. "My brother will not grow fat, will he?"

Katla and Aud laughed as their mother puffed out her cheeks and rounded her arms, mimicking a wide girth.

"Go outside...away from cooking. Gather herbs and berries near the barley field." In motherly kindness, she shooed them from the longhouse.

The trio grabbed bronze-banded buckets in search of the land's bounty. Helena missed her family much, but could voice no complaint to her treatment. She failed miserably at cooking, turning bread to stone, stewed fruits to mush, and even bruising tender greens. She had her talents. Time would come to display them.

The pouch remained under her bodice, a constant reminder of home, however kind these Norse. She was destined for a different life. Home. She would return when the time was right. No amount of tears or anger at her fate would make that day come any quicker.

Sestra was right: fighting didn't help.

Katla and Aud swung their buckets as they ambled into the forest. They chattered while picking at bushes, sometimes dropping to their knees to pluck a wild onion. Freedom from duller tasks lulled them deeper, deeper into dense forests untouched by a woodman's axe. Katla and Aud kept to their task, but the fine hairs of Helena's neck pricked.

Something watched them.

Something, or someone, lurked behind ancient, shadowed trees. She swung full circle, checking here and there.

Nothing.

Her unease grew. "Aud? Katla? Let's return t—"

A scream tore the air.

"Run!" Aud shrieked and flew past Helena, her sun-browned feet thumping the earth as she disappeared in waves of barley.

A large, upright figure growled and snarled in the shadows.

"Katla?" Helena cried. "Katla! Where are you?"

A strange creature, a wild-eyed mass of human bulk in bear hide, slid from behind a tree.

The man-beast snarled at her. Drool dribbled his beard as he hefted an ax, twirling the weapon as if it were a simple stick. Katla's bucket rolled across the clearing. The maid cowered in the dirt.

"Here!" Helena swung her arms wildly and ran into the clearing. "Over here."

Her heart banged her ribs. The massive man-beast growled at new prey. Beady eyes glittered black within a hollow, decaying bear head. The rest of the hairy pelt draped down his back. Katla whimpered and crouched by a bush.

"Helena..." Katla's voice quavered. "My ankle...I twisted it."

Helena sucked in shallow breaths. "Can you run?"

"I...I think so."

The man-beast's unearthly stare swiveled from Katla to Helena. A slow, spittle-flecked smile formed within the bear's head, revealing rotting teeth. He settled on Helena, and the knowledge pierced her bones with numbing iciness. He would go after her.

"When he moves, run."

Katla pressed her shaking hands to the ground, a cat ready to spring. The creature weaved as if in a trance, watching Helena. Bending, she gripped a jagged rock but kept eye contact with the attacker. Her other hand searched dirt and curled over a palm-sized stone.

"Katla..." Helena rose slowly.

Their predator snorted. His boot pawed the ground as if he were a bull. The black hide-head tilted, and the bear snout pointed at her.

"Run!" Helena threw the stone with all her might.

Katla sprung up with a screech and ran.

The man howled when the stone struck. Blood squirted from his face. A meaty fist covered his nose.

Helena threw the second rock—and missed. Her breath bellowed from her chest. She turned to run. Green everywhere blurred her vision. The clearing's edge was close, so close. Ahead...the barley field...the men...Halsten and the other thralls. But her feet failed her.

Helena slammed onto dirt. Unforgiving ground jarred her bones. A sharp rock poked her thigh. Her cheek pressed cool earth, but she tasted blood and copper. Spread-eagle, she looked down: her foot was caught in a twisted root.

Her fingers clawed dirt and weeds. She scrambled to her knees. Behind her, the brute laughed at his downed prey. Chills swept her skin. Grasping a tree, Helena scraped her palms on bark. She turned to see the giant swaying on his feet. A sickened unsteadiness replaced his predacious glee. His hands shook. The ax loosened in his grip and slid lower.

Like grains of sand slipping through an hourglass, what happened next was but a breath of time.

Metal glittered by her feet—bronze—a forgotten bucket, her last weapon. Desperate hands grabbed the bucket and hurled it.

Thwack!

The bucket banged his shoulder, knocking the bear-head askew. The man-beast wobbled and dropped, smashing a knee on rocky ground. Bone crunched, a loud crackling sound, and the attacker roared. His meaty hand slapped the earth. When he did, a yellow stone embedded in his armband broke off and rolled toward Helena's feet.

More noises. Behind her.

Halsten and the thralls crashed through brush. Men brandished scythes and sticks at the fallen attacker. Helena slumped against the tree. The copper tang was stronger in her mouth. Every limb ached and shook.

The menacing man-beast grabbed his ax and swung it at the band of men. The men danced a few steps back but held the clearing.

Then the attacker roared, pushed himself upright, and fled into the shadows. Thundering, crashing sounds in the distance followed a fading, unnatural howl.

Sweat trickled down Halsten's face. Each man's eyes darted from the darker forest to Halsten. No one wanted to give chase.

Halsten swiped his forehead. "Let him go."

Helena's fingers sifted the grass, finding the stone. The clouded yellow piece stuck to her palm—'twas amber. She gathered her wits and breathed slowly. One of the thralls, Marc, a young ironworker of Normandy, touched her shoulder.

"Are you hurt?" Concern filled his eyes. He crouched beside her and put an arm over her shoulders.

"Aye, but not in the way you ask." Her knees jerked and quivered under her skirt. She couldn't stop shivering.

Marc's dark eyes were soft as he nodded, the unspoken bond of slavery between them. He brushed back hair that stuck to her sweat-damp cheek, but his hand dropped when Halsten approached.

Helena raised her cupped hand to show Halsten the stone. "This fell off his armband."

Halsten's eyes narrowed in quick scrutiny, then he shrugged and scanned the other side of the clearing. "A chip of amber. 'Tis nothing." He glanced at Marc. "See her safely back to the longhouse."

Stolen from her home, her face cut, and today's attack—'twas too much. Fat tears rolled down her cheeks. Shoulder-wracking sobs followed one after the other.

"Hush now, Helena," Marc said, rubbing her arm.

When her sobs lessened, Helena leaned into Marc and closed her eyes and let him lead her from the clearing. The yellow stone stuck to her palm until it dropped in thick weeds.

...

Berserker. Halsten and the thralls whispered the word until Mardred came near. The Norsewoman's upset hushed all discussion. That such evil visited her farm hurt like a tender wound. The shock of that day brought Helena some respite. Mardred insisted she rest.

The rest drove her mad.

She itched to work. Unaccustomed to idleness, Helena didn't think she'd be so quick to *want* to return to her labors. But there was only so much kindly attention she could take. Even Halsten laughed one morning when she hurried to haul water before any could stop her.

"Ready to be up and about again, eh?" He waved on his way to the field.

They had an understanding. Halsten expressed his thanks to Helena, and she implored him to speak to Hakan.

Would he ask for her freedom? So deep was his gratitude that Halsten told her, aye, he'd speak to the chieftain.

Helena watched him on his way to the fields when Mardred linked arms with her.

"Want to work, do you?" Mardred grinned and pointed to the bucket at her feet. "I have a task. 'Twill take days and little cooking on your part."

She motioned to a loaded cart manned by two sturdy thralls, and the Norsewoman's natural weave skirt swirled as she headed toward the gate.

Helena jogged to catch up. "Where are we going?"

"Today, you prepare Hakan's longhouse. 'Tis down river...two or three pilskudd from here."

"Pilskudd?"

"Aye. Pilskudd." Mardred stretched her arms to hold an imaginary bow, letting loose her bowstring. She arced her arm in the air and whistled. "Pilskudd."

They walked a long while in companionable silence on the sunny day. Birds chirped and oxen hooves clip-clopped the earth behind them. Helena's fingers rubbed an uneven seam on her apron and she ventured the daring question.

"Can you talk about the berserker?"

Mardred's easy gait slowed. "The berserker."

The Norsewoman followed the flight of one bird chasing another and said nothing. Mardred's keys jingled with each step, and when she spoke, her voice was weary.

"People claim they are shape-shifters. But, as you saw...they are men wearing old animal skins on their heads." Mardred's fingers curled tightly on her apron. "Warriors chew mushrooms they get from Raven women, healers who live deep in the forests. These mushrooms make them crazy. A cut to the arm...they don't feel it." She shrugged her shoulders. "Useful in battle. Many chieftains use berserkers when they go raiding. Such warriors stay at Birka's outpost."

"And this was one of those men. But why? Why here?"

Mardred shook her head. "I know not. More attacks are happening around Uppsala." Mardred absently brushed a wisp of blonde hair from her face. "Many in Svea say these attacks are Odin's wrath because our king rejects the gods for another belief. King Olof wishes to do away with the blot."

"The blot?"

"Aye, blot...blood. The ninth year sacrifice: nine cows, horses, pigs, goats, and men." Mardred scanned the road ahead as if such a thing was commonplace.

"A sacrifice of men," Helena gasped and jerked to a stop.

"Aye," Mardred nodded. "This happens."

Mardred cocked her head at Helena, bewilderment writ on her face. Then she smiled.

"Oh, nay, Helena. *You* wouldn't be a sacrifice. Only male thralls, and troublesome ones at that." A firm nod punctuated the last statement. "Surely, this happens in other places, too?"

"Nay." Helena's shoulders hunched against a shiver.

"Mayhap Hakan has said as much." Mardred played idly with her keys. "This is what the king wants to abolish. The ninth year blot comes this year...ah, look—" Mardred waved her hand with a flourish. "—Hakan's farmstead."

Helena was glad for the change of subject. Mardred's brisk fingers pointed here and there.

"Hakan's longhouse. Not the typical longhouse of a chieftain. He is modest. Look." Mardred scurried ahead to a narrow home built lengthwise into a hill. Thick grass grew on the roof. "And, he has a barn almost as large as his longhouse."

"Over there is the entrance to the thralls' longhouse. And, there..." Mardred turned a quick glance to make sure Helena followed. "...that smaller door leading into the slope? That is the root cellar, and beyond...the weaver's shed." Cocking her head, Mardred asked, "Do you weave?"

"Aye, Mardred, much better than I cook."

Mardred laughed heartily. "Then let's poke about and see what we find."

Clutching the rings chained to her waist, Mardred paused. Her gaze measured Helena, a narrowing of the eyes before she sighed and passed the clanking ring to Helena. "I may as well give these to you. You are as close to the lady of the house as Hakan will have."

Entering the longhouse, the women met clouds of dust. Mardred sputtered and coughed. "I'll leave you to look around while I set the men to work."

Helena batted thick air and waited for her eyes to adjust to dim, dusty light. She rolled up animal skins covering each window and opened the shutters to let sunlight bathe the room.

Two hearths, one in the floor and another built into the wall, overflowed with ash. Chests were stacked near a rough table and benches. A large bed dominated the far end. One heavy, ornately carved chair sat in the middle, a lonely throne. Cobwebs hung from wall pegs and shields. A few spears dotted the walls, all caked with dust.

"You have your work cut out for you." Mardred entered, followed by the men carrying chests.

Helena dove into the distracting work, dusting and washing. She hung dried herbs, scenting the air pleasantly. With the keys in her possession, Helena tested each chest's lock. Treasures ranged from sturdy pelts to dried spices, flat pans and more bronze-banded buckets in need of polishing.

In one chest, she found a heavy green glass smoother for flattening seams. Who would think the fierce Norse so vain about their clothes?

"Look at this, Helena." Mardred cooed as she unfolded linen thick as a cloud from an open chest.

"What is it?"

"Eider down bedding."

Mardred buried her face in the softness. Helena found more down-stuffed pillows and set them on the bed. Both women admired the linen luxury.

Mardred clucked her tongue and said in gossipy tone, "Astrid will be full of envy." She gave a satisfied "humph" and sank into the rich bedding. "I envy *you* this luxury."

A bolt shot through Helena. *She thinks I will sleep there?*

Mardred closed her eyes, swishing her arms across the linen's softness. "You won't want to rise on cold winter morns."

Helena busied herself folding cloths. "Who is Astrid?"

Mardred hitched up on both elbows.

"Fairest woman in all of Svea, and a grasping witch. Years she was married to my brother. Then one day she was not." Mardred shrugged, as if this were commonplace.

Helena folded another linen and watched the Norsewoman trace circles in the down cover. Silence was the best enticement to loosen Mardred's tongue.

"A woman calls witnesses to her home to divorce her husband. She announces three times that they are no longer married, first at the lintel and then by the bed. Our custom is, young children stay with their mother, and boys go with their father when they're older."

She warmed to the topic and wagged a finger at Helena.

"This is what plagues my brother... causes his head ailments. He wants much to have his son. But Astrid knows that when Erik goes with Hakan, the gold will stop. So, she delays and asks for more of *this and that*—" Mardred flopped her hand back and forth, mimicking a childish voice. "—as a condition to release the boy permanently."

Mardred's eyes took on a sage light as her arm swept a wide arc over the longhouse.

"All this is yours to care for and oversee. My work is done, but you have much ahead of you. Come bid me farewell." Mardred stretched from the bed and headed toward the door. "You can explore my brother's many hidden treasures later." Mardred winked. "He has many surprises for the one who takes the time to look."

7

Helena tested a key on a small chest blanketed with dust. Rusted hinges creaked as she raised the lid and found shiny silver ingots the size of a man's fingers. How long had this chest sat, forgotten? Another chest held two richly jeweled chalices fit for a king. In this same chest, someone had wrapped a boy's tunic around child-sized ice skates, as if these were just as valued. She turned the chipped elk bone skates over in her hands.

Erik's.

A rough carving of a horse in wood, the work of a child, completed the cherished trove.

What manner of man lives by his sword, yet keeps tender remembrances of a little boy?

Her favorite find was a harp, a close replica to one she had played at home. Stroking the strings soothed her. Every spare moment, Helena strummed her idle pleasure. Music held memories of home.

Helena loved fixing the longhouse with no one to gainsay her. Wiping her hands down the front of her apron, she took in the glorious day. The sun shined bright, the air smelled of fresh pine boughs, and the grass beckoned like a soft carpet.

Gamle and Selig worked the barn and fields. Both men had served Hakan and Mardred for years. Gentle in demeanor, they enjoyed Helena's music while at their labor. She climbed atop the longhouse and sat over the lintel, dangling her legs over the edge. She closed her eyes, and her fingers strummed soothing notes of home. One Frankish melody after another floated through the air.

...

Hakan, as bone weary and dirt-covered as Agnar, passed by the rune stone that marked his farmstead. His body ached and his head pounded. He'd sleep on molded fodder and be glad.

The sight that greeted him promised nothing of moldy hay.

Someone worked a plow in one field. Rich, black earth churned into neat rows. His barn's lintel carvings shined with a new coat of red, blue, and yellow on the weathered doorway. Docile beasts nipped at flowing grass in a newly fenced meadow. He had wandered into a dreamland, drawn by hypnotic sounds of a glossy haired siren atop his roof.

That siren's long legs swung from her perch above his door, her dark braid coiling at her hip. Agnar's hoof clomped the earth, her reverie broken. Pain knocked at Hakan's head and...

His Frankish thrall?

She scrambled to her feet, her mouth rounding as she stared back at him.

"Lord Hakan, you are home." She scurried across the roof and into the yard.

Hakan slid from his horse, wincing as his feet touched ground. Gamle raced from the barn and took Agnar. Hakan rubbed his temples as he gave another quick survey of his land, but grimaced anew when daylight pierced like shards of iron to his head. His stomach swirled from the pain. The rooftop siren, wide-eyed and clutching a harp, approached him with keys jingling from her waist.

"Welcome home, my lord. I didn't know you'd be back so soon."

He squinted at her. "My bed."

"Come, all has been made ready." Her voice was breathy and low.

He followed the sounds of soft, jingling keys to his longhouse, and he met pleasant aromas. Stew simmered in a pot. Flat bread browned in a pan. On his table, wooden bowls heaped high with wild berries. Then, he scanned the walls.

"Pine boughs on my shields?" If his head didn't hurt so bad, he'd laugh.

"They freshen the air." His thrall smiled as she moved to the hearth.

He remembered the longhouse before—bare and dusty. Now, hard-earned luxuries, objects of long ago trades, pieces he had forgotten he owned, were on display. Someone had been busy, very busy, nosing through his things. Hakan rubbed his forehead. Tension overpowered anger at his thrall's prying. He needed his bed and her gone.

"Your head ailment?" Helena asked, as she removed the bread from the fire. "Mardred told me about them."

He grunted, sure that Mardred had given his thrall an earful. Hakan removed *Solace* from his back, the iron clattering on the table. With pounding head and sore limbs, his bed drew him like lodestone. He stretched across clean linens and able hands moved over his calves, untying and removing his boots.

"Does the pain fill all of your head? Or just behind the eyes?" his thrall asked in hushed tones.

"Starts behind my eyes and moves over my head." Waving a hand at the window, he groaned, "The light..."

He draped his forearm over his eyes, blotting out daggers of brightness. His thrall's footsteps pattered on the earthen floor. Heavy wood shutters scraped shut, and welcome darkness came. His hand flopped onto the cool linen coverlet.

The bed dipped from the weight of someone next to him. His thrall's soft hand pressed his forehead and slid to his cheek.

"Leave me," he growled.

The cool hand withdrew, but she did not. He winced as more sharp pains shot through his head and receded. He needed her gone. Sometimes things turned ugly...he turned ugly.

"Best you leave me. I can be...unpleasant," he rasped.

A rustle of cloth on cloth, then the warmth of her frame drew near.

"My lord," she whispered. "Is the pain *only* behind your eyes? Or has it begun to move?"

"There's a harpy in my head who's unsheathed her claws. By Odin, why the questions? Leave me." But his words had no bite. He was weak as a lamb.

"I can help you."

He tilted his head and squinted at the maid through his lashes. The move roiled his stomach worse than churning seas.

"My father was...*is* an apothecary," she said. "There's a remedy, ergot, a spur that grows on certain grains. I saw it here when I cleaned your root cellar. Ergot cures head ailments."

Hakan rubbed the heels of his hands across his forehead. "Thor's hammer knocks my skull. If you've a healing potion, *get it.*"

His head ailments marched with vengeance once the ache moved behind his eyes.

"My lord, the ergot can also be a dangerous remedy. Mad grain, we call it. The cure can be worse than the ailment."

"Aye?"

"Your arms and legs might burn from within, or you'll imagine seeing things. 'Tis not *so* bad. But...you could lose a limb, go mad, or—" He heard her suck in her breath. "—death. But, this is only if the quantity is incorrect." She

70

touched his shoulder. "I would use only the smallest amount."

"You plan to kill me?" He asked, opening one eyelid.

Terrible pain, cramping, and the need to retch gripped him. "Get your potion," he rasped.

Footsteps left the longhouse. Keeping his head still, the agony eased. Mayhap he should bear through it as he always did and sleep it off. 'Twas a dangerous idea to trust his pretty thrall. Her welcome today was friendly enough. If she poisoned him, she must know his death would not mean freedom...'twould mean her own end.

What had she said? Too much, and he died. Too little, and he lost a limb.

Ah, the havoc one woman could render. Sweat pricked his forehead and trickled down the side of his face. He ought to stop grousing at her; he was at her tender mercy. Under him the bed dipped, the frame creaked, and in the shadowed haze, a soft hand touched his shoulder.

"My lord, open your mouth and swallow."

A pasty lump slid over his lip with little effort.

"We'll know the potency soon." Her whisper hovered near his ear.

A cool cloth stroked his brow. He waited in darkness, his breath slow. Hakan couldn't fathom time or space, save the pain in his head and the roil in his stomach, an ugly twin to his head ailments.

"Do you feel heat in your limbs? Does the pain ease?"

The voice floating in the dark spoke to him. His Frankish thrall. His belly churned less. Heavy drowse seeped into his frame from head to toe.

"The pain lessens," he mumbled, keeping his eyes shut. "My legs...tired."

"Good." A cloth gently swiped his cheek and neck. "Mardred says these head ailments happen after you see your former wife. That they're caused by guilt and anger."

"Mardred talks too much," he groused, shifting on the cool linen eiderdown. His head and limbs numbed as after

71

drinking a pleasant elixir. "Too forward. Thrall...should know her place."

He tried to smile. Hakan opened one eyelid a slit, but Helena was a hazy nymph at his side.

"Forgive me," the nymph whispered as she began to remove herself.

He grabbed her wrist, not wanting to lose her closeness. "Stay..."

"Such kindness for one in need of *my* help," she said, tart-tongued.

He chuckled softly. "Deserve that." Hakan kept his eyes closed, but his grip on her slackened. "Please stay. My head...improves."

"Harp music is a soothing balm for head ailments such as yours. Would you like me to play?"

"Aye, play for me."

Soothing music floated, as much an elixir as sleep's drugging potion curling over him. The bewitching thrall surprised him. What other talents did she offer?

...

Helena awoke to the acrid odor of burning meat. The harp pressed her chest and gouged the hard stone in her neck pouch.

A steady pulse of breath broke the silence. Lord Hakan slept. She wiped sleepiness from her eyes and, uncurling from the great chair, let her vision adjust to the dim interior. Quickly, she removed the stew pot outside the door. Gamle had kindly left an earthen pitcher full of creamy milk on the doorstep. She lit soapstone lamps inside and prepared the meager cheese and bread.

There will be no fine white linen and glass or slow-roasted pork as befits a chieftain's homecoming.

Helena plucked Selig's tunic from the mending basket. Back and forth went the rhythm of her stitches, but her eyes flicked to the bed, studying Lord Hakan in the half-light.

He is nothing like my betrothed.

Guerin, soft and scholarly, stood about her height, while Lord Hakan towered over her, his massive shoulders and body hard as stone. Guerin's long tunics slumped and wrinkled about his frame. This man stretched out before her wore a long sleeveless leather jerkin to his knees with no trousers. His legs, long and well-muscled, caught her gaze. Coin-sized scars whitened his knees and dark slashes marked sun-browned legs. The bed creaked when his arm flopped. She jumped, and felt a flush rising.

She rolled her eyes and thought of Sestra. "I'm turning into her."

...

Hakan awoke with a powerful need to quench his thirst. He scrubbed both hands across his face and sat upright. The Frankish thrall glanced up from her sewing. A hint of charred food filled his nostrils.

"Have you burned my homecoming feast?"

"My lord, I thought you'd sleep through the night." She set the shirt in a basket and rose from the chair. "Are you feeling well?"

"Aye." He rubbed a whiskered cheek and grinned. "Your potion worked miracles."

"'Tis a powerful remedy."

"You haven't poisoned me." Hakan flexed arms and legs, inspecting them. "I have my limbs."

She stiffened visibly. "I would not harm another, especially someone weak. I am a merciful woman."

"Unlike we Norse, you mean?" The bed creaked as he stood up. "Mercy," he snorted. "A rare trait among your sex."

Hakan removed his warrior's belt and dropped it on the bed. Helena motioned to the table, but her dark blue eyes snapped with rebellion.

"Your food."

He strode to the table and dipped his hands in a bucket, washing away traveler's dust. His thrall stood attendance, but her eyes held the same hawkish stare that had pierced him on the ship. He wanted things to go better with her.

"I insulted you, when you have done me a kindness." He slid over the bench and waved a hand over the table. "Will you sit with me?"

'Twas his best effort at an apology—she'd get no more. She hesitated. He'd not force her, but both heard her stomach growl and saw her cheeks turn pink.

"*Please.*" Hakan smiled as he removed a cloth covering a bowl of cheese. "You cannot deny your hunger."

The maid's shoulders eased their stiffness and she slid onto the opposite bench. Good. She set a ripe berry cautiously to her lips, watching him with wary eyes.

"Why didn't you eat?" Hakan tore into the bread and offered her the inner, soft portion.

"Mardred said 'tis a lack of respect to begin without you." She accepted the bread. "Remember, I was not born to this."

"You would go hungry with food here?" His hands swept over the table. "I'd wager the men have eaten." He smiled, shaking his head. "Mine is not a royal house. Do what I ask of you and show respect ...otherwise live as you see best on my farmstead."

"Only within the farmstead?" She picked up an earthen pitcher.

"Where else would you go?" He scooped a handful of berries into his mouth.

"Home," she said easily as golden ale poured from the pitcher into his drinking horn. "When you were gone, I saved Katla's life. Such an act must be worthy of reward. The reward of my freedom?"

He raised the horn in salute. "Saving Katla's life was more than worthy of reward. But, here you stay." He studied her carefully. "I hope you'd save the maid's life without thought of reward, because you are a...merciful woman."

Helena blushed, he was certain, to have her own words repeated.

"I was taught to bear kindness for all." His thrall's chin tipped high. "Katla and Aud have been good to me." Her hands lifted in appeal. "You must know I want to return home. Don't most thralls wish this?"

"This is your home now." He spoke with the same hardness he used with his men. "You don't know me well, but in time, you'll find me fair and just." He pulled a hunk of soft cheese from the bowl and smiled to soften the sting of his edict. "I'm thankful for your remedy today. How could I let go of a thrall with such a skill?"

Her mouth pulled a taut line and she picked at her bread and cheese. "What I thought would set me free, chains me."

"You don't look like a chained woman."

He said the words as encouragement, but a pang of guilt touched him. Saving Katla was worthy of great reward amongst his men. Such bravery was expected of stalwart men, but facing him now was no trained warrior.

She was as fair as any Norsewoman. Red embroidery decorated her loose neckline—the standard of freewomen, not thralls. The neckline drew his eye to lush womanly swells...curves his hands itched to explore. He drank in her every move, following subtle shifts of her body in the fine linen tunic and liking the way the cloth clung to her.

They ate in silence and Helena poured more ale into his drinking horn. Her long, chestnut braid fell forward and she tossed the dark rope past her shoulder. Her slender arms were lightly golden from the sun. Was the skin lighter beneath the armband that marked her as his? Would her skin feel as fine as Abbasid silk if he touched her? Her cheek had healed well; a dark pink line crescented her cheek. Even that strip of skin needed exploring

Hakan rubbed both hands through his unruly hair. He needed a good dunk in the cold river to rid himself of these thoughts. There were plenty of willing women to sate baser needs. He didn't dally with thralls—a legacy King Olof had fostered in his youth. Many chieftains did, putting their peaceful homes in peril. He watched Helena leave the table in silence and open a shutter to stare at the sky.

"Do you like our Norse skies?" Hakan asked, aware of her hands twirling a loose tendril falling across her face.

"I do," she said with a soft, dreamy lilt. "The sun doesn't set...it hides beyond that horizon." She lifted a hand, tracing the outline of distant trees. "Trees darken against the sky's purples and blues. 'Tis my favorite time."

The moment, oddly intimate, played on him. He recalled the day he had purchased her from the Danes. Aye, that strange sense, a curling vine, stretched and grew within his chest. When Helena went to extinguish the soapstone lamps, the spell was gone.

"If you don't need me, Lord Hakan, I'll sleep now."

Hakan wanted the spell, the pleasant connection to return.

"Are you tired?" He flipped open an unlocked chest near the bed and pulled out a wooden board and small leather bag.

He plunked the game on the table and waved his hand over the pieces.

"Backgammon?"

"'Tis a game? I do not know this backgammon." Her pink lips pressed together.

"Come." He motioned for her to sit opposite him. "We Norse have many pastimes to entertain us when work is done. I'll teach you," he coaxed. "One friendly game and you'll see we're not so different here."

She returned his grin and moved to the table.

Hakan set the pieces on the board. "You can speak to me of your home."

The way his thrall's eyes softened, Hakan guessed she found him a little less the barbarian. He *would* sway her from this discontent. She *would* accept her new home.

8

Lolling against a birch tree, Hakan followed the steady movement of warp and weft. Helena created a swath of wool from the creaking loom, a castoff of Mardred's that he had moved from the pit house into shade. Many days she worked the wooden structure with the talent of a harpist, weaving cloth the way a musician wove songs.

"You'll make me a very rich man." Hakan smiled.

"You are a rich man already." Helena's fingers strummed steady movement across tight strings. "Wait for the next flax harvest. My fine linen weaves will amaze you."

"Amaze me?" His whittler's knife slid down the wood piece he shaped.

"You'll be fat with profits. Last season, my linens gained some fame in Paris," she said with pride. "The secret is not to boil the flax for very long. Too long and you ruin the shine. Truly, I love working with cloth."

"I noticed." Hakan chuckled to himself, recalling the ship.

"Oh?" Her eyebrows arched as her hands kept working.

"On the ship," he added. "The mending. What I meant as punishment was your pleasure. You're as happy to have needle and thread in hand as weaving." He wiped the knife's edge in the grass.

Hakan rested his elbow on a hitched knee. He was impressed with her knowledge. Never before had he cared about such things as turning flax into linen, boiling wool and the like, but with Helena, 'twas an art form. She produced beautiful cloths of softest quality that made Mardred rave, and then his clever thrall made the sturdiest wools, sail cloths fit for a king's ship. He didn't gainsay her requests. Last week he had labored at *her* bidding, hauling great bales of wool.

She turned the greasy mass into sails. King Olof had charged him to replace a lost Knorr ship, a casualty of the rebellion at Aland. Under Helena's capable hands, the dirty wool had turned into fine sails.

Those sturdy cloths stretched across one green meadow, bright stripes of color, drying in the sun. Sails, natural weaves and vibrant reds, puffed and billowed, catching air, but large rocks pinned them. He smiled to himself and slid his knife over the smooth birch stick in his hand. Helena was a maid of many talents.

"You smile because you know I'm right." She crowed her victory. "You see the results with those sails and know I'll not disappoint."

Nothing about her disappointed him. In truth, he never thought a woman could stir his interest again or be so easy to wile away the day.

"Nay, I smile because a once mighty chieftain has been reduced to bowing and scraping to his thrall's whims. But, I'm grateful."

He meant to tease, but the counter-weights ceased clacking. She studied him behind the loom's warp strings.

"How grateful?"

"Enough to share the spoils." His knife slowed. "Trade some for yourself."

"Truly?" Her face lit at the offer.

"Aye, if the quality is of such renown, perhaps you can get a house thrall for churning butter, making cheese and bread. I need one these days." He couldn't help the jest, wanting nothing more than to smooth matters with her.

She laughed and threw a skein of yarn at him. He deflected the skein, and the yarn rolled in the grass. Hakan turned again to the wood in his hands. The loom thinly masked her face, but he caught the way her fingers rested with the lightest touch at the tiny pouch she wore under her tunic.

"You've never told me the price for my freedom." She dipped her head a fraction and unbound hair slid past one shoulder. "But, if my weaves are well received, I would amass enough to trade for my freedom."

"Helena." A warning note threaded his voice.

"I wish to return home...you must know this...to return to the people I love." Her voice was little more than a whisper. She gripped the loom's frame as if she pleaded with him behind a dungeon's barred door.

"To your betrothed. The one who let the Danes steal you," he said, as the sting of her choice burned him.

Broken pottery shards, the loom's counter weights, clanked again. Her back was stiff, and she was closed to him. Hakan tossed his whittling to the ground. He would work the fields. At least flax was not so moody and mysterious as the wants of women.

"Unhappy with that?" Helena nodded at the discarded wood. The loom was a stringed veil, half-hiding her face.

Hakan's palms pressed the soil, poised to push him off the ground. But he met her blue gaze, and her distress hit him as hard as Sven's elbow jammed to the gut. A breeze ruffled Helena's unbound hair. Strands around her face had lightened from the summer sun.

"The carving...a spoon for you." His gruff voice downplayed the offering.

"Ah," she nodded. Her voice dropped to soft, soothing tones. "I noticed some small carvings...the chest that holds your chalices. Did you carve those?"

"Nay. Erik did."

"Your son."

He did not like this meekness, nor that he caused it. He wanted the maid who bested him in games and laughed at her meager cooking efforts.

"Aye." He paused. "Erik. He is eight winters now."

"I am sure he'll grow to manhood and be as fine a man as his father." Her direct gaze was followed by a tender plea. "Please. Don't go to the fields yet."

She called him a fine man. His heart swelled. And, she who had vexed him a moment ago, now comforted him. The tension in his arms eased as he settled back against the tree.

"A son must know his father. Erik sees little of me." Hakan's voice was flat. "The one thing I feared is happening. I grew to manhood without my father, and so will my son, if things don't change."

"You have said little about losing your father."

The loom forgotten, Helena hugged her legs to her chest, resting her chin on her knees. Old wounds lost some of their sharpness when he shared them with her. He was not as quick to keep the past in darkness.

"They died in a fire on our farmstead when I was eight. Mardred was already married to Halsten. They restored the farm, Skardsbok Gard, after the fire. The king took me in." Hakan raised one knee and rested his forearm there. "Olof raised me as if I were his own son. Gave me my first sword. Alas, Queen Estrid birthed Anund Jakob when I was fourteen. 'Twas time to go *a viking*. See the world."

Hakan stared at the slow-moving river that bordered his fields as visions of the past danced before him.

"I almost willed death to take me," he said, letting the dark past tumble into light of day. "Sven came to my aid. Many a time he saved my skull, and I his."

Helena's eyebrows knit together. "When did you have Erik?"

"After some years, I returned to Svea, a man of success. Sven and I decided to build our own long ship. I became chieftain, and he my second." He shrugged at this. "Plunder, trade...'twas all the same to us." Hakan grinned. "Mayhap I was chieftain because Sven would rather knock heads than use his own."

Her bold eyes sparkled and a smile curved her lips. A tiny bird swooped between them and pecked the ground. Hakan picked up the birch wood piece and knife again. For all of Helena's impulsiveness, she knew when to hold her tongue...when listening mattered. Too many maids chattered endlessly when quiet would do.

"One summer, the most beautiful maid in all Svea married me. And the next summer she was swollen with child, but all was not right."

A lump clogged his throat. Dust of the past stirred—retelling was not easy. Hakan drank long from the ladle in the water bucket beside him, then offered it to Helena.

"Nay." She rubbed her arms and one hand caught on her thrall's band. Her fingers traced the carving etched deep in silver. "We don't have to talk about this, Hakan."

"Better you hear it from me." He again picked up the unformed wooden spoon and knife. "I want Erik to live here. I'm surprised my meddling sister did not speak of this already."

Helena smiled. "Remember, I was learning how to cook at the same time. That kept her very busy."

He grinned and his knife slid across the birch wood. Fragile slivers curled under the blade, dropping to the ground. He was glad to have something in his hands. He would finish this and never speak of that time again.

"All was not well when Astrid's belly swelled with Erik," he said, his voice hoarse. "I was happy to have my own farmstead. But Astrid wanted me to take Mardred and Halsten's farm. By rights, Skardsbok Gard belonged to me, but after the fire, I didn't want to go back." His knife slid back and forth over the wood.

The small bird returned, picking up a wood shaving in his tiny beak and flying away. A breeze played with the fine, paler hairs that framed Helena's face. Her eyes were large blue sapphires shining for his benefit alone.

"What did you do?"

"I built the finest longhouse on the other side of Svea. 'Twas not enough. I bought thralls. Astrid did not have to lift a finger. I wanted to work the land like my father, but my being a farmer *shamed* her." The words tasted as bitter gall on his tongue. "She wanted a powerful chieftain...status in Svea."

He paused and stared at his now flourishing fields.

"I let her think I was more than I was, a failing of youth. Such was my need to impress her, to convince her to marry me instead of Gorm." At Gorm's name, the knife jammed the wood. "She chose me. Soon, she learned I gave equal share to all who served me, not keeping a chieftain's share. She railed at that." Hakan shook his head at the memory and flicked the chunk to the ground.

"I preferred the company of my men. Anything to bring peace. Mardred assured me some women don't do well carrying a babe in their belly. Best I go away and come back bearing gifts."

He and Helena exchanged smiles at Mardred's wisdom.

"That didn't work?" Helena asked, her chin still resting on her knee.

"Nay. Whatever I brought, she thirsted for more. I wanted to please her for giving me Erik." He smiled. "I wanted more sons and daughters. I was happiest to be with Erik, though all he did was drool on me." His joyous memory vanished. "By next summer, something was very wrong."

Small shavings of wood flew from his knife and his jaw clenched. "I am certain Astrid was not faithful. By rights I should have flayed her back, but I couldn't. The mother of my son would not be treated like an unfaithful..."

Bitterness spilled from him, but Hakan let the acrid poison disappear like mist. His frame eased, drained of the bottled anger.

"When I returned from one of my voyages, she had divorced me," he finished, but the flat words held no sting.

"Then what happened?"

Hakan shrugged. "A Norse woman gets half, the home and all that's in it. But I gave her everything: the thralls, livestock, all save my weapons and long ship. I wanted Erik to lack for nothing."

"And how did you come by this farmstead?"

"Olof," he said, a wry smile beginning to grow. "He thought I needed to live on *this* end of Svea."

"A wise king," she laughed. "But by the heavy dust I found, you spent little time here."

"When Astrid and I parted, we agreed Erik would come with me when he was older. 'Tis the Norse way." He rolled the whittling knife in his hand. "Now you know why I've come home."

"Mardred explained to me about the son living with his father when older. But why is Erik not with you? This is what plagues you, the reason for your head ailments." She waggled a finger at him. "Do not deny it."

"Aye," he acknowledged.

"And he's not with you now because..." her voice trailed, inviting him to finish.

"Because Astrid hides him from me." He stopped whittling. "I want him *before* having to take the problem before the assembly. She does that to goad me."

"Then, we must find a way for you and Erik to be together. Now."

Helena said the words with such resolve; her agreement was another unexpected pleasantness. He was about to say as much, when both heard a trotting horse. Sven rode past the farm's open gate and behind him, a dark-haired boy on the verge of manhood drove an ox cart. 'Twas Marc, Halsten's blacksmith.

Sven bellowed across the sunlit yard, "I leave you alone for a sennight and this is how you wile away the time? Sitting under a tree with a fair maid?"

Sven swung his leg over the horse's head and landed on both feet with a thud. "At least bring one out for me."

Hakan waved to a spot in the shade beside him. "Join me?"

Sven settled against a bale of wool and stretched his legs before him, crossing them at the ankles.

"Have you food to share with a weary traveler?" He grinned at Helena.

She wrinkled her freckled nose. "I might find something amongst my burnt offerings."

Hakan watched her departure, her gait long and easy. Sven also watched, and once Helena was inside the longhouse, he turned to Hakan.

"Astrid was greedy with the tribute furs. She took all the mink." He spat on the ground. "Gorm was nowhere in sight."

"As I expected," Hakan shrugged.

"He's hiding now that you're back." Sven's bushy brows lowered. "You're too good to her. She's nothing but—"

"Don't. Astrid is the mother of my son. Would you have me leave Erik wanting?"

"I hate to see you taken by a—" he stopped.

Hakan flashed a warning glare.

"A *viper*, such as she," Sven finished carefully.

Hakan plucked a long blade of grass. "I will have to go before the Althing."

"A public spectacle." Sven grimaced.

The subject dropped with the arrival of Helena, a tray in hand burdened with food and ale. Hakan jumped up to help Helena, taking the tray from her hands.

"Thank you, my lord."

"You should have called me. This is too much for you to carry."

Helena's eyes sparkled at him. "You've spoiled me. There will be no end of talk from Mardred when she hears how much you've labored for me."

The easy banter continued as she served the fare, pouring horns of ale for both men. Helena set the pitcher down and started to leave when Hakan called her back.

"Don't leave. Join us. You've worked hard this day. Rest with us."

Helena waved toward the fields and the laborers there. "But, the men—"

"Can wait. Please. Sit."

Settling on the grass, Helena nibbled fruit. Hakan, knowing her preference for water, passed the full ladle to her before settling back on the tree.

Sven's shrewd eyes beetled from Hakan and Helena. "I hate to interrupt your peace, but pressing problems bring me here."

"Of what?" Hakan cradled his horn between both hands.

"Have you not heard? More berserker attacks...closer to Uppsala."

Hakan tipped his head at Helena. "Helena and my nieces were attacked."

Sven stroked his beard and watched her thoughtfully.

"None survived the latest attacks. What happened?"

"I told Halsten and Mardred everything, as did Aud and Katla." She shook her head and crossed her arms against a phantom chill.

Sven leaned closer. "What do you remember?"

Helena's words sketched the details of the attack. Squeezing her arms, her hand traced the design on her armband, and she stared at the creatures emblazoned in silver.

"There is one thing...in all the upset..." She glanced at Sven and shook her head. "'Tis nothing, I'm sure."

"What is it?" Hakan asked.

"The berserker wore an armband."

Sven's dark eyes narrowed. "Do you remember the design?"

"A sea serpent." She squinted and looked at the ground. "With slashes throughout its body. Here." Her fingers scratched the design in dirt. "Like this."

Hakan absorbed the sketch: roughly Jutland Norse in style, an animal with rounded eyes and a serpentine body slashed with stripes. Helena drew talon-like claws gripping the ends of the S-shaped design. The final detail, that odd S, was familiar. Helena dusted off her hands.

"And, something else...an amber stone. Nay, two amber stones." She canted her head, as one does when recalling a hazy memory. "The stones made the serpent's eyes. One broke—"

"Are you sure *this* is what you saw?" Hakan asked, pointing to the design.

"Two pieces of amber? Serpent's eyes?" Sven leaned in close, almost menacing.

"Aye, I'm certain." Helena inched back. "Why?"

"You were scared." Sven frowned, his voice threading with doubt. "You've seen much since you came to Svea, many armbands."

"I saw what I saw," she snapped. "*This—*" She pointed at the serpent etched in the earth. "—was on the arm of the man who tried to kill me."

Hakan set a calming hand on her shoulder. "We believe you."

Sven's deep voice boomed. "'Tis strong proof. The attacks are the work of at least one chieftain. I must return to Uppsala and tell Olof."

"Because of the armband, you know this?" Helena's brows pressed together as she glanced from one man to the other. "A chieftain of Svea?"

Hakan nodded at Sven, then turned to Helena. "I need to speak with Sven alone."

She rose to her feet and dusted off her tunic. "Who would do this?"

Sven's eyes burned black. "Gorm."

9

H akan followed Helena's slender form as she moved through the yard. She hauled two buckets and bore the look of one distracted—looking but not seeing. What was on her mind? She stumbled on the path, and he started to get up, but Gamle rushed from the barn to carry the buckets for her.

"She's a thrall." Sven crossed his arms, warming to his gibe. "They're known to toil and labor…makes life easier for us."

Hakan glanced at Sven, but he was drawn to the maid laughing easily with the other thralls.

"What?" Sven chuckled. "You've nothing to say?"

"I want…" Hakan's words trailed off as his eyes tracked Helena. How could he explain what he failed to understand?

"You '*want*' what?"

Hakan glowered at his friend and refused to rise to the bait.

"You want her. And because Olof taught you *his* code of honor, you'll not touch her." Sven flicked an insect off his arm. "Just be done with it. Take her. Like an itch that needs scratching. She's *your* thrall."

"There are times I wonder what sits between your ears."

Sven shut his eyes and lifted his face to the sun. "You never danced attendance on Astrid. Not like this."

Snippets of years past flashed across his mind, all hazy and blurred.

"Skalds will weave a new tale. The great chieftain bows low before his thrall, and spurns every highborn Norse maid from Jutland to Trondheim." Sven chuckled at his own words. "But, unlike you, I cannot wile away the days with a fair maid."

They walked to the barn, but Sven's words nagged at him.

"I like Helena, aye. She serves me well. She lacks Astrid's cold nature, nor does she have Mardred's excessive need to talk," Hakan reasoned. "Like being with the men...only not."

"That's it. You look at her and see someone like me: big, hairy arms and a beard with bits of last night's stew." Sven rumbled with laughter, slapping Hakan's back. "To be sure, Hakan, next time we go to battle, feel free to carry my hammer. 'Tis much for me to carry."

Hakan punched Sven's shoulder and both laughed at the jest. The Erse thrall, Selig, led Sven's horse from the barn. Sven mounted his steed and the saddle creaked under him.

"When I return, be ready to practice for the Glima wrestling." Sven rubbed the shoulder Hakan punched, and his eyes lit with mock seriousness. "A feeble hit. Your farmer's ways have weakened you. And don't think that I'll spare your pretty face for any maid." Sven tipped his head toward the fields. "No matter how pleasant the maid may be."

Helena trudged again up the path, the buckets balanced easily in her grip.

Sven cupped his hands and called out to her. "Farewell, Helena. Take care of my friend. See that he is well-rested."

Her head tipped as she yelled across the distance, "Farewell, Sven."

The pleasant grin faded from Sven's features, replaced with bear-like gruffness. "I will speak to the king about the berserker's armband...ask around Uppsala, too."

Hakan slapped Sven's mount. "Go quickly."

Sven kicked the horse into a gallop, stirring clouds of dust and air.

Hakan watched Sven disappear past the gate and kept his feet planted. He would not rush to carry the buckets for her. Mayhap he *was* too easy on her. Sven's jest about dancing attendance nettled him. But the maid came to stand beside Hakan, placing both buckets on the ground. A faint sheen covered her freckled nose.

"What did he mean about being well-rested?"

One look at her dark blue eyes and Hakan's resolve melted. Wisps of hair blew around her face as they always did by mid-day, whether her hair was braided or unbound. They played about her cheeks now. Her warm friendly manner enticed him.

"Hakan?" Her arched eyebrows pressed together when he failed to answer.

He liked the familiar way she said his name, as one well known. He was simply Hakan to her. His hand reached up to a lock of hair, running the silk between his fingers. That night on the ship, the first time he touched her hair, floated across his mind.

"Aye?" He tucked the strands behind her ear. One finger skimmed the inner curve of her ear, tracing the softness of her plump lobe.

Helena's lips parted. Her dark blue eyes glowed under fluttering, thick lashes as a blush pinked her cheeks. The past week there had been accidental touches, times brushing close. But this was no accident. His touch had purpose.

Helena swallowed hard. Was she as spellbound as he? Closing her eyes, she tilted her face into his palm like a cat rubbing into a caress. Benumbed by the softness of her skin, Hakan stroked her neck...the edge of her tunic neckline, the long delicate collarbone. His fingers stopped at the leather thong she always wore and slid beneath it.

Helena stepped back, her eyes rounding.

"Please." Her voice was breathy and low. She shook her head as if to knock away the alluring moment.

Hakan lifted his hand to touch her, but her hands shielded her.

"Don't." She tilted her head away from him.

"What's this?"

Her eyes implored him. Hakan warred within himself. Never had he found such delight and ease with a maid. Yet, Sven's words nettled him, hanging in the back of his brain. Mayhap, he made too much of this ease between them, and she was an itch to be scratched.

"My lord," she said, smoothing her palms down the front of her tunic. "I have something of great importance to discuss."

"Aye."

Helena hooked her fingers under the leather necklace and pulled a worn pouch from her tunic.

"Inside this pouch is a stone...my dowry," her voice faltered. "My father saved the life of a wealthy merchant passing through our town. In his gratitude, he gave my father this—" She tipped the pouch upside down and a necklace dropped into her hand. "—and my father gave it to me as dowry, so that I would be acceptable to Guerin and his family."

She grabbed his hand and set the simple pendant in his palm. Hakan splayed his fingers, judging the gold link chain and rough red stone. The jewelry had middling value. Her eyes on him were full of hope.

"I couldn't let the Danes take it. I...I had expected to be rescued and return home." She motioned to the necklace. "If I returned home without it, I'd have no dowry."

"And your Guerin would not marry you." Hakan kept his tone even.

"'Tis our way." Helena's face tightened. "Sestra told me to trade it for my freedom on the ship, but I couldn't part with it then." Her shoulders straightened. "I think Guerin would have me with or without a dowry."

"There was a question in your mind about that?" Hakan scoffed and glanced away. "Your betrothed. The one who let raiders take you...who failed to rescue you."

"I know what you think of him." She swallowed and raised a hand in entreaty. "Surely you understand someone wanting to go home?"

"Because you are so desperate to leave this place," he said, his voice blade-sharp and mocking. "Because I treat you poorly."

Helena's lashes fluttered, and she studied the necklace in his hand. She tipped her head at the red-eyed dragon on his silver armband and pressed on with stiff persuasion.

"I noticed you have similar stones...your sword, your armband." She inhaled as one does before making a risky request. "I would trade this for my freedom."

Hakan's eyes narrowed. A savage force rose in his chest, and some of it spewed from him like the brute she called him on the ship.

"By all rights, this is mine." His fingers curled around the chain. "When I bought you, I can claim all that was on your person."

"You could trade it for other thralls to replace me," she wailed.

"Is that what you think? That I trade people without a care?" His voice was harsh and graveled.

"Isn't that the Norse way?"

Her bitter, wrenching question struck a chord, as if dousing him with icy water. Her vulnerable blue stare and quivering chin thawed something inside him, playing on him. Nay, this wasn't about thralls who come and go. He believed, or wanted to believe, that part of her found the same joy and ease with him as he did with her. Was it not shared between them?

92

"'Tis the Norse way for a master to use his thralls as he sees fit." His bold gaze traced her body. "You've not been so abused. Nay, you've been treated very well. Would you not agree?"

He was a fool, wanting to strike back at the unknowing hurt she rendered. The maid cringed at his rudeness.

"Aye, you treat me well, my lord."

He saw wetness on her lashes. She turned her face to the fields, and another piece of the riddle that made Helena fell into place.

Hakan cupped her chin. His thumb stroked her scarred jaw. "Your pouch, the stone is the reason for this. Magnuson said as much."

She nodded, sniffling and swiping at tears that rolled down her cheeks.

His thumb brushed a tender stroke over her cheek's curving pink scar. "The stone almost cost you your life. Why?"

Hakan, with great tenderness, stroked her face. The salve had done its work: smooth, touchable skin remained. But the salve only healed skin deep wounds. Some wounds lurked deeper than the Dane's cut. What ached beneath the surface? More fat tears rolled down her cheeks.

"I am a peasant maid." Her voice quivered. "When Guerin wanted me, I felt…" Helena sniffed and chewed her lower lip. "I was suddenly important. A woman of value. Without it…"

Her vulnerable admission was a tender spot for her. Couldn't she see her worth was higher than any stone?

His thumbs wiped away her tears. "Keep the pendant. It came at a great price. Wear it for all to see."

Hakan took her hand in his and set the necklace in her palm. He curled her fingers over jewel and chain.

"Aye, Helena, the stone could buy more thralls. But 'tis metal and stone. They do nothing for me."

Her lashes, spiked with wetness, fluttered at him. Bewilderment writ on her face, he soothed his voice as if calming a babe.

He shook his head. "I'll not trade you for that."

"I don't understand." Her eyebrows knit together.

How could he explain what he didn't fully understand? He was on shaky ground. From the corner of his eye, part of a red sail caught a strong breeze and fluttered. Selig replaced the rocks that tamped down the sail before the whole cloth blew free. The vibrant red waved at him, a banner by which he could escape explaining why he would not let her go. Hakan waved his arm at the sails drying in the meadow.

"Look what you've accomplished in so short a time. You promised me great talent weaving fine linens...to expand my wealth." Hakan's arms folded across his chest. "Strong sails for my ships. This I understand." Tilting his hand toward the jewelry in her own, the corners of his mouth turned down. "Stones do nothing for me."

A thousand glittering stones couldn't equal her worth. He stared into the depths of her blue eyes and called himself a coward for not admitting this to her.

Helena sniffed again and clutched the pendant, returning it to the leather pouch. "Is there no custom? No means to gain my freedom?" she asked, her voice hoarse with emotion.

Hakan sighed. "There are ways."

"Mardred told me a thrall can earn her freedom after some years of service. Is this true?"

"Aye." His arms stayed crossed, unmoving. He'd give no more.

"Then, may I strike such an agreement with you?"

"Such as?"

"I want to earn my freedom." Her eyes pleaded with him.

Hakan shifted his stance, cagey about giving an inch. His neck and shoulders knotted.

True, many a valuable thrall gained freedom after years of service. Most stayed.

"Serve me well for seven years, Helena, and you'll be a freewoman."

"The time cannot be shortened?" She clasped her hands together. "Seven years," she groaned. "So long."

"I will not be swayed on this."

She canted her head at him, doubt clouding her features. "But, will you keep your word, my lord?"

"What makes you doubt me? The way I've mistreated you?"

Helena flinched at his sarcasm. She was not satisfied. Seven years must feel like one hundred to her. Her fingers plucked at her apron, and she kept silent. A stab, like a hot brand, hit him. This was rejection. An arm's length from her, Hakan shut himself away as if in a distant fortress. "I require your respect. For seven years."

Pain flashed from her eyes. She dabbed at their corners and nodded.

Hakan needed to move. He needed something to ease the itch that plagued him. He needed to keep a good distance from her. His ax leaned against the barn. He grabbed it and swung the heavy tool over his shoulder.

"I have to clear some trees," he announced. The field did need widening, and he needed wood.

The tree line would keep him a safe distance from her, yet he could keep an eye on the longhouse. And the loom where she would sit. Hakan walked to the edge of the yard and something pushed him to needle her.

"I expect fresh bread at my table tonight. See to it."

Her eyebrows shot up at his harsh command. He hadn't spoken to her that way since the journey to Svea. Her body visibly bristled at his tone. He waited, and Helena bowed her head in exaggerated servitude. Hakan whistled on his way to chop wood, pleased at gaining the upper hand.

Much could happen in seven years.

10

"Ahhhh," Hakan's painful grunts pleased her.

"What? Is the pressure not to your liking?" Helena's oil-slicked hands pounded his bare back.

Three days of chopping trees from sunrise to twilight had taken a toll on Hakan's frame. He groaned with sore muscles from labor so different than his warrior's sword play. Three evenings he walked into the longhouse after a douse in the icy river. Three evenings he shoveled food into his mouth and dragged his aching body to his bed. Nary a word was said between them.

Helena could have banged every pot and he would have slept. And she was vexed enough with the lout to try.

"Uh." Hakan groaned into the bearskin rug. Helena smacked meaty shoulders, bearing down with all her weight.

Three days she vented her small rebellions: blackened bread crusts, over-salted stew, his bed left unmade, meals served late, and of course her favorite...cool silence. If she made headway with him, he showed no sign: Hakan was stolid and unmoved.

This eve he had grimaced as he lowered his bulk onto the bench. His calloused hands rubbed his neck, and a pang of mercy made her brush aside his hair and touch the spot. The tender remedy, a tiny peace offering, was the first they had spoken since his abrupt refusal of her pendant. Now, with Hakan's jerkin lowered to his waist, Helena leaned over wide-set shoulders, smashing her churlishness into unyielding brawn.

"I warned that pain comes before the pleasure with this cure, my lord."

Angling his head, Hakan spewed words as she thumped his back. "You...oohf..."

Thump.

"...need...not..."

Thump.

"...work all thhh—"

Thump.

"—ache from my back..."

Thump.

"...at once...ahhh." Another groan muffled in the pelt.

"But, I must." She pressed the heel of her hand into a difficult knot. The flesh, glistening with oil, smoothed under her hands. "'Tis necessary to remove the soreness of your labors."

He wheezed as her fingers kneaded his neck and shoulders, the knots lessening little by little under her skilled hands. Though still angered, there was certain pleasure in touching him.

"Ohhhh, that's perfect." Hakan crowed his pleasure. "Aye, Aye... right there."

Her fingers pressed into the bulging muscles, hard and tense from labor.

"Your hands work magic on my aching back."

Helena glared at the back of his head, certain he toyed with her, for her hands were none too gentle.

"I don't know why you insist on hauling logs when there are horses and *thralls* to do such work," she said, slipping in the barb. "Let your chattel build that longhouse."

"Would you have the new thralls sleeping and eating in here?" Hakan looked at her from the corner of his eye. "Interrupting our *pleasant* evenings?"

He smirked at her before burying his face in the heavy pelt. Helena rose to her knees and bore down with all her might. Halsten had brought four new thralls to the farmstead. They slumbered in the barn until another building for thralls was constructed. Helena crouched lower.

"I don't know why that matters, my lord." She gasped the words as she strained over him. "I'm no different than those thralls. I should sleep in that longhouse with the other slaves."

"Back to that again? I thought we settled this. Seven years and you're free." Rising on an elbow, he slanted a wicked grin over his shoulder. "Mayhap I should increase the time? What Norseman would deny himself the pleasure of good service like this?"

Helena pressed his shoulder with all her weight; she barely nudged him. His blonde hair fell about his face. Hakan laughed heartily and resettled himself on the pelt. Yet, the Norseman must have known she paid a small price in pride to humble herself and be the first to speak. Nay, even more to render care to his aching muscles.

"Peace, Helena, peace."

Her hands slowed, making smaller circles along his spine.

"Aye, peace." She sighed. "You'll like this better."

Her fingers splayed from his spine across his ribs. Back and forth. He was at her mercy in so many ways. She ran the place, ordering everything as Mardred did her own farm. What irked her was that she was no closer to freedom.

Helena stroked bronzed skin over thick brawn and long sinews. He was an unmoving wall in both character and flesh, but she reveled in the feel of him under her hands. For all his impassive silence, she was certain he missed their ease, especially in the evenings. She brushed the hair from his nape. The light touch brought a wave of gooseflesh across his back. Hakan's shoulders flexed under her fingers.

"You... must be glad not to cook anymore. Olga will ease your burdens." Strain edged his voice.

Her hands hovered over him. Hakan wanted to pacify her. The notion sat well with her.

"Aye, I'm glad to have her here."

Olga, an older Rusk woman, bent her sturdy arms to many tasks on the farmstead, freeing Helena to weave and experiment with dyes for fabrics. Helena looked after Hakan's longhouse and his needs, while Olga cooked for the others. The Rusk woman even made the butter and cheese and cultivated the vegetable garden that Helena left sorely neglected.

Hakan interrupted her reverie. "Did you learn this from your father as well?"

"Hmmm," she hummed, recalling home. "Nay, a band of Jews came through our village. They travelled with an old man from the far eastern lands of the Khazars. He knew much about the rhythms of the body. He and my father spent hours trading knowledge. I listened and learned."

She poured oil into her palm. "He believed many of the body's ailments can be found in sections here." She scratched small circles around the bones of his spine. "One man, bent with pain, came to see us. The old man from the east made small ink dots on his skin, then tapped needles into the dots. This made the pain go away."

"In Byzantium, I remember hearing of—."

Someone pounded on the longhouse door.

"Father? Are you there?"

Hakan sprung from the bearskin and slipped his arms into his leather jerkin. He ran to the lintel, but the door burst open. A flash of white-blonde hair and a boyish, summer-browned face launched at Hakan.

Erik.

His thin arms encircled his father, but when he pulled away, dark blue eyes idolized the great Norseman before him.

"Father..." He cried, sniffing and gulping air.

99

Hakan's arms closed, surrounding the boy. Dropping to one knee, Hakan kissed the top of Erik's head.

"How did you get here?" The snort of the horse outside the door answered that question. "Where have you been?"

"I had to run away, Father. She says she'll never let me come to you." Erik wiped his tears on the shoulder of his tunic. "Mother used to say, 'someday, someday...'" His voice rose to an excited pitch. "But I know she means *forever*." He wailed his discontent.

Helena read the strickening emotions that played across Hakan's face. This was what he wanted. He spoke so often of having Erik by his side, the completeness of this. Hakan had told her of the hole that gaped inside him, had hinted at his fears that his son would grow up fatherless just as he had. And now the small arms of the son gripped the father, as if never to let go.

After the sobs subsided, Hakan turned to Helena. She nodded and moved on silent feet, setting the table. Olga's spicy cider would please the boy. Muffled sobs filled the longhouse. Hakan's large hand stroked the smaller blonde head. Helena touched Hakan's shoulder, gesturing to the table. Grabbing a soapstone lamp, she closed the door on her way out to care for the horse nuzzling grass.

They will need privacy.

Father and son needed much time together. Tethering the horse to one of the inner posts, Helena set the soapstone lamp on a barrel, making a bed in fresh hay for herself. Doing this she heard laughter close by. Feminine giggles and a man's voice floated in the air.

I will go to the river and come back later.

She needed to be alone. Helena made her way to the long dark ribbon that edged the farmstead. Thick trees lined the river, with only a small clearing and rocks to ensure privacy. She lifted her tunic skirt above her knees, and with slow steps walked into the cold river. Fine silt slipped over her feet. Wind blew through the tallest trees, a hint of nature's song.

She tucked her skirts about her knees, then glanced at the heavens. "I'm not much of a conqueror."

A peace, however, seeped into her bones as she took in the sky's vastness. When was the last time she had prayed? The half-lit summer night, unique to the Norse, soothed her, a mixture of dark sun and bright moon. The sky never went full dark.

"Aye, seven years. That isn't so long, is it?" she whispered as water gently moved downstream. Air stirred, coiling around her like a blanket.

Seven years of labor to return to a man who had failed to fight for her.

Hakan's judgment of Guerin haunted her. She bent over clear water and dug her fingers into gritty silt. Tiny specks sparkled, grains of earth that looked like valuable gold but weren't—much like people.

As she leaned, her leather pouch dropped from her tunic. Helena splashed her fingers clean and yanked the burdensome tie from her neck, dumping the dowry piece in her hand.

"'Tis mine to wear." Helena slid the chain over her head and hefted the uncut stone in her hand. If only a fine craftsman could cut and trim the rough edges.

A twig snapped in the darkness. Startled, her hands opened on reflex. The pouch dropped and floated away. Her skirt dragged water. Footsteps. Someone watched her. Her heart was thick in her throat. Those footsteps moved through trees closer to the river. Another berserker?

A male voice called, "'Tis me."

"Hakan," she snapped, as she lifted her soaking hem from the river. "You gave me a fright." She trudged ashore and splashed water at him.

He laughed and sidestepped the wet arc. "And you gave me a great deal of pleasure. I cannot remember such a display—" He folded his arms across his chest. "—not since a bath on my long ship. And as I recall, I vexed you then."

"Shouldn't you see to Erik?" She moved close enough to smell his leather jerkin.

"He sleeps. He liked the cider best." Hakan placed an open palm to her soft cheek, whispering, "Thank you."

She was about to ask why but guessed a multitude of things: a cinnamon-flavored cider drink that would delight a boy; understanding the need for a private moment between father and son; and mayhap putting three churlish days behind them.

His knuckles stroked her cheek. "You know what I need when I need it. The peace you bring to my farm...being with you is like breathing life-giving air."

Her breath hitched high in her chest, catching there. How could she be irritated with a man who said such things?

Helena set her hand on his chest. The strong thump of his heart beat under her palm. Her thumb brushed the flesh exposed at the neck of his leather jerkin. The notion struck her that she touched him often enough: when his back needed rubbing, a cloth tunic fitted, or a cut cleaned and wrapped—always with a purpose, never just for the joy of touch.

This was enthralling. And dangerous.

"I made a bed near the horses. I should go." Her voice was thick and hoarse.

"Your hair...you comb it every evening."

Helena's brows lifted in surprise. She could recount many details about him, but didn't think he noticed such things about her.

Hakan pulled out her whalebone comb from behind him. He had tucked the comb into his belt. "I thought you might want it." He grinned.

Helena perched on a rock. "Please," she whispered over her shoulder. "Will you comb my hair?"

Hakan untied her braid and his fingers splayed through her tresses, unwinding the plait. Shivers danced across her back, dandelion soft. He set the comb to her head, and the strokes began, like one slow caress after another.

102

Night birds swooped over trees. Insects chirped. The river's gentle flow sounded in the clearing. The backs of Hakan's fingers grazed her nape, sending a tremor through her body. Slowly, up and down the comb went. Up and down Hakan's hand followed.

He was not chieftain any more than she was thrall under the moonlight.

Both were spellbound. She craved more, but caution to not want this so much made her break the hypnotic silence.

"What will happen? With Erik?"

"I'll keep him with me for a time. Astrid rides on a boar hunt north of Svea. I'll send a message to the servant charged with Erik's keeping that he's safe with me." Fatherly pride tinged his voice. "And we will build the ship for King Olof, practice swordplay, throw the hammer... I'll teach him some wrestling. When he is older, he'll wrestle the Glima." Hakan chuckled. "And one day he'll defeat me."

They both laughed at that. Helena couldn't see it, but she knew Hakan's face shone with fatherly pride.

"This feels good to know that I'll wake up tomorrow to see my son."

"As well you should."

"Shall I re-braid your hair?"

The mighty Norseman startled her again, to do something so tender.

"Nay, I'm tired." She cupped the soapstone lamp and faced him. "I made a bed for myself in the barn."

Hakan shook his head and yawned. "You sleep inside with us."

Back in the longhouse she sank tiredly into her bed of pelts and eiderdown near the far hearth. Erik was curled in the middle of his father's vast bed. Hakan laid a bear pelt beside the bed, then he moved from one lamp to another, blowing out the flame. Before the last light was out, Helena watched Hakan brush a lock of hair from the boy's forehead. All fierceness washed from him, and the tender expression on his face tore at her heart.

How long could this last?

11

"What will we do today?" Erik asked before he stuffed a large bite of sweetbread in his mouth.

"We could check the forest pitfalls for moose and reindeer and practice throwing spears." Hakan strapped *Solace* to his back and asked with mock-seriousness, "Is your mount able?"

Crumbs traced the boy's mouth. "Vlad is brave and strong." Jamming another hunk of bread into his mouth, Erik almost knocked the bench over in his fervor. He angled his words around bites of bread. "Do you have a sword I could use?"

The young boy, taut with excitement for adventure, didn't wait for his father before running out the door. Hakan retrieved a small wooden sword hidden behind a shield and slid the toy weapon into his belt.

"We'll need food," he said and grabbed spears from the wall.

Helena set provisions on the table. "'Tis ready." Then, she moved around the table.

"You will come with us?" Hakan leaned the spears against his shoulder and tried to measure her mood. "'Twould be typical to have a..." His voice faltered.

"A thrall to serve you." Helena supplied as she cleared the table, not looking at him.

"I want you with us."

Hakan stood in his longhouse, master of his domain, but couldn't shake the suspicion that his thrall had gained equal footing with him. When had that happened? He had asked her to join him like some besotted fool. Busy at her labors, she gave him a kindly smile and shook her head.

"This day belongs to father and son." Helena balanced dishes and nodded at the door. "Your horses await."

His own thrall dismissed him, reducing him to a tongue-tied youth. The notion grated such that Hakan hoisted the spears and walked into the day's bold sunshine without a word. In the yard, he passed the spears to Gamle, while Erik peppered him with questions. When everyone was mounted, Hakan pointed to the northeast hill.

"We go that way." He gripped Agnar's reins, but from the corner of his eye he saw her.

He was attuned to Helena, the pattern of her walk, the way the air changed when she drew near. Wiping her hands on her apron, she approached him. She came so close that Agnar shielded her from the others.

"I came to bid you good day," she said, then kissed her fingertips and touched his boot.

Helena's blue eyes rounded as her hand seemed to melt back to her side. The sweetness of the gesture, so natural, startled them both. A broad smile split his face.

"'Til the eventide."

...

A large pig, liberally spiced with pepper and tangy green leaves, roasted slowly over the pit. Potatoes and baby onions simmered in a tripod pot, and Hakan's favorite fennel bread cooked slowly without a hint of burning. Olga worked the feast, a celebration of father and son. Helena watched the

106

efforts to the music of pottery shards clacking on her loom, and hoped father and son had enjoyed their day.

"If only a maid would have a doe-eyed look for me."

Sven had ridden into the yard and leaned over his horse's shoulder.

"Sven." She rose from the loom, tossing her braid behind her. "I didn't hear you."

"I could tell," he smirked. "Thinking of him, are you?"

"Nay," she said, clearing her throat at the lie. "They are off, Lord Hakan and Erik."

"Erik?" His brows twitched with surprise. "Has Astrid given him to Hakan?"

"Nay. The boy ran away." Helena rubbed her hands down her apron, unsure how much to reveal. "Hakan will return him soon."

"Will he?" Sven mumbled as he dismounted and passed the reins to a thrall. Then his nose caught the air. "I smell a feast. Am I invited?"

"Of course. Olga and I planned a feast fit for a king to celebrate Erik. You're always welcome here."

Sven strode into the longhouse whistling his approval at the white linen tablecloths dotted with glassware.

"This will be a fine feast." He crossed thick arms. "I'd best take the sauna soon to be clean enough for this." Sven strode to Hakan's heavily carved armchair and settled there. "Have you ale?"

"Aye, but tonight, mead." Helena poured ale and set the horn before Sven.

"Mead. I'm impressed." He downed the ale and held out the horn for more.

"Mardred and Halsten, their entire household will be here," she said, refilling the horn.

"'Tis well you do this for my friend and his son." Sven shifted and leaned forward in the chair.

"Thank you."

The pitcher balanced on her hip, she waited. Sven leaned close. His studied her with an intent that defied his jovial nature.

"You're a curious one." He raised his horn as if to honor her. "Will you sit?"

Helena lowered herself onto the bench, resting the cool pitcher on her knees. "What do you mean?"

Sven's gaze swept over her. "Rare beauties in distant lands have crossed Hakan's path."

"And you tell me this because..." Her chin tipped, not wanting to hear him wax long on Hakan snared by the wiles of other women.

Sven's meaty fingers stroked the horn's rim. "You aren't the fairest maid, but your eyes, your form, would make a Norseman think twice about leaving home." He tipped his head at her cheek. "You're a comely maid even with the scar."

"Why Sven, you pour such fine compliments." Her hands wrapped around the pitcher, and she was tempted to douse the oaf.

His dark eyes speared her. "You're the first woman to capture my friend's eye in a long time."

She started to rise. "Kind words, but—"

"Don't leave. I'm no silver-tongued skald." He snorted, draining the horn. "He's taken with you. Watches over you like a wolf...gives you the run of his farmstead. You wear Hakan's keys."

Her shoulders tensed. "I work the same as the other thralls."

Sven pointed to the large key ring hanging from her waist. "Nowhere else in Uppsala is a thrall so honored. You keep the keys to his farmstead, the chests holding his riches. Some husbands don't trust their wives as much."

Helena knew little of the comings and goings of Uppsala. She had only seen the town when she had arrived. The lay of Sven's words was new territory.

"Take care of my friend. Give him happiness. By Odin," he said, swiping a hand across his mouth. "He's had little of that." Then, his dark eyes narrowed with warning. "He won't take marriage vows again. Don't place your hopes there."

"I seek to please him every day," Helena said vaguely as she rose from the table to gather soap and linens for Sven.

The hulking Norseman's warning of no marriage pricked her. Did she hope for that? Sven's voice rumbled behind her.

"There's sure to be more unhappiness in his future. Trouble will come to Svea."

When she turned around with soap and linen in hand, Sven stared out the open window, lost in thought. But then he slapped his thigh and sprang from the chair.

"Enough talk. I'm for the sauna."

Sven's words puzzled her. A prophecy of doom? She shook her head, brushing off the Norseman's mysterious words. Erik was here, home with his father for now, and the celebratory feast drew near.

Before Helena closed the shutters, she leaned against the opening. This captivating, pagan land was growing on her: bountiful fields, newly dropped lambs with tender legs testing the meadow, yellow butterflies fluttering in hazy sunlight.

How could a perfect place ever be touched by darkness and evil?

...

Father and son filled their days with hunting, swordplay, wrestling, and riding. This morn, light burst through every door and window, yet the boy slept soundly. Helena crouched by the fire, the wooden spoon Lord Hakan had carved for her clanking softly as she stirred a pan of eggs. Cheery meadow flowers filled an old, warped bucket atop the table. Hakan stood near the table, one boot propped on the bench as he watched his son sleep.

"Will you wake him? I must ready the horses to return him to Astrid."

"Can't he stay another day?" Helena gathered the apron around the hot handle.

"'Tis hard to say this, but his mother needs to see him," he said, his voice rough like metal on rust.

Helena set the pan on the table but her eyes shined at him. "You're very thoughtful."

"Or a fool." He shrugged. "I hate to bring the matter before the Althing, but I know the outcome. Time and custom are against Astrid." He noticed Helena's fingers toying with her red pendant, worn openly outside her tunic. "Your necklace."

"Mardred disapproves. She claims 'tis too bold for a thrall." Her face flushed as she finished, "She claims people will think unsavory things of me."

"Don't be bothered by Uppsala's gossips." He nodded at an open shutter and the meadow beyond. "We are far from them."

Hakan left the longhouse, his long strides taking him to the barn. Was it that easy to shut out the rest of Svea? He shook his head, not willing to let a few gossips interfere with his peace.

What of Helena's?

Hakan brushed away that nettlesome question under the mindful list of tasks that demanded doing. First, he needed Sven, who snored on a bed of hay, to awaken. Hakan tapped the toe of his boot on Sven's leg. The snoring Norseman mumbled and shifted in the hay. Grabbing a bucket, Hakan tossed fresh water, drenching his friend.

"Good morn."

Sputtering, Sven sat up, rubbing his face. He glared at Hakan under dripping strands of hair. "You're too free with buckets these days."

"And you're too free with my mead," Hakan chuckled. "Time to rise."

Scratching both hands over his chest, Sven ran his hands through his hair. Pieces of hay fluttered to the ground. "There. I'm ready to break the fast."

Hakan saddled Erik's horse, shaking his head. His friend's quick recovery from morning churlishness never ceased to amaze him. Sven stretched his back and twisted at odd angles, as one testing sore muscles.

"My back tells me you are ready for the Glima." He groaned about aches and pains as he picked up his small ax and tied it to his belt. "And, may I never have to fight you again."

"Sore?" Hakan cinched Erik's saddle.

"I know enough to meet you with hammer and ax, if we ever face each other in battle." Sven leaned his shoulder on a post and cracked his knuckles. "What are you about today?"

"I return Erik to Astrid." Hakan rubbed Agnar's muzzle. His morning's chore buzzed about him like a bothersome bee.

"The boy got here but a few days ago."

"He ran away to be with me. I would have him live with me, not runaway when his mother's back is turned." Hakan breathed deeply of the fresh hay and morning summer air and grabbed a currycomb from a hook.

Sven snorted and crossed his arms. "That one cares only about her own welfare. She's off with Gorm."

"Mardred and Halsten said she spends much time with Gorm, but the few times I've been to her farmstead, he's not been there."

"Like a coward." Sven narrowed his eyes at Hakan. "Some say he'll marry her."

Hakan combed Agnar's flanks. "Erik said Gorm's name a time or two. Says he sees Astrid often."

"They deserve each other, as only one viper appreciates another." Sven leaned an open palm against a wooden beam. "Gorm's presence at her longhouse is all the more reason to have Erik in yours."

"I will talk to her one more time. Mayhap now she'll see reason. If not," Hakan's jaw worked, "the Althing."

Sven's boot toed a pebble. "The fall season brings about many decisions, my friend."

The currycomb slowed its progress over Agnar's flank. "What do you mean?"

"The Ninth Year blot. King Olof."

Hakan didn't answer. So caught up was he with Erik, Helena, and the farmstead, that he hadn't bothered to give a second thought to what happened outside his gates.

"Many fear an uprising in Svea." Sven kicked the pebble into scattered hay. "Olof has made no bones about what he would do with the temple and our siddur, our Norse way of life."

"He is *King* Olof." Hakan's strokes slowed over Agnar's ribs. He stared hard at Sven. "And worthy of respect for the peace and prosperity he's brought. Not many kingdoms can claim that."

"Aye, aye, *King* Olof he is, but many think he's turned into a weak old man, unfit to rule." Sven's fingers absently rubbed his small ax. "A man is only as good as the power he holds. Many in Svea grumble about his Christ-follower beliefs. They fear he threatens our ways."

Hakan watched Sven with keen eyes. Alarm, as in days of old, days of court intrigue in distant, arid places, made him see Sven with new, wary eyes. Was it the way Sven's fingers rubbed his weapon? The agitation on his face? With careful motion, Hakan hung the currycomb on the hook.

"Did you tell Olof about the berserker wearing Gorm's armband?"

"I did." Sven's eyes glittered darkly. "He bade me keep quiet about it. For now, we do nothing."

"*Nothing?*" Hakan repeated the word so sharply that Agnar snorted and sidestepped.

"More evidence of his growing weakness." Sven spat on the ground.

Hakan stroked his steed's neck and tried to weigh this news. He did not want to think the worst of the man who had taken him in as an orphaned boy.

"Olof waits for the right time to act, not charging off in haste. 'Tis wisdom, not weakness."

Hakan defended his king, his friend, but doubt clouded his mind. He bent to raise one of Agnar's hooves.

"Many say his belief weakens him. But—" Sven stopped the bitter thread and raised his hands as a sign of peace when Hakan glanced up at him. "I know. The king loves you as if you were his true son. You know him better than Anund Jakob." Sven spat again on the earthen floor. "And there is no peace between them."

Hakan lowered the hoof. He didn't know about discord between Olof and his son, but neither did he ask. Standing upright, he dusted off his hands.

"Is there something you want me to know?"

Sven stared outside the barn a moment. "You should have been king."

Hakan's body jerked at the odd pronouncement. "I neither want, nor need, to be king."

Sven's eyes remained hooded, as if he calculated Hakan's answer, while staring at the fields. He let his hand drop to his side and all signs of turmoil vanished. He slapped Hakan on the back.

"What are we doing out here with horses and cows? We should be inside with Erik and a certain fair maid." Sven gripped his shoulder with an exaggerated groan. "Do you think she'd rub some oil on my hairy shoulders? I ache...right here. I hear she has talented hands for these things."

Brittleness edged Sven's forced humor. If Hakan didn't have this matter of Erik and Astrid to deal with, he would have pressed his friend. The pair walked back to the longhouse, but the hair on Hakan's neck stirred. He was mindful of the naked absence of *Solace* at his back.

12

The metallic song of swords played a rhythmic melody as Sven and Hakan practiced battle moves. Spears scattered the earth, some broken and split, attesting to the day's labor.

"You grow stiff with neglect, Hakan," Sven jibed through labored breaths. "Or do you rage over returning Erik to Astrid through *Solace*?"

Hakan brought his sword down hard. Sven swung his blade up, grunting from the force of iron meeting iron.

"She demanded more gold from me." Hakan's sword slid the length of Sven's and he stepped away. The recounting tasted like ash in his mouth. "Astrid would *sell* her own son. Our talk was heated, ugly. I would never deny her time with Erik."

"It has always been thus, my friend." Sven dove to strike, but Hakan jumped aside.

"Nay, not like this." He hefted his shield, and moved the wooden circle with menace. "I agreed to her demand, and with her next breath she demanded more."

Sweat dripped from Sven's brow, and he studied Hakan like a wily predator. He grinned and lurched at an opening, but Hakan was ready and parried the blow, knocking his friend back a step.

"Still think me stiff?" Hakan swung *Solace* in a wide arc and attacked from the side.

Sven backed away, the whites of his eyes growing. Then, roaring like a bear, he lunged to deliver a mighty blow. Hakan pivoted to avoid the attack. Sven, stretched too far, left himself exposed. Hakan saw the advantage, yelled a battle cry, and knocked his friend's sword to the ground.

The mighty blow caused Sven's weapon to fall and his shield slipped, the disc rolling away. The sword clanged as it hit the soil, and the man it served followed.

Oooommmmfff.

"Stiff? Nay," Sven spoke between bellows of breath as he lay on a patch of grass. "I think you angry."

Tipping his sword point in the earth, Hakan's chest heaved. "Because I will do what I want least and go before the Althing to gain what I want most. I'm certain of the rightness of that plan."

Sven nodded silently from his place on the ground.

"Call it a day?" He extended a hand to Sven.

"Nay." Sven's arm flopped over his eyes.

"You want more practice? We've broken half my spears, split the handle on my best hammer. You want *Solace* next?" Hakan managed a half-smile, leaning on his sword.

Chest puffing up and down, Sven spoke between gulps of air. "I meant 'nay' to getting up." He moaned. "Roll me to the sauna, will you?"

Hakan chuckled. "You are determined to work us into battle-readiness. But tonight is the Glima. I need to save myself for that."

"Aye. Couldn't let you go soft with your farmer's ways." Sven's hand flopped at Hakan. "Next time, I'll send Inge the Red. He's better with the sword."

"Trying to convince me to go a-viking again? I've had enough adventure for a lifetime. My life is here."

His eyes surveyed all that was his. A farm long neglected was growing—nay, flourishing—and prospering in the warm Norse summer. Under that same Norse sun, Helena walked from the small vegetable garden, a bucket dangling from her hand. She and Olga chatted and smiled, the older woman's hands moving with enthusiasm. He was glad of their friendship. Olga helped Helena. He could only hope Helena sought her help in *all* matters.

...

"Lord Hakan watches you again."

Helena looked across the yard and waved at Hakan.

"His eyes feast on your every move." Olga waved and smiled at the men. "There is wanting in his eyes."

Their footsteps moved leisurely across the path to the longhouse door.

"Olga..." Helena gripped the bucket with both hands as she glanced to where the men relaxed.

"This must be very hard." Olga's round face was full of compassion.

"Hard?" Helena leaned against the lintel frame. "Nay, being with Hak—I mean Lord Hakan, is very easy. The difficulty is not knowing."

"What do you mean?" Olga's brows knit together.

Helena was sure discomfort was writ plainly on her face as her gaze flit under lowered lashes to the men.

"Ahhhh..." Olga tipped her head to the space behind Helena. "Shall we go inside?"

Olga took the vegetable bucket from her hands and set the burden on the table. The longhouse cooled Helena's skin, tight and flushed from awareness of the chieftain who stirred her. They slid onto a bench and Olga folded her hands in her apron.

"I was not much older than you when I was taken from my home. I lived near Talinn. Men came from Jutland, raiding, killing." Olga closed her eyes. "I served a wealthy Rusk merchant who used me for his baser needs. He was neither cruel nor was he caring. Soon he tired of me," she said flat-voiced. "When he died, I was sold to another Rusk trader who made his home near Birka. There I met Vlado."

The older woman's blunt, grey lashes fluttered. Her eyes lit with joy at Vlado's name.

"A thrall is not to seek her own happiness, but please her master." She patted Helena's knee. "'Tis the way of things."

Helena played with her braid's feathery tip. "You never wanted to return home?"

"There was no more home for me. All was destroyed. What could I return to? No father. No mother. No brothers. All were gone." She turned to Helena, a depth of years shining from her pale blue eyes. "I learned to find happiness when and where I could. Do you understand?"

Helena nodded, but Olga's words set a new burden on her slender shoulders. Seek freedom? Or surrender? Hakan's keys, his armband, marked her as his. But, there was no peace in the knowledge of that kind of belonging.

The older thrall's work-rough hand touched hers.

"Do you understand? You have happiness here." Olga pointed at the earthen floor. "Lord Hakan is taken with you. I'd say he loves you."

"What?" Helena snapped to attention.

"Aye. Look at the way he treats you, the way he watches you as if no greater treasure exists."

"Nay. 'Tis Erik he treasures most." Helena played with the red stone hanging from her neck.

"A different kind of love, a father for his son than a man for a woman. A son will grow into manhood and make his own way in the world. Children leave. True love does not." Olga paused. "You don't make your bed with him?"

"Nay, I sleep there." She pointed to her small bed near the hearth. "He says he'll never marry. Besides, 'tis unlikely a chieftain would marry a thrall." She remembered the bucket on the table. "Especially one who can't cook," she finished, trying for humor in the awkwardness.

Helena rummaged through the bucket, glad for the ruse of examining the vegetables than facing Olga's knowing eyes.

117

After a moment, the Rusk thrall headed to the door. Helena gave her a distracted wave, but Olga tarried in the light and made a humming, pensive sound.

"Hold what you have. Treasure it, Helena."

Helena's fingers slid through the rich, dark soil that settled at the bottom of the bucket. The grit, darker than Frankish soil, caked her fingers. Olga's words rung in her head, but the older woman disappeared before Helena could ask: What should she treasure?

Freedom? Or Lord Hakan?

...

Laughter and music filled the night. Uppsala throbbed with life, and the giant longhouse, the one with three Norse gods guarding the entrance, was the hub. Every shutter was open, as were the giant double doors that welcomed all. Bone-flute melodies and goatskin drums mixed an alluring rhythm that drowned the senses and spilled into the streets.

Helena rode on the front of Hakan's saddle, wrapped in the warmth of his arms. He had made unusual requests before they had left his farmstead, but now they rode in rare silence to Uppsala.

He requested she wear her hair unbound.

She did that to please him.

He asked her to wear a fine blue tunic of the softest wool.

She did that, too.

He bade her wear a slender silver headband.

She did.

His gifts were of an embarrassing generosity, elevating her beyond thrall's status, but Helena couldn't deny him and was garbed thusly. What was he after this eve?

The fear of being swallowed up by these Norse roared back with all the noise and revelry before her, and when Hakan lowered her from Agnar, her feet rooted on the spot. Wraiths of smoke lingered and swirled, giving the structure a dream-like mien. After Agnar was settled, she and Hakan stood, side-by-side, not as master and thrall, at the entrance of Uppsala's meeting house to celebrate the mid-summer festival. Helena looked every inch a highborn Norsewoman—save the scratched thrall's band that squeezed her arm.

Hakan tugged her into the building, hailing his men. Emund, Nels, and the handsome rough-souled warrior, Brand, all raised their horns in greeting. Older children worked a spit that turned roast boar over a fire pit. Hakan gently pushed up her chin.

"Your mouth." He tapped her nose and smiled.

She smiled at him, but couldn't shake the slight tremors that coursed through her limbs.

Hakan was every inch a chieftain this eve: broad-shouldered and powerful in his new black leather jerkin with black trousers and wolf-skin boots that laced up his calves. Strong muscles stretched over each limb. A loose thong caught his hair at the base of his neck. He was a man of land and sea, nothing like her betrothed.

Hakan was solid sunlight to Guerin's docile night.

The unbidden comparison snared her, for Hakan won easily. His warm calloused hand grazed her arm, as he searched the room for a place to sit. Long tables made a giant rectangle in the middle, while rougher benches lined the walls for lowborn freedmen and thralls. From a throng of men broke Sestra. Her right hand balanced a pitcher on her hip, and she had two pitchers clutched in her left.

"Helena," Sestra cried out over the din.

She broke from Hakan and went to help her friend, grabbing two earthen vessels.

"Bless you," Sestra cried, having some of her burden removed. "My feet pain me already." She spun around, eyeing the benches. "Ah, there's an opening. Come."

They wove through the crowd and found seats behind a barrel. Sestra plunked the heavy earthen pitcher on the barrel.

"You look well." Sestra leaned back, assessing Helena.

"I've followed your advice."

Cinnamon eyebrows arched high. "And what advice is that?"

"Not to fight." Helena folded her arms over her chest and her fingers absently traced the etched armband.

Shrewd eyes narrowed on Helena. "And?"

"'Tis all." She leaned close enough for her friend to catch every word over the room's loud revelry. "Lord Hakan asked me to wear this finery and I did not gainsay him." She shrugged. "I weave. I clean. I mend. Like all the other thralls." Helena plucked at the fine fabric. "'Tis hardly what I wear every day."

Sestra's lips puckered. "You don't look like a thrall, but if you're willing, I could use your help. Now, we work." And she picked up a pitcher for Helena. "Later, we talk."

Helena moved about the crowd and poured spiced cider to revelers tipping horns and cups her way. When she came to Emund and Nels, the two young Norsemen nearly tripped over their feet when she poured the cider for them.

"Lord Hakan is looking for you." Emund pulled her around an over-large Norsewoman and pointed. "There. See? At the center table. You must go to him."

Helena wended her way through the crowd, holding the pitcher with two hands lest someone jostle it and splash cider on her tunic. She would return the garment in the morning and this whole business of the finery would disappear, for the clothes and jewelry came at a price: women, both high and lowborn, studied her with wary, skeptical eyes, while some of the men were bolder in their appraisal.

"Helena," Hakan called to her, rising from the bench. In quick strides, he was at her side. "I lost you."

"I saw Sestra—"

"What is this?" He frowned at the pitcher and took it from her. A boy passed by and Hakan stopped him. "Take this."

Hakan grabbed her shoulders and pulled her closer. "I didn't bring you here to serve. You serve only me. Do you understand?" He gave her a shake. "There are dishonorable men, Helena. Once they know you aren't a highborn woman..."

Her fingers grazed the silver headband. "Then, this is to keep me safe?"

The noise swelled and the crowd pressed them close. Hakan pulled her into the shield of his chest and whispered in her ear, "'Tis to honor you. It pleases me to see you in finery."

His lips grazed her ear lobe, not quite a kiss, but warm shivers slid down her neck. Hakan pulled back but his grip was firm.

"Remember, I protect my own." His lips quirked as he repeated the words once said on Uppsala's streets. "You will be safe with me, but you must stay with me."

An ale-addled warrior leered at her.

She clasped Hakan's hand. "I'll not leave your side."

He led her through the smoky, crowded room back to the table. Sven took up much room as he leaned toward another Norseman. There was barely space for one, much less two.

"Sit, Helena." Hakan motioned to the small opening on the bench.

Helena gathered her skirts and settled on the bench, Sven's bear-skinned tunic brushing her. The table was laden with platters of meat, breads, whole-roasted vegetables, and baked apples. Most ate with their hands; this rousing festival did not call for glass finery. Hakan loaded a shallow bowl with smaller meat slices, some of the choice vegetables, and a hunk of bread that he buttered.

"We share." And he set the bowl between them.

Somehow, the crowded hall, and even more-crowded table, seemed intimate. Her legs brushed Hakan's as people pressed on either side. Helena dipped her head to ask a question and the tip of her nose grazed his arm. Skin and brawn pulsed alive and warm against her mouth. She brushed her lips high on the thick muscle that covered his shoulder. 'Twas impulsive. She had not so much as held

121

Guerin's hand, much less touched her lips to him. Hakan's ale horn stopped mid-way to his mouth and his ice-blue eyes turned a curious shade darker when he met her gaze.

"Finally." Sven spoke over her head to Hakan. "The Glima begins."

Hakan raised his drinking horn to his friend. "Will you wrestle?"

"Only if I can bring my ax and hammer, but for some reason that is frowned upon here." Sven laughed at his own jest and tipped his head at a far table. "Wives cry foul when their men are gravely wounded. 'Tis supposed to be a test without weapons."

Hakan raised his hand in greeting to the flock of matrons. "And I'd rather face Sven's war ax than run into those hens and their unwed daughters."

Sven groaned between bared teeth, giving something of a smile as he waved greetings. "'Tis the wife of Lord Anund, no less. Come all the way from Aland."

Helena batted Sven's arm. "Why not go talk with her? She may be the mother of your future bride."

"You've never seen Lord Anund's daughter." Sven's false smile slipped as he eyed Helena. "I have."

"When did you see her? The maid's never left Aland." Hakan spoke over Helena's head. "She's just come of age. 'Tis her first time in Uppsala."

Sven shrugged and his meaty fist waved vaguely. "I can't place the time."

Just then, Emund entered the ring and faced another young Norseman. Their chests were bare and glistened with a sheen of sweat as they circled. Emund rose on the balls of his feet, his boots looking as if they barely touched ground. Men yelled advice and cheered.

Sven and Hakan bantered over her head. Both strove for her attention, trying to outdo the other with a witty comment or explanation of a wrestling move. Emund won easily, pumping his fist in the air in victory.

"Are you enjoying this?" Hakan leaned close.

"Aye, the people of Svea are hearty in all they do." His nearness brushed a wave of pleasure down her arm.

"Not so different from life in your fair country?" He leaned his arms on the table's edge.

Her fair country...the mention of home made her think of Olga's story of loss and the uncertainty of her own parents. Did they survive? Here she sat in a great hall, feasting, and the notion that she thrived and they might not nagged at her. Helena couldn't let herself be content to wait seven years. She touched his arm.

"Would you reconsider my freedom?"

Hakan stiffened under her hand.

"That again. You've much time—"

Someone yelled the chieftain's name. "Hakan Lange. Champion of the Glima. Ready to be bested?"

The cavernous longhouse thundered with his name. "Hakan! Hakan! Hakan!"

Fists pounded the tables until he rose from the bench and waved to the crowd. Emund stood awkwardly in the middle of the tables as the rest of the room exploded with applause.

"Young Emund is about to learn a hard lesson." Sven crossed his arms and a deep chuckle rumbled in his chest. "This'll be quick."

Hakan moved around the tables and entered the arena, giving a wolfish smile to Emund. He was stripped to his waist, wearing black trousers and black boots. Felling trees had made him taut and sinuous. The men traded banter as they circled each other, their stares fierce.

The two grappled, shoulder to shoulder. Their feet pressed the dirt floor. Both levered their weight and size against the other. Hakan was too much for Emund. He braced on one leg and slid the other foot behind Emund's ankle, tripping him.

Emund's back slammed the dirt. Air huffed out of him. He raised a flat palm in the air, the sign he yielded the match.

Tables exploded with applause and cries for more. Hakan threw his head back and loosed a victory shout.

"Hakan wins again." Sven stood up to cheer his friend.

Hakan waved off the demands for a rematch as he picked up his jerkin. Helena watched him hone in on her and smile, and then he disappeared into the crowd. Beside her, Sven grumbled the names she dreaded most.

"Astrid. Gorm."

He motioned at the entrance. Crowds parted as they did for women of her ilk: those rare, beautiful creatures perfect in every way.

Helena's heart sank.

Tall, with hair so blond 'twas almost white, her crown of glory flowed thickly to her waist. Astrid's features were slender and refined, as if she were carved from birth by the most caring artisan. The noblewoman near floated across the room, heading their way.

As she rose from the bench, Helena forced a tense nod to the approaching lady. But there'd be no kind greeting in return. Astrid split Helena in two with her chilly eyes. A tall man, handsome and older, followed. Silver threaded his red hair, shorn close to his nape in the Norman style.

Hakan returned from the arena and set his hand on the small of Helena's back.

"You're welcome to sit here. We're leaving."

"So soon? I would've thought you'd stay until sunrise, telling stories of old glory and plunder." Astrid's perfect eyebrow arched.

"What I do is not your concern."

"'Tis unusual for a chieftain to have a thrall seated next to him, and one so richly garbed." Astrid's bright blue eyes took in the finery, resting on the red stone, then moved higher. "And a scarred one. People talk."

The woman's cruelty stung, but Helena tipped her chin high. Driven by a bedeviling urge to strike back, Helena wanted to make this Norsewoman believe the gossip, to rub her face in it. But how? Beside her, Hakan's voice rose over the din.

"Worry about the company you keep these days, Astrid."

"How goes the farming?" Gorm asked, but to Helena's ears 'twas a taunt.

"The farmstead flourishes," Helena said, entering the fray of words. "I'd invite you to see for yourself, but something tells me you're not welcome. Ever."

Gorm's silver-grey eyes rounded at her outburst, but then he tipped his head at her in barest salute. The corners of his well-formed mouth turned up in a small smile.

"Where did you find her?" he asked Hakan, as his slight leer slid over her.

Hakan tensed beside her.

"'Tis my fault we leave early." Helena slipped an arm around Hakan's waist and leaned in like a cat.

Astrid's perfect lips puckered, creating tiny lines around her mouth.

Sighing, Helena traced one finger across Hakan's powerful arm. Her languorous, solitary finger stroked the valley between tense muscles, and her voice dropped suggestively.

"We really must be going." She gave Astrid a sly glance as if sharing a secret, one woman to another. "I'm sure you understand."

'Twas worth it to see the ice queen's mouth gape. Astrid recovered her grace, but her eyes narrowed to testy slits. Helena held her head high, her hand clasped in Hakan's as he led her through the smoky hall. Once past the open portal, neither let go.

...

"How many mistakes does your God allow one man to make?"

Startled, Helena glanced across the longhouse. Every inch a Norse chieftain at leisure, Hakan sprawled in his great chair before the fire pit. He leaned his head against his fist, looking mesmerized by the fire's embers.

"His forgiveness cannot be numbered." She bent over the chest and returned the neatly folded blue tunic. Leather hinges creaked in the silence as she shut the lid.

Helena walked with care toward Hakan. He shifted and linked his hands loosely in his lap, stretching his legs before him. The Norseman had brooded on the quiet ride back to the longhouse, and his odd question made no sense.

"Do you regret your long voyages from home?" She leaned against the table's edge, bracing her arms behind her. "I mean, when there were troubles. Is that why you ask? You seek forgiveness?"

Hakan faced her, and the look in his eyes glinted with danger. His smile alarmed her. The territorial wolf was back.

"You think I have guilt over Astrid."

Her feet shifted underneath her. "I'm not sure what troubles you."

The wolf prowled, though he sat in a great chair. His uneasiness made her skin tight and her heart race. Hakan was a handsome man, very appealing to all of the fairer sex tonight, with his black jerkin stretched across broad shoulders. He had shaved for the Glima festival, and his blonde hair, lighter from summer, loosened from the leather tie.

"Many thoughts trouble me tonight, but Astrid's not one of them." In the dim light of the longhouse, his white teeth gleamed against his tanned face.

"Does your head ail you?" She clasped her hands together, comfortable with the role of nurturing thrall.

"Nay, but 'twould please me if you sat close to me and played your harp."

"Music would be pleasant." Skittish and studying him under the veil of her lashes, Helena retrieved her harp.

She sat cross-legged on a pelt near his chair. 'Twas easy to strum a soothing song and lose herself in the delicate notes her fingers plucked. But when the last note faded, the restless wolf stirred on his throne, unpacified.

126

"Why did you play that game with Astrid? Letting her think more goes on between us?"

Ice-blue eyes pinned her, yet, 'twas his voice, dangerous and soft, that did things to her.

"I...I don't know." Her own voice faltered as warmth flushed her skin.

Glowing embers molded his face with dim light. Hakan leaned forward, resting both elbows on his knees. His sinewy hand plucked the harp from her, placing it on the ground.

"Why?" Hakan's fingertips tilted her chin.

Tingling flares struck Helena all over...like sprays of orange metal shooting from a smithy's hammer strike. The air, her dress, all hung heavy on her frame. If he didn't touch her so, she could think better.

"I...I didn't like how she treated you."

"You know you played with fire. My control hangs by a thread." Hakan brushed the hair from her face and whispered, "You are so beautiful. How did I find such a treasure in all my travels?" The corners of his lips curved up. "Someone to help with my Frankish."

He caressed her cheek, her forehead, tracing her eyebrows, even the tendrils surrounding her face. She shivered, mute under those fingertips that made a slow trail over her lips, her scar.

"And we always speak Norse, you and I, never Frankish." He smiled at that.

"Because you wish not to leave this farm." *And you'll never let me go—no matter if I serve seven years or not.*

She flinched at that truth, but Hakan must have misread her.

"This scar does nothing to lessen your beauty." He spoke with fierce protectiveness. "If I could take back the pain you've suffered and put it on myself..."

Such thoughtfulness...she would not correct him. Hakan's fingers played over her hair, her face, floating over her skin with the barest touch. Growing bold, Helena put her hands on his boots, the fur soft to her skin.

"Come to me, Helena. Come to me as a willing woman, not a thrall."

Hakan's words doused her as if with cold water. She pulled away, remembering Olga's words earlier that day: *Soon he tired of me.* Helena squeezed her eyes shut a second. The longing in his eyes overpowered her as her mind tangled with powerful yearnings.

"I feel hard pressed to stop," she whispered. "But what of when this passes? Will you tire of me?"

"I make no promises but that I will take care of you."

She licked her lips, sorely tempted to sit in his lap and toss home and freedom aside. This connection between them wove like taut threads, cinching tighter each day. The tension would make her snap, yielding easily to him. But Hakan's next words filled her with heaviness. With a slight shrug, he spoke in the same even tones as when he had asked if she could swim that night off Jutland's shore.

"You live in bondage to me, but I treat you better than many Norsemen treat their wives. I'll never speak marriage vows again. What I offer is the best I can give." Then, as if knowing his words stung her, Hakan cosseted her hair.

Her hands rested on his boots. 'Twould be so easy to give in and let the mysteries of this attraction unravel between them.

"I would take care of you," he whispered in a hoarse voice.

His eyes darkened with promise if she yielded to the temptation of pleasure. But Olga's story played on her mind. What was meant to influence Helena to relent instead filled her with resolve. Though she sat at Hakan's feet, her back went stiff and hard as any shield he used.

"I am grateful you've never forced yourself on me...that you give me many freedoms. But, my lord, you do not give me the freedom I crave most." She folded her hands in her lap. "I decline your offer and will take care of myself."

A mere hands-breath away, his pained eyes fixed on her. Hakan jerked out of the chair, leaving the longhouse in rapid strides, the magic of the moment lost.

13

Lord Hakan possessed a great treasure that he failed to share with her.

With heavy heart and rag in hand, Helena slammed the heavy green glass smoother on fine linen stretched across the whalebone board. Tendrils stuck to her cheeks and forehead from the heated glass as she pressed out wrinkles with all her might. *How could he?*

She should have given herself to him.

She wanted him as much as he wanted her.

She would tell him today, if he would stay long enough for them to speak.

Tonight he would stay. The king was to visit, or so the king's man said who tarried in the yard, waiting for Hakan.

Since the Glima, Lord Hakan had buried himself in hunting: bear, deer, moose. He dragged one carcass after another to the farmstead. Then, he had gone upriver, trapping with Sven. Gone three days, he had just returned and unsaddled Agnar in the barn.

Her curious gaze strayed to the king's message.

Stick-like marks were scratched in neat rows, but 'twas no matter. She couldn't read in any language, and the rare ability awed her. Hakan knew this, yet he failed to share that treasure with her. She set the smoother atop orange embers and fed her curiosity. She picked up the wooden slat, and the pad of one finger traced the indented lines.

"What are you doing?" Hakan called, striding through the longhouse.

She jumped and held out the wooden slat. "The king's man brought this."

"I saw him." Hakan scowled and took the king's message.

He went to his great chair near the hearth and read the message. Did the message bear glad tidings? She couldn't tell, for he bent over the hearth and scraped a layer of wax into the embers. He held the board over the mild flames until the wax began to soften. With the tip of a sharp-edged stick, Hakan etched his own message to the king. Helena hovered close, examining his calloused hand as it moved the stick swiftly over soft wax.

"You read and write." She folded her hands into her apron.

He glanced up from the board. "I do."

"And you never told me." *And never offered to teach me.*

"I did not."

He focused on the board, and she could have been little more than a bothersome gnat. His head was bent to the task, while the stick moved with quick precision. She leaned in closer.

"I wonder if—"

"You'll have to wait."

He tossed the stick into the fire and went to the lintel, beckoning the king's man and calling loudly for Gamle and Olga. Dismissed, Helena leaned against the table's edge and rested the heels of her palms there. At a loss, she watched his broad back fill the doorway.

Hakan passed the wooden board to the king's man. Olga came from the root cellar, wiping her hands on her apron. She scurried across the yard with Gamle when she saw Hakan's face. Hakan issued clipped commands too quick and low for Helena to understand. She stared at the earthen floor and drummed her fingertips. Why such urgency?

"Aye," Olga said, her head bobbing in deference. "A feast. This eve."

Filling the doorway, Hakan turned to Helena. "Make the longhouse ready. King Olof dines here tonight."

Helena grabbed the tunic, her peace offering, from the whalebone stretcher. "I've been working on this for you."

His eyes, icy and distant, scanned the garment. "'Twill do."

Hakan left for the sauna while Helena prepared for the king's visit. She stretched the best white linen cloths across the table and cleaned and polished Rhenish glassware. She unrolled thick beeswax candles from cloths hidden in chests.

Then, she was left with the tunic to finish. The linen came from young flax thrice boiled. The bolt of cloth from which she made this tunic was a soft, clean white, not the usual oat-colored linen, and felt like silk.

Blue, yellow, and bright red threads had been stitched into the fabric in the same style as the symbols on Hakan's armband. Small, tiny seams, her best work, made the cloth appear to be knit together by air.

Now, laboring over the seams to flatten them, perspiration beaded on her forehead. The strength of her arms, her heart, went into perfecting this garment. And now he would greet a king in it. What more could he want?

...

"What more could she want?" Hakan tossed a cup of water onto the pile of sizzling river rocks.

"What?" Eyes shut, Sven reclined on a bench in a stupor from the heat.

"Helena. What more could she want from me?"

"Not this again. How many times must we go over this?" Sven rubbed large fingers through his unkempt hair.

"She greets me as if nothing happened. As if she didn't spurn me. I come back from hunting to find she's sewn a tunic fit for a king. I never asked her to make it for me, yet, she smiles as if…" He let his words trail and wiped sweat from his face.

"Aye, 'as if' what?" Sven asked.

"Nothing," Hakan grumbled, and poured more water on the pile of stones where steam hissed and curled.

"As I said in the forest," Sven said, cracking his knuckles. "You should bed the maid and be done with it."

Hakan wiped a rag across his nape and shoulders, removing the forest's grime.

"When will you cease to think of women as vessels to meet your needs?"

"Because they are," he snorted, and his eyes were narrow slits. "Give her something she wants, then. Mayhap she'll run to your arms."

"That's the problem. What does she want? She lacks for nothing and asks for nothing."

Except for her freedom—the one thing I'll not give.

"Then count yourself lucky." Sven spoke through a yawn, "Every woman wants something. Garments. Jewels. A fine steed."

"Nay, she wants only to return to Frankia. I already promised her she could return in seven years."

"There you have it. Promise her what she wants but don't yield when the time comes."

"You would have me lie to her."

Sven scratched his chest. "Remember, my own mother was a thrall. My father promised her safe return to her Saarmi people, if she served him for a time." Sven managed a lazy half-grin. "Obviously she stayed."

"Unlike your father, I won't marry."

"Then try promising to set her free sooner than seven years. Make an agreement, one so difficult to achieve, she'll have hope and not vex you with pleas for freedom." Sven wiped dripping sweat from his face. "The maid will fall into your bed soon. I see the way you look at each other." Sven grabbed a folded linen and wiped it across his face. "I'm glad you're not tied up in knots anymore over the king's

133

teachings...honor with women and thralls. Women need to serve their purpose in this world."

Knots? His shoulders and back were full of them. Hakan watched Sven discard the used cloth, dropping it to the ground. He would never use Helena in that manner. Yet, his mind churned with the question: What could he promise her?

...

"You must go." King Olof's grey eyes bore into Hakan. "You're the only one I trust."

Aromas of roast pork and warm oat bread filled the longhouse—a fine spread that was hardly touched. Helena cradled an earthen pitcher, cool from the root cellar on her hip. Yet, none gave her the nod to fill their drinking horns. The air thickened with hushed words of a furtive mission.

King Olof was every bit the imposing leader this evening. A penannular ring, the size of a man's hand, clasped his red cape about his shoulders. His silver-white hair shined, tied at the nape of his neck. Several men awaited his pleasure outside the longhouse, their jests and laughter muffled noises beyond the closed door.

Inside, Hakan and Sven listened as the king outlined his request.

"I need you to go after these men," said King Olof, his smooth voice edged with desperation.

Hakan speared his meat with the tip of a small knife.

"I've served you many years. But what you ask..."

The king set his hands on the table. "You need to set things right in our kingdom, for Erik's future. Jakob rebels against me, despite everything I do." Olof's pained eyes pierced Hakan. "I should have made you my son."

"Olof..." Hakan winced at the king's admission.

The strong warrior leader of Hakan's youth crumbled before him, and the discomfort of that nettled him. Was it the tremors of an old man with numbered days? Or the tremors of his kingdom, his home, full of peace all his life?

"He rebels against everything." The king studied his trencher of food. "And Gorm has spread his evil influence. I sent my most loyal guards to investigate what you reported...berserkers serving Gorm." His hoary brows snapped together. "They didn't return."

Sven splayed meaty hands on white linen. "Mayhap they face delays."

The king eyed Sven. "Their broken, bloodied weapons were delivered to me."

Hakan set his knife on the trencher, unable to eat.

The king's eyes bored into Hakan. "You see the import of what I'm saying? Gorm's behind this...behind an uprising in Gotland. If the chieftains of northern Gotland take their rebellion south to Paviken...many will die."

Paviken was the only trading post on the island of Gotland, a rich, thriving outpost for traders of every stripe. Should word travel of unrest in Svea, the region would be laid bare for any man of ambition. Hakan spread his hands open before the king.

"You would have me travel to northern Gotland, a wild, open land that I know little about, and hunt down rebellious chieftains and their berserkers in forests they know well?"

"Aye."

"This could take a long time, a *very* long time. This fall...the meeting of the Althing...Erik...." He sighed. Too much hung in the balance: loyalty to his fatherly sovereign and safeguarding Svea's peace pitted against his own peace and the bone-deep need to be the father his son needed. "You have other chieftains who would welcome this battle."

Olof searched Hakan's face. "If I weren't so troubled, I wouldn't come to you." The king rubbed his lined forehead. "I wish there was something I could do to sway the assembly, but..."

"The Althing is for all men, justice tampered with by none." Hakan finished the king's words. "And yet, this same justice wrongly binds you."

Hakan sat in silence as the play of trust and mute appeal spread across Olof's face. 'Twould be easy to gather his most trusted, able warriors. They grew restless from their respite and eager for the prizes of battle. None had yet to give their loyalty to other chieftains, or so he had heard.

The uneasy notion of Hakan the Tall as farmer was not believed by even his own men.

Plunder from the northern Gotland chieftains would lure them from their summer rest. Yet, Hakan had grown used to the lightness on his back. His eyes flickered on *Solace*'s gleaming iron length on the far wall.

"There is this." Olof tossed an arm ring on the table.

The shiny silver band swirled and rotated in fast circles before it stopped. Sven and Hakan examined the ring. Dried blood cracked the surface, but the style, the design, was unmistakable.

Gorm.

Hakan and Sven nodded recognition. The Dane's serpentine mark was clear on the armband.

Then, Olof pulled something else from the pouch at his waist. Gripping it in his closed hand, he stared hard at Hakan. "With Gorm's armband and my men's bloodied weapons, there were these."

The king placed the items on the table with a reverent touch.

He set a plain trefoil brooch, save one modest blue stone in the middle. 'Twas one half of a pair of silver brooches. Hakan instantly recognized the favored pieces his mother had worn on her shoulders, gathering the cloth at her shoulders in summer's warmth.

Where was the other brooch?

The king's age-spotted hand laid an amulet of Thor's hammer. Two notches scored the top of the hammer. Blood rushed in Hakan's ears. His chest hammered with a heart ready to burst. Beside him, Sven growled like a bear.

"What's this?"

Hakan's stomach clenched in knots as he touched his mother's favored brooch and the amulet his father had worn faithfully every day to honor Thor. Both pieces had been missing since their deaths. Helena stood on the far wall facing him, her dark eyes huge orbs in her head.

The king's voice came low. "Gorm grows careless. Or bold in his treachery. He's no longer a rebellious youth spreading disorder in Svea. He's a dangerous man."

Hakan picked up his father's amulet and traced the iron edge.

"The truth is finally known."

"Aye." The king cocked his head to the side. "I fear he may be in league with the Danes."

Hakan stared at his sovereign as the very truth of what he had witnessed as a boy came back to him. Olof's coin-colored eyes wavered.

"And you think the unrest is the work of the Danes?" Hakan asked.

"Possibly," Olof answered and raised a placating hand. "I know I said the Danes were too busy devouring the Saxons to care about Svea, but you were right. Gorm's in league with someone. Who, I'm not sure."

"And Gorm's in Gotland now?" Sven spoke up after a long silence.

The king nodded. "I believe so. He disappeared during the mid-summer festival. That's when I sent the second man to find him, and days later, these were delivered to me." Olof gestured to the jewelry on the table.

"I'll do it," Hakan said with firm promise.

"I thought you'd agree." The king rose, leaving his fare untouched.

He strode to the door with a stronger gait, as if placing this burden at Hakan's feet gave relief. Olof placed an aged hand on the heavy door and looked at Hakan.

"I was wrong to withhold the truth, but as king, I had my reasons." His sage voice carried across the quiet longhouse. "May you find it in your heart to forgive me."

As quickly as he came, the king left.

"Ale?" Helena stepped out of the shadows, hefting the pitcher.

Her soft smile was a welcome balm, but both men declined. Sven, his brows thundering, rose from the bench and turned to Hakan.

"I go to Uppsala to alert the men. When do you want to leave?"

"Tomorrow. With the morning tides."

To his own ears, his voice was hollow and empty. He pushed away the food and stared at the waning summer sky through the open shutter. Helena cleared the dishes and quietly washed them. Hakan removed *Solace* from the wall and took his whetstone from a chest.

He seated himself at the table's bench, rubbing his neck from phantom weight. He wearied of the vicious cycles of kingdoms and treachery. The amulet and simple brooch, relics of his past, sat atop the white linen.

Aye, Gorm would pay as justice demanded, and so would the warriors and chieftains in league with him. Sliding his whetstone slowly down his word's edge, he lusted for this fight yet hoped 'twould be the last.

Behind him, a cool hand touched his neck. Helena. He didn't push her away. Her skin smelled of warmth and summer, yet when her hair grazed his arm, he needed some distance. In his grief, she enticed him, aye, all the more as he was raw from the evening's news.

Hakan shifted on the bench, leaning *Solace* on his leg. He reached over and held up the bloodied armband.

"Recognize this?"

"I do," she said, and he heard river-deep stillness in her voice.

Even her voice gave him pleasure.

There was no mistaking Gorm's design: the amber-eyed serpent on the berserker who attacked her. But whose blood filled the etched silver?

"These are similar to what the Danes wear. No Norseman from here to Trondheim would wear them." His fingers pinched white against the bloodied silver band as he set it back on the table.

"Gorm flaunts this. He once lived here, but for as long as I've known him, has stirred up trouble. Never a man of Svea. Never truly a Dane."

Hakan lifted his sword and pressed his thumb's pad against the blade.

"What is it your God says? 'A house divided cannot stand.'"

Surprise lit Helena's eyes and her soft lips curved into a gentle smile. "Aye, 'tis a truth." She slid closer to him on the bench. "Where did you hear that?"

"My travels." He said wryly. "One hears the rants of holy men."

She picked up the serpentine armband, examining it. "How is Gorm a house divided?"

"'Twas rumored that he was in league with the Danes, being half Dane. But the Danes feared Olof's power, the way he unified Aland, Gotland, Svea." He scraped the whetstone up and down the sword, creating a strange metallic song.

Picking up the small brooch, she fingered the crude carvings.

"Hakan, you turned white when the king put this on the table. Why?"

"'Twas my mother's."

Helena gasped. Hakan's long, brown fingers gently covered hers, and he took the brooch from her.

"She wore it the day she was murdered. The day our farm was burned to the ground."

"Gorm?" Her voice was soft and coaxing.

"Gorm was responsible," he said, his voice hollow.

As a boy, he had cried and yelled Gorm's name 'til his throat went hoarse, but none would listen.

"You *saw* him?" Her brows knit together in question.

"Aye, but no one believed me. Witnesses claimed that Gorm was on a hunt with them...four days ride from Uppsala, when the fire happened." His thumb tested *Solace's* edge with too much pressure. A thick, red drop welled and slid down iron. "The problem with rule of law: we honor it even when it protects evil."

14

"Did you try to kill him?" Helena gasped at the cut and wrapped his hand in her apron.

"Words worthy of a blood-thirsty Norsewoman," he chuckled without humor. "I was a young boy, remember?" He watched as she dabbed his thumb. "'Tis a small cut."

She cradled his hand. "But I don't understand . . ."

Hakan pulled his hand away and squeezed his thumb. "'Tis fine."

Helena would not let his gruffness push her away, and she inched closer to him. She needed to touch him to assure herself that he was well.

"The burden you've carried all these years...no one believing you."

He shrugged off her concern. *Solace* reflected his ice-blue eyes, alight with a dangerous warrior's glint. "Gorm made himself scarce from Svea after that, but I searched for him on my travels."

"You want vengeance."

"Aye."

His jaw ticked, but 'twas the deep ferocity in his eyes that startled her. This must be a glimpse of what it was like to have him bear down with sword and ax. 'Twas pure violence. Death whispered at her neck that she could lose him if Gorm won this battle of wills.

"But your own life…" Her hand brushed her nape.

His brows slammed into a hard line. "I'm a Norseman, remember? We live by the sword."

Helena was not cowed, instead giving what he needed most: a tender, listening ear.

"I had gone fishing upriver. Mardred was with Halsten in Uppsala." Hakan stared at a flickering candle and rested *Solace* against his thigh. "There was smoke…screams. I ran as fast as I could, but the farmstead was on fire."

Hakan's large hands clenched. "I was eight winters, but I knew whoever did this, did it out of hatred…deep hatred. I was on my knees cradling my mother, when I saw movement in the trees." His fists ground into his thighs. "His long, flame-red hair."

"Gorm."

"Only one man in Svea had hair like that…red hair down to his waist. Gorm was barely into manhood, stirring up trouble, but always known by his hair. 'Twas his vanity." Hakan shook his head. "Never had he done anything like that. By the time others had arrived, nothing could be done. They took my accusation of Gorm as the rantings of a distraught boy."

Helena yearned to fold her softness around him, but he jerked his hands away when she reached for him.

"Later, Olof hinted that he believed me." His arms crossed tightly over his chest as *Solace* balanced on his leg. "He took me in. Gave Mardred a dowry to start her life with Halsten after much had been destroyed."

"And Gorm?" prompted Helena. "What happened to him?"

"Disappeared. He returned years later with a chest of silver ingots and his hair shorn. I had begun to doubt myself, let my mind weaken in what I thought I'd seen that day." He snorted and stared at the row of shields lining his wall. "Then one day Gorm walked into Olof's hall...boastful, arrogant."

"Did you try for vengeance?" Helena clasped her hands in her apron.

"I was powerless. Too young to challenge him, though I foolishly tried." The muscles in his jaw clenched, but he managed to finish. "Gorm was bigger, older, well-trained."

She raised her hands, wanting to touch him, a connection, to render comfort, but her hands stopped short.

"Olof stopped me. But I had to leave Svea. Olof had his young son, Anund Jakob. I was sixteen winters, so I hired out my sword arm to a merchant."

"But you still don't know why? Why Gorm would do such evil?"

He shook his head, and Hakan's eyes held painful secrets when he studied her. "Do you understand? Tonight, Olof admitted that he knew all along Gorm was responsible for the killing and burning."

"The king *knew* what Gorm had done?" She gasped. "And did...*nothing*?"

"Olof is king before he is friend or father," he said, his mouth twisting from the acrid truth. "He must have reasons for not seeking justice, but I'll find out."

Her fingertips flew to her mouth. "He likely knows why Gorm did such a terrible thing."

Hakan nodded, staring off into the distance. "Another secret Olof keeps, but I will find out."

"You feel betrayed."

"I don't *feel* betrayed. I *was* betrayed," he said, bitter-voiced. "Olof only tells me the partial truth now because he needs my sword."

The force of emotions bounced off Hakan like the heat of flames. Helena longed to stem the flow of anger and pain, but like poison that must drain, so must this tide of emotions.

Fatigue played across his features as he set *Solace* on the table.

"I'm sorry," she said, and rose to leave, but he grabbed her wrist.

"Stay." His eyes, shuttered and distant, couldn't hide all of the ache. "Let us be as we were at the beginning of summer. We can play backgammon or chess."

The pain in his voice undid her and she nodded, aware that she was again on shifting ground with a man she yearned to touch. Hakan moved quietly through the longhouse and pulled the game from a chest. He slid onto the bench and both of their hands moved, setting up the board. As small wooden pieces were set in place, so did part of the puzzle that made Hakan.

"You blame all gods, Norse and otherwise, for their deaths?"

Hakan's gaze shot up, narrowing into shards of blue. The storm in his eyes lessened when she didn't back down, and his face eased as truth's healing balm poured between them.

He shifted on the bench and took a deep breath. "I do."

Helena had no comforting words. Her brain could not fathom his pain, and despite her own sorrows, all felt puny by comparison. Her hair slid over her shoulders and she idly finger-combed the ends as the game began in silence.

Tonight would be a truce.

Tomorrow, *Solace* would gleam from his back once again, and troubles, new and old, would come.

...

"I won't be your second," Sven said as they approached the barn.

"Why not?" Hakan snapped at Sven, hating the way the ground seemed to shift under him once again.

A rooster crowed and animals stirred as morning stretched across the farmstead. Hakan swung wide the barn doors and waited, but Sven's eyes failed to meet his.

"Emund will be a fine second," Sven said as he stared toward the trees. "He is anxious to prove himself."

144

Why wouldn't Sven look him in the eye?

"Emund's good, but he's not you." Hakan crossed his arms. "What stops you?"

Sven matched Hakan's stance and finally faced him. "Gorm doesn't care that we know what he's done. Have you thought about that?" Sven jerked his head at dew-covered fields, ripe for harvest. "Someone needs to protect your farmstead. Mardred and Halsten's, for that matter."

Hakan glanced at the rich fields but said nothing. So lost was he in the haze to exact justice against Gorm that he lost the mindset to protect what was his. Sven spat on the ground.

"Would you leave defense of your farmstead to a few skinny Flemish thralls? And what about Erik?" Sven's dark eyes hardened with truth. "How will you protect your own if you're not here?"

"Gorm's in Gotland. Not here." Hakan said the words to reassure himself.

"Olof *believes* he's in Gotland. What if he's not? Gorm smells Olof's weakness. He moves openly, doesn't care about stealth." Sven lowered his voice and jerked his thumb at the longhouse. "Who will protect Helena? You saw how Gorm looked at her at the Glima."

Hakan eyed the longhouse where she slept safely, peacefully in her own bed. Gorm touching her...a haze splayed across his vision. Sven had the right of it. He jabbed a finger at Sven.

"You. Sleep. In the barn."

Sven grinned as he set a heavy paw over his heart. "I'll treat her like a sister."

"I mean it, Sven." Hakan pointed to a pile of hay inside the barn. "You sleep there."

"As you wish." The hulking Norseman, his trusted second in battle for years, smirked and bowed obeisance.

They moved through the doorway into the barn's cool dimness. Animals, restless for open meadows, stamped their feet.

145

"The maid means much to you, Hakan. I'll see her safe." Sven stroked his beard, grinning. "But if you were a lesser warrior..."

Hakan couldn't help but smile. He dumped a ready bucket of oats for Agnar and spied the empty stall where Vlad, Erik's horse, had stayed.

"Erik." Hakan's chest clenched. "What about him? Even you can't be in two places at once."

"Last night, I asked Jedvard to keep watch over the boy."

Jedvard, an older white-haired warrior of Birka, could best Sven and Hakan at once. He was more hulking in size than Sven but without the clumsiness. His every move was fluid, if slower from age. He had hardly said a score of words since Hakan had known him, but 'twas enough that he cast his loyalty with Hakan and Sven.

"Something's not right." Hakan crossed his arms and his boot brushed stalks of hay into a stall. "What you say rings true, but I can't shake the sense that all moves too fast." He shook his head, not liking this unease. "But, who else can I trust?"

Sven pounded Hakan's back. "Good. I'll protect them with my life."

Through the farmstead gates came the men, their horses galloping hard on mist-dampened earth. Emund, Nels, Ingvar, Inge the Red, and others followed, their faces hungry for battle, excited for the task ahead. Sven had the matter right: the men were bored with idleness. Hakan waved his men to the barn and prepared to leave.

...

Helena stretched, drowsy and content. She flung back the pelt that covered her and grabbed her ivory comb. Her braid worked loose in the night, but with a few slow strokes she worked the tangles from her hair. Weaving a careless braid, she finished and slid her silver band high on her arm—a daily act that had become second nature. Olga bustled into the longhouse, bringing with her the sweet aroma of fresh oat bread.

146

"Good day to you, my lady." Olga beamed as she set the cloth-covered loaf on the table.

Helena shared her smile and wrapped the farmstead's key chain about her waist, feeling warmth all the way to the soles of her feet at Olga's use of "my lady."

Olga wiped her hands on her apron. "I thought you'd sleep the morning away and miss saying farewell to the master. But—"

"Farewell?" Alarmed, Helena jumped to her feet. Her comb tumbled from her lap.

"I thought you knew? Sven was here before the sun rose. The warriors have already come and gone. Lord Hakan leaves on some errand for the king."

Last night. The king. The arm rings. The brooch. Gorm.

Olga's voice floated behind Helena as she rushed out of the longhouse. At the door of the barn, Hakan cinched Agnar's saddle and gave instructions to Hlavo and Gamle.

All three turned at the sound of running feet approaching the barn. She stopped short of Hakan, panting from her sprint across the yard. Sunbeams poured between them, playing with dust moats and bits of hay that floated in the air. Strands of his blonde hair captured a halo of light, such that he looked like a hero of ancient lore.

"You're leaving," she said, her voice bleak. "And you didn't wake me to say good-bye."

Hakan dismissed the men with a glance. "We played games late into the night. I thought to let you sleep." He kept one hand on Agnar, and his voice was clipped and purposeful. "The sooner I go, the sooner I return. Sven will see to your safety. He'll sleep here in the barn."

"Oh."

Helena didn't move, but her sadness must have reached him.

"Helena." Hakan crossed the distance between them. His knuckles stroked her cheek. She placed her hand over his, accepting the caress.

147

With the bone-handled knife tucked in his boot, sword strapped to his back, and axe tied at his waist, Hakan was a chieftain ready for battle. Fear, the haze of it like when the Danes had attacked her village, skittered across her skin.

"Break the fast with me," she pleaded softly.

He hooked a finger under her chin. "You've convinced me to do many things I've not done before." He looked at the trees where her loom sat idle. "Like spend a summer day in the shade, and now you want me to keep my ship, my men, waiting. What will you have me do next?"

He paused as if drinking in the sight of her. He hadn't shaved, and his jaw bore several days' growth. She itched to know the feel of those blonde whiskers. Her lips parted with bold, unspoken invitation. Hakan brushed her cheek, when the clatter of hooves disturbed them. Sven rode into the yard, his horse prancing and circling from what surely was a race to the farmstead.

"I waited for you at the road's fork. When you didn't show..." Winking at Helena, he leaned on his pommel. "But I see what delays you."

Hakan led Agnar from the barn, looking like a lad caught dawdling from his tasks.

"I'm dragging my feet when I need to be about the king's business, but my stomach growls." He stood in the clearing and called to Gamle to take Agnar, when Helena laid a soft hand on his arm.

"You will stay?"

"I'll break the fast with you." He took her hand and kissed the open palm. "Time missed can be made up with fair winds."

"Then I'll gather some eggs," she laughed. "What's on the table now is meager fare when Sven visits."

She grabbed a basket inside the barn as Hakan and Sven walked to the longhouse. Their voices floated across the yard as she went to gather eggs.

"You've never missed a sunrise departure. The tides won't favor you..."

148

She quickly gathered eggs and, with the basket full, headed to the longhouse. Looking ahead, Helena noticed Olga had opened all the shutters. The door and windows were wide open to the morning's breezes. Yet, as she approached, her ears picked up Sven's booming voice to Hakan's deep, smoother tones. She slowed, clutching the basket with both hands.

"She's softened you..." Sven sounded disapproving. "No doubt your sword gathered dust when I wasn't here to help you practice."

"Practice? You worry overmuch about my fighting skills."

Outside, Helena approached the doorway but stopped. Her hair fell across her face; her hasty braid needed tidying. She set her basket on the ground to re-braid the mess. Leaning near an open window, Helena ran fast fingers through her hair as their banter drifted overhead.

"But, I like her," Sven's deep voice boomed.

Helena smiled to herself, knowing they were discussing her. She made three sections with her hair.

"Even though she makes me a farmer?"

"She makes you a *happy* farmer."

Leaning her back on the outer wall, she beamed at Sven's words. Helena heard garbled words. Sven must be chewing and talking at the same time.

"But, no matter how many babes you plant in her belly, you'll never marry again. And you'll never be *all* farmer. Too much warrior's blood flows in your veins. Look at how you answered Olof's call," Sven's voice rumbled. "You'll have her in your bed soon...no matter your code of honor."

Helena's legs went weak beneath her and she leaned onto the longhouse. Hakan didn't reject Sven's notion of planting babes in her belly. The wooden wall held her upright as the fine morning disappeared. The sun glared too bright. Flies buzzed an irritating dance too close to her face.

Was there any man a woman could trust?

Her mind flashed on Guerin, fleeing for his own safety that fateful day. And now, Hakan and Sven talked of baser

149

wants, the wants of men who used women to feed lust alone. She clenched her half-formed braid and left it undone.

"Erik will want to follow in his father's footsteps. He's almost of an age…"

Helena walked into the longhouse, subdued by what she had overheard. Both men nodded at her and spoke of Gotland as she moved to the hearth. She couldn't stop the whirl in her head, but noticed Hakan had already buttered a chunk of bread for her. He nudged a bowl of berries to her spot on the table and kept talking with Sven. Such thoughtfulness flowed between them. 'Twould be so easy to give in to desires of the flesh.

But you are only a thrall.

"Eggs?" she called to the men as that brittle truth of her place in Hakan's life rang in her head.

Hakan glanced her way. "Aye."

"And for you, Sven?" Her tone was over bright as she plucked an egg from the basket and began to toss it up and down.

Sven's head pivoted from the full basket, to the egg she hefted in her palm, and then to Helena's face.

"I'll eat whatever you put in front of me." He grinned uneasily, eyeing the egg. "You'll not toss that at my head, will you?"

"This?" Helena held the light brown egg between thumb and forefinger. "Why would I do that?"

Sven glanced from Hakan to Helena. She cupped the egg and let it roll across her palm.

"Helena." Hakan's voice threaded with warning. "Twould please me greatly to have my eggs *cooked* this morn."

She gave the egg a small toss and it plopped into her palm intact. "As you wish."

She knelt by the fire and cracked several eggs on the pan's edge. The men faced each other, bewilderment writ on their faces. Sven tore off a hefty chunk of bread and popped a piece into his mouth. Helena stirred the broken yolks with the wooden spoon Hakan had made for her, viewing the men out of the corner of her eye.

"And what else would please you greatly?" she asked Hakan, tartness seeping from her.

"I have all I want." He looked at her as if she were touched in the head.

The yolks gelled under the wooden spoon. "All, save your son."

Hakan's brows snapped together. "Aye, all would be well with Erik here."

"And if I managed it, giving you Erik, would you give me *whatever* I wanted?"

"Of course he would, wouldn't you Hakan?" Sven coughed, clearing his throat. "'Twas all he could talk about on our hunts, how he wants to please you."

Hakan folded his arms, studying her. "I see the lay of things. You sound like Astrid, pushing for what you want. Is that why you asked me to tarry this morn?"

She flinched at the insult.

Hakan glared at Sven. "And someday your brain will catch up with your mouth."

Sven grimaced and tried turning the tense air with humor. "Helena, I've just been insulted."

She wrapped the pan's handle in her skirt and carried the egg-filled pan to the table. Her gaze was only on Hakan.

"Is that true? Did you talk about me when you went hunting?"

"Aye."

His voice was steady, but she noticed his pulse beating rapidly at his neck as she set the pan before them. He appeared to choose his words with care. Funny how men measure their words to a woman, if they think trouble brews. Sestra would be proud at her quick study of men.

"And if I gave you Erik, would you give me anything I wanted? My freedom? Even return me to Frankia?" She scooped up eggs, ready to serve them.

Hakan smiled and nodded. He looked like a man who had found his way out of a dangerous bog. "If you get Erik before the Althing, then I'll gladly grant your freedom. I'll even take you wherever you want to go."

She held the wooden spoon mid-air. "Do I have your solemn vow? Your word of honor?"

Hakan nodded. "As Sven is my witness, you have my word." The corners of his mouth turned in a wry smile. "And you know my word is true."

Helena finished serving the men and slid over the bench to join them. They spoke of places to find Gorm on Gotland. Helena's ear blurred the details of their words, so stunned was she at the promise made. The men, oblivious as only they could be, went on with their plans.

The meal was quickly finished. Everyone rose from the table. Hakan and Sven stopped to collect their weapons, strapping them into place. Walking into the sunshine, Gamle brought Hakan's great black horse, holding him steady as Hakan and Sven clasped the other's forearm. Helena tarried in the shade of the tree by her loom.

"All will be safe." Sven's vow was serious as he glanced toward the tree.

Closing the distance between them, Hakan advanced on her, his iron helmet dangling in his hand. The wolf's ice-blue eyes narrowed on her.

"Helena."

Was there longing in his voice?

With the loom at her back, she'd nowhere to go as he towered over her. Helena opened her mouth to bid him a cool good-bye, but words were lost. Hakan grabbed her arms and gave her a fierce kiss, lips pressing lips. Her body tensed. Leather and warmth surrounded her. There was nothing soft about him or his kiss. The Norseman's calloused hands gripped her arms, and one hand squeezed the silver armband.

This was possession.

Hakan let go, and as quickly as the kiss began, it ended. He placed his helmet on his head, a kind of shield to her. Metal bands rimmed his eyes, and the nose guard covered the length of his nose, flaring at the tip. His face half hidden, sword at his back, Hakan became the Norse warrior and was nothing of the gentle farmer who had wiled away the summer with her. He touched his forehead in salute and jumped into the saddle. Agnar's giant hooves churned the earth in a fast gallop, kicking clods of dirt in his wake.

Helena touched her lips. 'Twas the first time she had ever been kissed.

...

All oarsman, stripped to the waist, glistened with sweat under the sun's unrelenting heat. The dragon lady's giant red and white striped sail caught scant winds in the drive to Gotland, but the oiled wool reminded him of Helena.

'Twas the same heavy cloth that had dried in his meadow while he had sat in the shade with his maddening thrall. Keeping his eyes upward, Hakan's foot knocked over a bucket. Picking up the errant vessel, a bronze band was hot to the touch from sitting in the sun. Hakan set the bucket on a barrel and a memory flashed.

The stop in Dunhad.

Helena had used this bucket to wash herself. She had spoken to him then in the same bittersweet tone he had heard this morning. Hakan grinned at the memory of her surprised look when he spoke Frankish. A man needed the upper hand with the weaker sex. 'Twas the balance of nature.

He understood what had irked her then, but why this morning?

Hakan crossed his arms and stared at the open sea. That vow about Erik couldn't haunt him. Never would Helena get him from Astrid. There was that promise of seven years. A lot could happen between a man and a woman in seven years.

The kiss this morning marked the beginning. He would woo her when he returned.

Women made intriguing riddles, not to be taken for granted, cunning warriors of the wiliest nature.

He glanced at the bucket once more. "What are you up to Helena?"

15

Helena marked seven days since Hakan's departure—seven days of plotting. Boiling and preparing flax kept her busy from dawn to dusk, but gave ready moments to ponder the soundness of her plan. Everyone labored in like manner except Sven, who would come and go mysteriously, never explaining his whereabouts, not that any dared ask.

He took the evening meal with her, but nights ended with Helena sewing while Sven napped in the great chair. Her plan was bold, and, watching the Norseman slumber in Hakan's chair, 'twas time.

Helena pricked her finger, then snapped her needle in two.

"Ouch," she cried.

"What?" Rubbing his face, Sven sat up.

"Look." She held out her hand, rolling the broken ivory across her palm. A drop of blood welled up on her fingertip, close in color to her red stone pendant.

"A broken needle." Bleary-eyed and grumbling, he settled back in the chair.

"Aye, but 'tis my best and smallest one, perfect for stitching the best tunics."

Sven grunted at the fractured implement, but his face stayed blank. Helena dumped the ruined pieces in the fire and quickly pinched her bloodied finger to her apron.

"See this seam." She raised the tunic she had been laboring over and held the garment under his nose for closer inspection.

He squinted at the shirt, looking but not seeing. "A fine stitch, aye."

"Notice the small stitches inside? Now turn it over. They're hardly noticeable. This gives the appearance of the cloth holding itself together."

Sven's meaty hands took the superfine cloth and turned the fabric over for rapid inspection. Then, Helena picked up the tunic of a field thrall, setting another layer of her trap.

"Now, look here." She turned the garment inside out and pointed to a crude seam, tutoring Sven with patient explanation. "Do you see the obvious stitching? 'Tis made with a larger needle."

Opening a small case, she dumped its contents. Three bone needles clattered across the table. Holes for thread varied in size, but not so small as to match the well-sewn garment crumpled in Sven's lap. His pained gaze swept from the table to Helena.

"What does this have to do with me? You need me to purchase some trinkets for you?"

"*Trinkets?*" She chafed and snatched the linen tunic from him. "I need you to take me to Uppsala tomorrow. Unless you know the difference between elk bone and whale ivory needles?"

His forehead wrinkled at these words, and she pressed the advantage.

"I thought not." Helena set her hands at her hips. "I prefer ivory, 'tis stronger, and of course, I need a very small needle, otherwise you'd have to go back to the shops for me. Really, Sven, I'm not sure I can trust you to purchase the right one."

"Please." He held his hands up in surrender. "Tomorrow...after we break the fast." His bushy brows flattened in a hairy line. "Did Hakan leave you coin for the likes of this?"

She tapped the keys tied to her waist. "I have the means to reach his coin."

Sven glowered as he glanced from her face to the keys she controlled, but she anticipated the lay of his thoughts.

"I shall keep a careful count of what I take." Then, Helena tapped her chin. "We can even bring some of the cloth I've finished. Take it to Frosunda to trade for Hakan. He wanted to sell them this fall. She'll be most pleased with the lichen dyes I've been experimenting with..."

Sven's eyes glazed over from her rapid chatter. He rose from the chair and went for the door, but Helena's words spilled like a rushing river to his retreating back.

"...there's a wonderful purple that she's bound to like. And there's my madder dyed wools. Even better, Frosunda will have excellent needles. We'll have to take the cart..."

Sven pushed the door and stepped through the portal but poked his head through the opening.

"Tomorrow."

"Good, because tomorrow I'll..."

He shut the door, damming the wave of words. Helena's lips curved into a smile.

"...begin my return home."

...

Svea's marketplace teemed with life. Skies blustered gray and chill, but this failed to stop the robust Norse. Horses' hooves clapped a rhythm on hard packed earth while children made games of jumping over the few small puddles left from the night's light rain. Helena gave Sven what she knew he wanted: the companionship of a silent female on the ride to Uppsala.

Their cart lumbered down Uppsala's main road, where weathered buildings lined the street. After pulling up to

Frosunda's shop, Sven moved to unload the large chest at the back of the cart, only to be nudged away by Helena.

"Sven, Sven," she said, waving at him to put the load back in the wagon. "We don't take all our wares in for Frosunda to see. If we do, then she's apt to think all is hers for the taking. I'd rather bargain piecemeal."

Sven leaned an elbow on the chest and scratched his cheek.

"To tempt her into wanting more." Seeing his befuddled look, she explained, "And to gain a better price, since there are other traders. 'Tis a rare day to make the best deal on the first try. Much bartering and shop visits will be had today."

Sven's faced paled as if she threatened torture.

"You and Hakan have bartered before," she chided.

"Helena, I'll be—" His head swiveled around, taking in a row of places lining the waterfront "—there." Sven pointed to a small tavern where two men idled at the door.

He moved quickly to escape women discussing the merits of fabric and needles. Pleased at his exit, Helena placed both hands on the wagon and studied one end of the road and then the other.

Where is she?

Her quarry was nowhere in sight. Brushing loose strands of hair from her face, Helena smoothed her skirt and ventured inside the small shop.

Perched on a bench with needle and thread, Lady Frosunda sewed. She was the perfect image of Norse womanhood: tall and blonde, just like Helena's prey. Her shop reflected the woman, orderly and warm. A brazier glowed hot with embers near her feet and cloth hung from wooden pegs across the wall. Atop a table, green glass smoothers squatted in a row alongside scissors and needles of every size.

"Helena, welcome." Frosunda rested the mending in her lap. "What brings you to my shop today?"

Helena's shoulders eased, glad that Frosunda remembered meeting her once at Skardsbok Gard.

"I have some cloth that might interest you. We spoke of my weaver's skill, and I promised to show you my cloths first."

She motioned to the cart outside the shop. "Come look. I've been working all summer. I'm sure you'll be pleased."

Frosunda followed Helena to the cart, and Helena's heart beat faster in her chest. Could she trust this Norsewoman? Despite her nerves, she lifted the key ring with a steady hand and unlocked the first chest. Frosunda inhaled sharply at the array of lush colors and soft weaves, plunging her hands into the chest. Fine fabrics spilled from her hands as she tugged on cloth, testing its strength.

"How did you get the linen so soft?" she asked with breathless awe.

"The retting process."

Frosunda dug deeper into the chest, pulling out rich reds and greens.

"How did you create these colors?" She examined closely the weave's weft and warp. "Mardred told me you were talented. But I had no idea."

"My father was an apothecary, and he liked to try—"

Frosunda's thrall approached the wagon, cooing over the jewel-hued fabrics.

"Mistress...these are amazing." The thrall pulled out another length of cloth, waving it like a standard. She nestled the weave across the back of the cart.

This was exactly what Helena had hoped would happen.

Lure the stinging wasp with the beauty of flowers.

A small crowd of women gathered, chattering and fingering the cloth, but Frosunda shooed them away, claiming the entire chest. She sent her thrall back inside and beckoned the ladies come another day. When the last of the onlookers drifted off, Frosunda shut the lid and placed a possessive hand on the chest.

"I want it all."

"The entire chest?" Helena shook her head. "I don't think I can trade *all* to you. I did promise to visit other merchants."

Frosunda set her other hand on top, fingers splayed wide. "What will it take?"

Helena chewed her bottom lip. The risk of her plan required twists and turns like an intricate construction, one layer dependent on the other. Right then, ravens fluttered and squawked in the road, then flew across the harbor. A young woman, a thrall of Eyre by the looks, stepped off a Norse ship. One man bumped her none too gently from behind as though she were slow-moving cattle. Her chin dipped low, and her drawn face dulled with the bearing of a lifeless woman.

Freedom was as dear as breath.

"Lady Frosunda, I need your help."

The Norsewoman's golden eyebrows rose almost to her hairline at the blunt plea.

"Nay," Helena said, giving the woman a reassuring touch. "'Tis nothing that could cause you trouble."

But, 'twas a lie.

Helena gave the street a quick glance and waited for two prattling Norse maids to pass.

"Tell me," Frosunda coaxed, tipping her head closer.

"I need to meet with Astrid, the former wife of Lord Hakan." Helena spoke above a whisper. "You know of whom I speak?"

"Of course, I know the woman." Frosunda's blue-grey eyes flashed as she straightened her posture. "She purchases my wares regularly."

"Has she been here of late?"

"Aye." Frosunda canted her head sideways, warming to the conspiracy. "Why do you want to speak to the likes of her?"

"Let's just say I want to make a trade with her, a trade that will bring happiness to all."

Judging by her furrowed brow, the mysterious words did little to satisfy Frosunda, but she was a merchant above all. The trove of mouthwatering cloths was too enticing. Lady

Frosunda studied the battered chest her hands touched with ready ownership.

"What do you want me to do?"

"I want you to tell her there are swaths of like fabrics at Hakan's farmstead...you would suggest she go see for herself."

"That's all? Tell her about your cloths?" A puzzled frown clouded the lady's features, and she shook her head. "I don't think she'd *ever* set foot on Hakan's farmstead."

Helena dug into the bottom of another chest. She retrieved a small burlap bundle tied with jute string. Opening the coarse package, she revealed her best linen yet. Frosunda's shocked breath whistled through her mouth. She grabbed both sides of the cloth.

"This blue..." Frosunda's voice trailed off. "Such a vibrant shade. It shines like silk. How did you do it?" Frosunda tugged and pulled at the fabric, even sniffing it.

The cloth was flawless.

"I mixed woad and indigo with lichen I found here."

Frosunda shook her head as her voice turned wistful. "'Twould take years for you to teach someone." She held the weave up high. "You are very skilled."

Helena, pleased with the praise, leaned closer. "Will you help me by showing that swath to Astrid?"

Frosunda gripped the blue cloth in both hands against her bosom. "I will."

Helena smiled, and wayward wisps of hair blew across her face as she lowered her voice again.

"And when you do, tell Astrid that you've seen cloth fit for a queen. Tell her I wouldn't sell them to you today, but that I have chests brimming with like fabrics, this same silk-like weave, all under lock and key at Hakan's farmstead."

"And for passing along this message, you'll trade all these cloths to me?" Her fingertips touched the chest. "And, Lord Hakan won't mind?"

Fragile lines around the Norsewoman's eyes tightened as she shrewdly assessed her beseecher. The merchant woman took a risk here, but in answer to that worry, Helena jangled the keys that hung low from her waist.

"He trusts me with his keys. The details of this trade are of no consequence to him. If I barter with Lady Astrid, *all* of what she trades in return will go to Lord Hakan."

Frosunda's lips pursed as she glanced at the key ring. She flicked unbound hair over her shoulder.

"I'll do it." She raised the vibrant blue cloth. "And this is mine for passing on this simple information?"

"'Tis yours to keep for helping me." Then, Helena tipped her head at the chest. "But this you must purchase."

"Agreed."

Frosunda's firm nod and quick step away from the cart gave Helena pause. One layer to her plan was firmly in place, but the next layer was more fragile. Her heart pounded and her lips dried. 'Twas almost too easy.

"Wait." Helena licked her lips. "Please understand, 'tis not just a message." She looked away, searching for the rights words. "Do it in a way that is...is—"

"Crafty?" Frosunda supplied. "Leading her to believe I share a great secret that benefits her above all other women of Uppsala?"

Helena winced at the truthful words. Halfway between the wagon and the shop, the Norsewoman's skirts danced in a brisk breeze. She set a hand on her hip and viewed Helena with knowing eyes.

"I've survived two husbands in Uppsala, the first forced on me by my father, and now I live a comfortable life. What I have has not come easily, but 'tis mine." Her chin tipped high. "Now, the esteemed thrall of Uppsala's great chieftain seeks my help. You want to see Astrid alone? So be it. I'll pass the message—" Her lips twitched. "—with careful intent, appealing to her vanity. 'Twill be one woman helping another."

A burden lifted from Helena's shoulder, a glimmer of hope that this could truly work. And within her frame, warmth spread from the knowledge that others saw how Hakan favored her.

"Now, can we go inside to discuss the price of that chest?" Frosunda asked, pulling open the door to her shop.

Helena lifted the chest from the ox cart, welcoming the burden. She carried it into the shop and set it on the wood floor. Frosunda gave directions to her thrall as if their private talk outside hadn't happened. This Norsewoman was not one to underestimate. Helena loosened her cape, a necessity on this cool summer day, and slung it over her arm.

"I need to see your smallest needles," she said.

Frosunda waved a hand across her store as she bent over a small coin chest. "Please. See if any of my wares interest you."

A display of wrist cuffs caught her eye, all dark material threaded with silver and some with gold. She fingered the pretty pieces, boasting intricate embroidery, remembering a dark blue band encircling Astrid's lower arms the night of the Glima.

Frosunda raised her head from the coin chest. "I offer threaded gold for Frankish and Saxon traders who come to port. You are Frankish?"

Helena fingered the designs. "Frankish, aye, but I've never seen the likes of these in my village."

Frosunda came to stand beside Helena. "Then you've not mixed with people of wealth."

The words held no sting. Frosunda was a proprietress. Her mind worked in measures of barter and trade, assessing opportunities. Helena played with the chain at her neck. Her body warmed the gold that touched her skin.

"A simple maid from a small village south of Paris doesn't see a lot."

One corner of Frosunda's mouth turned up. "You've turned more than a few Norsemen on their heads with your *simple* ways."

Frosunda patted a superior red and gold cuff. "I'll be glad to show you how to create such a cuff sometime."

Frosunda moved to a scale suspended from a beam over a table. The Norsewoman removed a small, iron ball from a metal plate on one side and stacked silver ingots on the other.

"You can make the thread, if you find a talented silversmith." Frosunda bent close to the scale, eyeing the plates for perfect evenness.

"No such skilled person works on Hakan's farm. Mayhap Halsten and Mardred's blacksmith—"

"What say you to twelve silver ingots? One for each length of cloth. They are excellent quality, but not so long." All business, Frosunda beckoned her over to discuss the price.

"'Tis fair." Helena nodded.

Frosunda balanced another ball on the scale when the door flung open. A voice boomed into the small space.

"What goes here?"

Frosunda's hands knocked the balanced scale. Iron and ingots shot across the floor, landing with a noisy crash. Helena dropped to her knees to pick up silver shards and the round metal counterweights.

The Norsewoman's lips drew a tight line. "I should've known 'twas you, Sven Henriksson." Taking angry steps toward him, she sniffed him. "What? There wasn't enough ale at the tavern?" Frosunda shook her head. "If it weren't for friendship with your mother, I'd ban you from my shop."

"Aye, but you'd miss me, Frosunda. Who else but Sven Henrikkson to give excitement to your well-ordered life?" He grinned in his good-natured way and gathered the metal balls that rolled to his feet.

The merchant woman sighed and took the ingots Helena picked up from the floor.

"Sven, would you be so kind as to move this chest to my back room?"

The Norseman hefted the chest and strode across the small space. The Norsewoman wrapped the ingots in burlap and took out another scrap of cloth. Something small went inside the scrap that she handed to Helena.

"These are three of my best ivory needles." Frosunda cupped Helena's outstretched hand with both of her own. "And I'll stick to our bargain. Every word of it."

"Thank you."

Sven came from the back room and bid Frosunda good-bye. He helped Helena climb back onto the ox cart and asked, "What was that about a bargain?"

Helena stretched her neck making a play at viewing the clouds.

"Oh, nothing...idle talk between women."

"And no more shops to visit?" he asked with rare quietness, glancing at untouched chests in the cart.

"Nay. We go home."

She turned to smile at him and ask about his respite at the tavern. The words came out, but not before she caught a sharp, assessing look from the man everyone took for an amiable oaf.

...

Three miserable days of rain and wind slowed life on the farmstead to a near halt. The storm was not so bad as to destroy the crops. Instead, the men idled with the coming and going of the wetness. Such was not the case for Olga and Helena. The looms and boiling cauldrons were moved inside the pithouse.

And, on the stormiest day, Helena's quarry arrived.

Cloths swimming in cauldrons soaked up color in roiling water. Helena stirred a large birch stick around a dark, red onionskin brew. Steam rose high, and sweat beaded her forehead, plastering hair to skin. She swiped the back of her hand across her face, and Olga chortled over the dye Helena smeared on her face. Laughing as they were, Helena almost missed the strange man at the pithouse door. Wearing worn, russet wool and clutching his cap between nervous hands, the man called to Helena.

"Please...H...H...Helena," he stammered. "Please come speak to my Lady." He kept wringing his hat through twitching fingers.

Helena followed the man past a horse-drawn cart, the sides of which bore ornate carvings. A large man held the reins, and his beady stare traced Helena's walk from the pit house to the longhouse. Passing through the lintel, she found Astrid admiring her reflection in a polished iron shield boss. The lady was a sight to behold, patting blonde tresses swept into elaborate knots and held in place with ivory combs. Her tunic was the finest purple wool, with saffron and red embroidery webbing the neckline. Rich cuffs of saffron and red weave dressed her delicate wrists.

"Ah, there you are. I hoped you'd be nearby." She played with silver earrings that hung from pinkish lobes. "I don't like to be kept waiting."

Astrid gave her a cursory glance. The noblewoman winced, a subtle display that she found Helena lacking.

Helena badly needed to bathe and don new garments. Smeared colors streaked her apron and tunic. Murky tints stained her work-worn hands. She splayed her fingers, and her nails were dark-rimmed from a lichen dye, though the effect looked more like dirt. She balled her hands into her apron. The sweat that pricked her body now wasn't from hot cauldrons.

Astrid picked up her skirt with dainty hands, and her feet, shod in doeskin boots, made a graceful path around the center table.

"I see Hakan's keeping his vow of a simple life," she said, sighing. "He always had the mind of a lesser chieftain." Astrid eyed the spacious eiderdown bed. "But he keeps some luxuries."

She peered at Helena and lips reddened by hawthorn berries pressed into a harsh line. Of course the question of the bed hung between them. Who slept where?

Helena almost wanted to laugh from relief. 'Twas so simple. She chided herself for acting like a startled deer. She was struck with the idea that somehow she was on equal footing with this highborn woman. Their mode of dress bespoke different lives, but all ended there.

Was Hakan the currency both wanted?

She couldn't work that puzzle as her guest demanded attention.

Astrid drummed long fingers on the table. "Well, don't just stand there. Aren't you going to invite me to sit? Offer me some mead?" A sharp-pitched sound that should have been a laugh came out. "We Norse are renowned for our hospitality, you know. 'Twas one of the things Hakan cherished about me most."

Helena walked briskly to the table. "Please sit. We don't have mead, but perhaps a fine cider or ale?"

Astrid did not take the great carved chair, but instead sat at the bench.

"Cider will do."

Helena fetched the earthen pitcher cooling at the windowsill and poured amber liquid into a Rhenish glass. The blonde beauty drank slowly, swallowing every last drop, then held the glass up to admire its blue and yellow designs.

"I understand you're a weaver of some talent. I'd like to see these fabrics you've created." She set the costly cup on the table. "If they're good, I'm willing to make a worthwhile trade." Her eyes glinted with avarice as they shifted from the glass to Helena. "A quiet trade to benefit you alone, thrall? Every woman, even the lowborn, needs her own coin."

The noblewoman's jibe to her station failed to hit the mark. Helena set down the pitcher and let the satisfaction of a well-placed snare settle. She stood tall and flattened her dye-stained hands on the table as she faced Lady Astrid.

"I thank you for the offer to better my lot in life, Lady, but I serve the pleasure of my master, Lord Hakan. I would not deceive him or steal from him."

Astrid's face pinched. "I see."

Undaunted, Helena continued. "He trusts me to trade honestly in his stead, and I won't abuse his trust."

Helena pulled up the keys hanging low from her waist and made a show of going through one key after another.

"Ah, this is the one." Metal clinked loudly, announcing she was no ordinary thrall.

Astrid's eyes narrowed on the massive key ring. Helena moved to a middle-sized chest that held the coveted cloth. She dared not vex the woman anymore, but the tense moment was forgotten when she unrolled bolts of fabric across the table. Astrid examined the linen weaves closely, and anger evaporated as her eyes rounded at the display. One splash of color after another unraveled atop the long, plank table.

"'Tis truly an amazing weave...the color. I've never seen a design like this. Not in all of Svea. Nor anything from merchant ships, even from Byzantium." She turned the fabric over in her hands. "Such a bold blue...shiny, like-silken threads are in the weave."

Her eyes, dark like violets, spread wide with unfeigned awe. Helena sat down at the table as an equal and basked in the pleasure of winning this woman's hard-won esteem. Something told her that little impressed Lady Astrid.

"Before the Danes took me, my father and I experimented with dyes. As to the weave, I've lived all my life at the loom. If I didn't have to tend our flock, you could find me at my loom or with needle in hand. Only last winter did my weaves come out so well." She smiled and curled a leg underneath her, getting comfortable on the bench. "I like to think my fabrics would have found their way north someday."

"I want it all. Name your price." Astrid's eyes looked like sharp stones. "And thrall, no one else is to have cloth of this quality."

The lady held the fabric possessively, as if it were already hers. Helena rose from her perch on the bench. This was becoming too easy. She retrieved the last bolts of fabric and rolled them across the table for Astrid's inspection. The

Norsewoman covered her mouth like an excited young maid as fine colors spilled before her. The time was ripe.

"These are yours if you give Erik to his father before the Althing."

"What?" Astrid's eyes flared. She stood upright, almost knocking over the bench. "Did Hakan put you up to this?"

"Nay," Helena assured her, "he knows nothing." Pointing to the swaths of linen, she said, "This cloth could be tree bark for all he cares. Strong sails of rough wool mean more to him. But, he knows 'tis important for a father to see his son."

"Thrall," Astrid's voice shrilled. "You outdo yourself with such forward talk. Do you have any idea who I am?"

Astrid's fingers dug like claws into the fabric before her. Those fingers could very well be on Helena's throat, yet she moved closer to the Norsewoman. Was not this meeting a gamble? Much like warriors who diced away all their coin while others left with bulging purses? She could win or lose all.

"Please, listen to what I have to say, and—" Helena grabbed the smallest span of cloth. "—this piece is yours…just for listening."

Astrid's eyes coveted the material. She snatched the cloth, a rich emerald green, and sat down. "I'm listening."

Helena slid onto the bench, and one hand rubbed her collarbone and neck, giving her a moment to gather her thoughts. Her pendant's chain rolled under her bodice, a comforting token.

"Lord Hakan plans to bring the matter of Erik before your annual meeting."

"This I already know," Astrid snapped

Helena cringed, afraid she had been too blunt. Her fingers twirled the chain at the top of her bodice. She needed strength and strategy to bargain with this harsh-tongued woman who held so much power, but plain talk was best.

"Then you know he *will* gain Erik, as is your custom. And what will you have?" Helena leaned bent elbows on the table and her head canted at the rivers of color splashed before

169

them. "I will give you all these cloths if you relent now. Before the Althing."

A sliver of a smile curved Astrid's lips. "And what if the Assembly never happens? Much goes on in Svea these days." Her cornflower eyes slanted across the rich colors. "These could end up in my possession by...other means."

Helena leaned closer and the table's wood dug into her. "I don't understand."

Astrid hummed, a smug smile on her face. "You're a thrall. You wouldn't."

Helena's fingers played with her necklace, rolling the chain in nervous habit. The bench creaked underneath her as she slumped in defeat. Did she want this trade too much? Astrid stood up and her busy hands skimmed cloth. The Norsewoman gave a rough fold to one bolt of cloth before moving on to another, and for all the world, she appeared to be a Norse matron making a purchase. She idly adjusted a comb in her hair, a comb Helena recognized from the night of the Glima.

"'Tis a pretty comb," she said, voicing her thoughts.

"Gorm gave it to me," Astrid said with pride in her voice, not bothering to look at Helena.

"And you will marry this man? Gorm?"

A frown marred Astrid's smooth-skinned face as she examined more fabric. "Someday."

"But you have known him a long time, have you not?"

Lady Astrid's red lips thinned, and she stopped viewing the fabrics to glare at Helena. 'Twas then Helena knew: the Norsewoman had much, yet so little. Men eluded her. Beauty so often snared a man, a trap to catch his eye, but Lady Astrid's beauty would never be enough to keep a man. Her heart was too cold and brittle.

"Have you ever wondered why Gorm hasn't asked you to marry him?" The unguarded words slipped from Helena's lips.

"What do you mean?" Astrid's fine-boned visage tightened.

Helena shrugged. "I speak only as one woman to another. I was betrothed to a man before I was stolen by the Danes." She pulled her necklace from her dress. "See. 'Tis my bride's gift...hidden when the Danes took me. Lord Hakan doesn't want it. He bade me keep it."

"'Tis not a gift for certain favors?" Astrid leaned forward and palmed the red stone, weighing it in her hand. Her gaze went to the eider down bed. "Then, you and Hakan are not..."

Helena shook her head so fast her hair spilled over her shoulders. "Nay."

The Norsewoman turned the stone side to side with uncalloused hands. Yet, her fingers bore no rings. No gifts from Gorm to grace her hands?

"I understand the wont to be married, and how irksome when a man's ardor cools. Nothing in life goes quite as planned, does it?"

"Gorm wants me," Astrid snapped. Yet, she let go of the pendant to plop her bottom in a most ungraceful manner on the bench.

The red stone swung back and forth. The table's edge bit into Helena's forearms as she leaned closer to deliver the sting.

"Yet, he *hasn't* made you his wife."

Stricken whiteness painted Lady Astrid's face. Helena's words had hit the mark. The highborn woman leaned on her elbows, her narrow-framed body slumped against the table's edge. Helena poured cider into the Rhenish glass and passed it to her. 'Twas a small gesture. The Norsewoman set the rim to her lips but didn't drink. She set the glass down, staring blankly at the cloths.

Helena chose her words with care. "You want Gorm to marry you, yet he evades you on this."

Astrid dropped her head into her clean, white hands and nodded like a defeated woman. Long fingers slipped into her crown of white-blonde hair, mussing neatly combed tresses.

"He makes promises that he easily breaks."

"Did you ever consider that you are mother to the son of his most hated enemy? Why would he want a reminder of his enemy under his nose in his own longhouse?" Helena gave the slightest shrug. "Some men cannot bear to care for the offspring of another man."

Astrid's red-rimmed eyes, glossy with tears, stared back at Helena.

"I've thought the same." The Norsewoman rubbed two fingers to her temple. "Since his latest return to Svea, Gorm watches Erik with much malice in his eyes. There have been times I've feared for my son in my own home." These last words came in a high-pitched whisper.

In that instant, Helena's heart softened to Astrid. The viper truly cared for her son, but was snared in a life of her own making.

"He visits you often?"

"My farmstead is far, the only one off a small bay a long ride from Uppsala. Gorm comes and goes without any in Svea knowing."

"I'm sure if Erik weren't around, he'd marry you."

If words could spill blood, then Astrid looked as if their talk bled her in a slow death.

Silence filled the longhouse, save for the patter of new rain outside the door. Helena's words were bold, even mercenary in their aim. Erik should be with his father, but she was pushed by her own wish for freedom. That truth niggled at her conscience, but the twinge passed. 'Twas too late to tread with care.

Wisps of the highborn woman's hair came undone from careful coils. Her red-rimmed eyes mingled hardness with some other emotion. Love? Pain? She folded an arm over her stomach and rocked gently back and forth.

"I will do it. Erik needs to be far from Gorm." Astrid rose tall from the bench. Some of her hair stood out, and lamplight behind her made her look wild and fierce. "And I *will* take all the cloth here." She swept her hand across the table. "And that." Astrid pointed at the pendant.

Helena covered the red jewel. "My pendant? Why?"

"We all give up something, don't we? Each of us—you, me, Hakan—gains something and loses something. I'm sure you have your reasons for this meeting." Astrid's smile was not the tender kind. Her eyes shone with a hard gleam. "You do want this, don't you?"

The stone, hard and cold in her fingers, had cost so much. Helena's jaw clenched as she recalled the cut that had curved across her cheek. The pain had healed long ago, but the mark remained. Wisdom, hard-won from her trials, spread its own kind of healing balm as she spoke sad words.

"No one goes away from you unscathed," Helena said, removing the chain from her neck and setting it in the Norsewoman's outstretched hand.

"Everything has its price." Astrid slipped the jewelry into her pocket and began to gather the cloth.

Helena planted both dye-stained hands firmly on the fabric. "The cloth stays until you deliver Erik."

Silence hung between them, save the rain's song outside. Slowly, the Norsewoman tilted her head in a show of respect.

"Aren't you the clever one." Then she patted her pocket where the red pendant hid and her smile held no warmth. "I shall enjoy this."

That venomous jab failed to spread its poison. How little the Norsewoman knew. To let go of the once valued stone...'twas freeing. With a lightness that eased over her form from head to toe, Helena dipped her head in obeisance.

"May the jewel do for you what it's done for me."

The message was lost on Astrid. She moved through the longhouse, her purple skirts swaying in her exit. Outside, grey skies poured steady, fat raindrops.

"Did you love him?" Helena asked. "Ever?"

Standing in the lintel, Astrid peered at the drumming rain and tucked the green cloth under her arm, one of her prizes of the day, and took her time before answering.

"I love Erik," she said.

The Norse beauty took a bracing breath and gathered her skirts against the muddied yard.

"In three days, thrall." And she was gone.

Weak in the knees, Helena sank to the bench. She viewed the longhouse, massive in size unlike her own village home. Norse implements surrounded her: shields and weapons, soapstone lamps and treasure-filled chests. Yet, intrigue and mysteries abounded in these north lands, so different from her once simple life. Today she had set in motion a new course.

Did she meddle where problems were best left to uncoil without her help? Rain and wind skirmished beyond the open portal. Their battle brought a damp chill through the open door.

A rainbow of fine, richly colored cloth covered the table. Helena touched the weaves. Creations of her own making, with minor flaws obvious only to her eyes: an overlarge thread here, a thickening of color there. A master of the craft controlled a dye's cast well.

Today's meeting spiraled with unexpected turns. Remnants of the conversation pieced together in her mind. One fragment pressed like a burr to her skin: *Gorm comes and goes without any in Svea knowing.*

Her fingers covered her mouth as the heavens poured outside.

Was Gorm here now, while Hakan tried to hunt him down in Gotland?

16

"**B**e the bear again," Erik pleaded.

Sven lay sprawled under the birch trees clustered near Hakan's longhouse. His tongue lolled out the side of his mouth, a mock bear felled in the hunt. The boy giggled at the mighty Norseman's feigned exhaustion, launching himself with a thud at Sven's chest.

"Come on, Sven." Erik drew out the Norseman's name in childish plea, stretching himself belly to belly over Sven's generous torso. "'Tis fun."

Sven lifted his head. "You have chased me down and slain me a score of times already, young Erik. How many more hunts must we practice?"

Raising his immense size from the ground, Sven tossed the laughing boy upside down over his shoulder. Erik's bare feet dangled to Sven's girth, and boyish haunches clad in light blue trousers wiggled.

"At least another score," Erik said, and his laughing face turned red.

"Helena," Sven bellowed in the yard.

"Aye?"

"Have we need of tender Nordic loin this eve?"

"Would that be Nordic loin of about eight winters?" Helena paused midst stirring a slow heating cauldron. "Aye, Olga could make a feast of it."

"Good." Sven swatted the backside of the laughing boy. "'Tis prime, or will be by the time I show him how to throw a Norse hammer."

Erik strained to flip over Sven's shoulder, but a meaty fist held him place. "We're going to throw the hammer? Do I get one of my own?"

"A smallish one." Sven spoke to the warrior-in-training at his shoulder. Then he touched his fingertips to his forehead in salute to Helena. "We're off."

Sven hauled Erik as if he were nothing more than a small sack on his shoulder. Helena gripped the heavy stick in her hands and watched them head to the meadow. Erik's boyish frame moved constantly, spilling joy like an overflowing cup. He jumped. He ran. He played at mock battles and hunts. Or he ate and slept.

In the sennight since Astrid's bond servants had delivered Erik, the boy did little else but move at high speed or be at complete rest. Nay, complete sleep. His eyes lit at learning everything about his father's farmstead. But weapons and the ways of war caught his eye the most.

Helena dabbed her apron to her forehead. Sven relished the role of teacher to the lad. If 'twere possible, his barrel chest puffed out more with pride at how quickly Erik learned the art of Nordic war, even fashioning two small wooden swords, one for the boy and one for himself to practice battles. The large Norseman played the skald, recounting Hakan's feats in battle, retelling of skirmishes in distant lands. With more than ten winters of adventuring, Sven had a never-ending supply of stories. Sven often let the boy win at sword play, dropping to the ground in huffs and puffs of dramatic display.

But the one battle Sven couldn't win was getting Helena to tell how Erik came to be at Hakan's farmstead.

Savoring that victory was short-lived with the present stench of candle making. Boiling fat to make tallow was odorous work. So awful the task, she labored outdoors, rather than trap the tangy aroma in the pit house with still more weaving to do. Helena's face scrunched in displeasure. Nearby, Gamle chopped wood. Chickens squabbled loudly that she missed the approaching horse and rider.

"I had not thought to be welcomed back with such a look," Hakan called out as he dismounted Agnar, looking gloriously dirty and safe.

"Hakan!" she yelled. Running through the yard, she near flew into his arms.

Helena buried her face in his jerkin, breathing deep of sea and leather and warmth. A canopy of branches swayed, fanning shade and sunlight over them, but new, tender heat pricked her skin. That impulsiveness shook her to the core. The reaction was pure and true, no matter what had been said before his leaving. She pulled away, letting her hands slip the length of his arms to catch his hands.

"I worried..." Her voice trailed as she checked him helmet to boot.

All limbs appeared intact, but not unscathed. A wide, bloodied cloth wrapped above one knee, and he favored the leg. Yet, the weight that had settled on her in his absence lifted. In meager moments, the air between them shifted. Her unbridled greeting stoked smoldering embers that would not be denied.

"Helena," Hakan whispered her name.

He removed the helmet and his eyes burned ice-blue. Her body read all too well the message in his eyes, and breath came heavy in her chest. Such stark hunger.

The breeze rustled his hair, more strands flaxen white from so much sun. She touched the unbound length, a slow treasuring exploration, and lowered her gaze to his chest. The darkening of his eyes was too much. Every inch of her pulsed awareness, from bare feet grazing his wolf skin boots, to his hard frame pressing close. These jumbled sensations overwhelmed.

"Your hair is overlong, my lord. It needs cutting." Her voice was thick to her ears.

Her palms made slow, light circles on his chest. The leather jerkin beneath her hands was a kind of armor that kept her from him. She braved a look at his face, and Hakan's full wanting melted her. His was an invitation to explore. Her fingertips traced his unshaven jaw, tingling from the abraded feel. 'Twas rough warmth...so like the man. Hakan dropped Agnar's reins and his calloused hands skimmed her bare arms, pausing at the silver manacle that claimed her as his.

In his eyes, a mix of need and...

"The day I left...the kiss—" he said, his voice deep and uneven.

Helena set two fingers to his mouth. "We'll not speak of it." She pressed against him and gave her own bold invitation. "I'd rather we try again."

Wolfish blue eyes flared, and his mouth sought hers, a tender touch, counter to the fierce possession at his leaving. Lips grazed, a brush of skin to skin, and a burst of curling heat shot through her.

Helena rose on tiptoe and her body sought his, wanting full contact. The scent of mint from his mouth, the graze of whiskers against her cheeks, 'twas an assault like rich mead to her senses. When her curious, questing lips parted under his, Hakan's mouth moved, seeking more. Her body hummed to the tune of his kisses, each growing more insistent, more needy.

A surge so powerful filled her, a shocking blend of enticement and torment.

She pulled away, but her hands clasped him, sliding down the length of his arms. Helena needed the strength of Hakan's warm flesh under her palms to ground her. Her heart thumped a rapid cadence, not easing its race. He could easily command her body with simple kisses. He already had.

The dangerous allure for more set a tempting trap. Hakan was an elixir that befuddled her. Her path, her purpose, had been so clear.

"I thought often of my return...of you," he said. "Not wise for a warrior who should keep his mind on other things." His blue eyes darkened and his breath came harder, too.

Helena stepped back and circled a hand low on her belly to quell the heat within.

"I smell of sea travels." The corners of his mouth drooped. "I planned to clean up in Uppsala, but once the ship reached harbor, I couldn't wait."

"'Tis not that—"

"Father! Father!" Erik yelled across the distance.

Boyish arms and legs pumped as he raced toward Hakan. Sven followed behind, slow moving as he carried wooden practice swords and hammers.

Helena pulled away. Erik buried his head against his father and wrapped his arms around his waist as if he'd never let go. Disbelief and shock writ itself across Hakan's face as he looked from Helena to Sven. Hakan set a careful hand on the crown of Erik's white-blonde head, the touch hesitant and unsure. But Erik's presence was real. Hakan's arms encircled the youth. The two held each other in silence broken only by the child's muffled sobs.

...

"Did you get him, Father?" Erik asked, sitting beside Hakan at the large plank table.

They shared a light repast, but a feast worthy of a king was planned for the evening. Erik questioned Hakan in between gulping hunks of sweet bread. Sticky globs of honey collected at the corners of his mouth. The spot he took on the bench had once been occupied by Helena. The subtle pang in her chest felt foolish...to be jealous of a child, especially since father and son had been long separated.

"Get who?" Hakan asked as he tore off a chunk of bread.

179

"Gorm."

Erik's blue eyes, so dark like his mother's, studied Hakan. Helena guessed the boy enjoyed the victory of knowing that news as she dipped her spoon into her stew. Sven and Hakan exchanged questioning looks. Erik's legs swung under the table and he swallowed another bite.

"Sven said you were after some chieftain not paying tithe to King Olof. But I knew different." The boy sat up taller, smiling his satisfaction. "Mother said that you were after Gorm." He turned the hunk of bread this way and that, scouting his next bite.

"Is that why she sent you here?" Sven asked from his side of the table.

"I'm here because of Helena." He swiped his mouth, glancing between his father and Sven. "Don't you know?"

"I've only just come home." Hakan leaned his forearms on the table, looking at Helena then back to Erik. "What have you heard?"

"One night mother was talking to her thrall, Britta. She said something about Loki needing his due and she had to give me to you." Erik gulped down his cider, gripping the wooden cup with both hands. "She talked about the king sending you after Gorm...and something about deciding her path. Oh, and that your thrall, Helena, convinced her."

Helena cringed at the word *thrall*. Echoes of the Norsewoman's scathing tongue had almost been erased from her mind. When Helena looked up from her stew, Sven and Hakan watched her. Sven was no longer the bear-like oaf as his eyes assessed her. But Hakan's face was impassive and distant, so like the early days on his ship.

"I like Helena," Erik said, setting his elbows on the table.

"And I like you, too, Master Erik." She tipped her head in cheerful deference.

"But, Father, did you find him?"

Gorm.

"I did not, but I found others."

"Because you're the king's best chieftain." Young blue eyes filled with adoration.

Hakan smiled at his son and tousled his hair.

"Sven's told me all about your adventures, fighting and raiding...building your own ship...fighting for King Olof." Erik's slender arm, browned by the summer sun, shot out in mock sword play. He slashed and swiped at an unseen enemy.

"Anything else?" Hakan asked, laughing.

Helena shifted in her seat under Sven's silent attention. Dark eyes narrowing, the Norseman measured her over his horn of ale. Did he guess what had happened at Frosunda's shop? Would it matter? Young Erik was home with his father. She smiled sweetly, then gave her attention to the boy who burst with news.

"Sven took me to Uncle Halsten's farmstead. We saw your knorr ship being built. Helena went with us. But, Sven got a little mad with that ironsmith from Normandy. Sven told him not to talk to Helena so much."

Hakan's brows rose a notch.

"'Twas nothing," she assured him. *Did it matter?*

Sven snorted. "Sniffing around her like a bull moose in spring. But, you can forgive the boy. A fine ironworker for one so young. Shows much promise, that one."

Hakan glowered at this news and speared an apple with his knife tip.

"'Tis a pleasant friendship. Nothing more." Helena swirled her spoon in the stew, chasing a carrot piece around the bowl. She stood up and said, "I need to check the cauldrons. And there is much to do for this evening."

One of the thralls had run to Halsten and Mardred's farm with the news of Hakan's homecoming. There was much to be accomplished concerning her everyday tasks, as well as the feast. When the time was right, she would talk to Hakan.

What would she say? The question kept poking as a burr to skin.

"When can we take a voyage?" Erik asked, like many children focused on his own wants.

"I just returned from a voyage. Give me a few days to scrape the sea salt off from this journey."

"Gotland's not so far. We can take a voyage to some place like Frankia? Frankia's far away, but not so far as Byzantum."

"Byzantium," Hakan corrected, but his eyes lit with possessiveness on Helena as she gathered her bowl. "I need to stay home and look to what is mine."

...

His son didn't stop a moment to rest, waxing long over Helena's descriptions of her homeland. Hakan wanted talk of journeys to Frankish lands to stop. With the boy here, would she hold him to his word? Not after those kisses. She must agree that staying was best. His farmstead was her home, and she'd finally accepted this.

One question swirled in his mind: How did Erik come to be here now?

But he'd not do the asking with Erik nearby.

Sven rose from the table. "There's plenty of daylight before our feast. Let's give your father a demonstration of what you learned. What say you, Erik? A mock battle or two before we take the sauna?"

Erik grabbed Hakan's arm and pulled him toward the lintel. "Sven told me good warriors go for the knees first. Cuts there are marks of Norse battle. Is that true?"

Hakan glanced back into the longhouse and found nothing painful about Helena's mark on his home. Green boughs lined the headboard of his bed. One of her embroidered cloths covered the bread bowl. An apron smeared with slashes of red and purple hung from a peg near his shields. A new tunic she sewed hung over a shield, an affront to any serious warrior, but pleasant to his eyes. He smiled.

She had been at work with her dyes again. He hoped that made her happy.

Hakan walked into the sunshine, his full heart sensing doom. He turned to see Helena's slender backside. Sun-browned legs struck ground under the soothing sway of her shorter russet tunic. She collected kindling in her apron, lost in the task.

When she turned around and caught him staring at her, she touched her fingertips to her mouth. He waved, knowing she recalled their kisses by the trees. There would be more of that. Much more.

From the practice field, Sven and Erik clashed wooden swords. Hakan turned again to Helena, but she failed to notice him, moving like one adrift in deep thought.

...

The farmstead hummed with the coming feast, a feast worthy of a chieftain's homecoming. Never mind that this had been a minor voyage. Hakan and Erik were to be honored. Gamle, dispatched to alert Mardred and Halsten, returned with news that at twilight the neighboring farmstead, family, and some warriors from Uppsala would join in the celebration.

Olga, Hlavo, Helena, and Gamle labored with fervor. Armor polished. Fowl prepared. New candles lit. Snowy linen covered the table. Sven and each family member would drink honeyed mead and Frankish wine. Aromas of cumin, pepper, mustard, and even costly cinnamon filled the air. Finally, Olga and Helena surveyed their handy work, well pleased with the results.

Wiping her hands on her apron, Olga blew a sigh of relief. "We did well today. But you. You are not ready."

Helena glanced at her equally soiled apron and the russet tunic saved for her most menial tasks. "'Tis not a feast for thralls, Olga, but for Hakan and Erik."

Olga leveled a long-suffering gaze on Helena and nudged her along.

"There is little time," she scolded. "Go to the pit house. You'll find a tub of water and soap. And there's a flagon of scented oil. Put it on your skin. 'Twill soften the day's work...make your hands as fine as any highborn woman's."

Like Lady Astrid. She ran her palms over her drab tunic.

"A clean tunic awaits you. To the pit house." Olga pointed at the large shed. "Off with you."

Entering the pit house, she found the tub amongst the cauldrons. On a barrel sat the earthen jar of oil scented from wildflowers. Raising the flagon to her nose, Helena closed her eyes as memories of her Norse summer swirled.

"That crafty old woman," she said through soft mirth.

Returning the vessel to its place, she noticed a folded tunic, the same one from the mid-summer's festival, and a plain, soft undergarment. The first night Hakan had touched her. She shivered at the pleasant memory. Fingering the fine cloth, Helena wrestled with the question: was she thrall or valued lady?

Hakan's one wish was finally fulfilled: Erik was in his home.

Did he need her? Would another thrall replace her someday?

Shirking the stained russet work tunic, she slipped into the tub and enjoyed the warmth. Let these Norse take their ice-cold dips in the river. She'd bathe in the Frankish manner. Helena lolled, unmoving, laying her head on the tub's wooden rim. Her hair floated on the water's surface like dark vines.

Would Hakan honor his word and return her home? Did he want her to stay? Unrelenting images spun inside her head. Kissing him. Touching him. Being touched by him. The easy companionship they shared. The light and joy in his eyes at the sight of his son. He had looked close to tears the moment Erik had embraced him.

She splayed fingers over her belly. When would she have a babe of her own? Sven's words sprang to mind, an ugly memory: *Plant a babe in her belly, that will make her stay.*

Nothing of love or the promise to wed. Touching her cheek, Helena found the faint line the cut had left. Her fingers followed the trail to the jaw, where the cut had been the worst.

Who would want a marred peasant woman?

A heavy tear rolled down her cheek at the craving of family...her own.

Voices outside and the wrinkled tips of her fingers forced the bath's end. She quickly washed her hair and stepped out of the tub. Helena removed the armband that marked her as Hakan's slave, rubbing scented oil on her arms. At first she thought to put the oil quickly on her arms, hands, and feet. She needed to serve the feast within the longhouse.

Tonight, there'd be no rush to serve. A peevish wish to dally, to look to herself, made her linger over the luxuriant feel of oil on her skin. She poured the scented balm everywhere. Even the most humble Frankish woman cared for herself with simple fragrant lavender oils. She missed the bounty of her homeland.

Sitting on a stump, Helena tended her hair with the crude elk bone comb. Outside in the yard, voices floated and mingled. People arrived for the feast. Her slow strokes stopped when Olga entered the outbuilding.

"I was worried about you." Olga wiped her hands across her apron. "Lord Hakan asks for you. He grows impatient. Nor can he stop talking about you. The fine sails you wove, the tunics you've sewn. And then there's your hand in bringing his son...all are curious, you know."

Helena smiled, stroking the comb through her hair. "I'm unsure what I'll say, what I'll do."

Olga grabbed the tunic. "Put this on. Sitting naked as the day you were born isn't the answer. You need to be by his side."

Helena slipped the undergarment and then tunic over her head. Olga tied one of the shoulders with a leather thong. No fine brooches to clasp the material this night.

Olga fussed at the shoulder. "The tunic is yours, but I can't be so bold as to fetch the brooches or the silver circlet." Olga's gnarled hand picked at a tiny nub of lint. "But, if you

185

wanted them, you need only ask. He'd give them to you. The master is so pleased with Erik's return."

Olga seated Helena again on the stump, running the comb through her hair. Sounding satisfied, the Rusk woman went round to face Helena and gave Helena a gentle shake.

"You could ask for whatever you want, and it'd be yours. Do you know that?" Olga's eyes searched Helena's. "I don't know how you did it, getting the boy here, but you did a good thing. You've done many a good turn for these people, what with saving Katla's life and returning the master's son to him. Go seek your reward."

Helena hugged Olga. "Thank you. For the rest you let me take, the bath, the oil. Your kind words."

Olga winked. "'Tis nothing but a little goodness for one so well-deserving. Besides, Hlavo and I might take a turn in the sauna with it tonight." A look of pure mischief played on her face. "The sauna is one thing I appreciate about these Norse."

Helena walked to the door and Olga called after her. "Do you know what you want?"

"I do."

...

Hakan felt Helena's presence as she entered the boisterous longhouse. He scanned the space within his home, to the side benches where all the thralls enjoyed their portion of the feast. Dishes clattered, voices hummed, a din of noise in his longhouse.

She stood at the end and talked with the Frankish boy, Marc. Hakan's eyes narrowed on the two. Helena should be in her usual place, near him at the table. On any other day, he sat on a bench on one side of the table and she on the other, facing him. Now, Hakan sat head of the table in his great chair like a proper chieftain, surrounded by the laughing faces of his family and loyal warriors. There was no room for the woman who took up so much space in his life.

"What ails you, Hakan? You look like you swallowed a nettle," Mardred asked, grinning ear to ear.

"He needs more of this fine Frankish wine. What say you, Hakan?" Halsten held up a pitcher of the costly red wine. "'Tis a day to celebrate."

Helena smoothly took the vessel from Halsten's hand, exchanging quick greetings. "Allow me to pour."

"You look pretty, Helena." Mardred's eyes twinkled. "We thought you collapsed from exhaustion at preparing so fine a feast."

Helena poured wine for Mardred, moving closer to Hakan. She smiled in good nature to Mardred's jest.

"As you well know, Olga bore the burden of this feast. But she's been a good teacher, as were you on the finer points of Norse fare." Helena topped Halsten's chalice once again and motioned to a wooden bowl brimming with fruit stew. "Do you like the sweet plum dish I made?"

"'Tis good," Aud said, evidence of the creamy purple pudding ringing her mouth.

"Delicious," Erik added.

"What is it made of?" Serious Katla stirred her spoon, examining the contents.

Keeping her eyes to those who addressed her, Helena held the pitcher with both hands. "A Frankish recipe of beaten eggs, fruit, cream, and a little honey. In my home village, we used strawberries, but I replaced them with the wild plums I found here."

"Strawberries?" Aud and Erik piped up, questioning the well-traveled Sven about the food.

Helena took the reprieve to return to Hakan.

Standing behind his right shoulder, she poured his wine in silence. He leaned back into his chair and breathed the fragrance of her.

"You smell of flowers," he whispered.

Helena drifted down the table before he could see her face.

"Helena, help me here," pleaded Sven. "Explain your Frankish fruits to these whelps. I lack the words."

"For once," said Halsten, laughing.

"Why not go there? Bring back some dried berries for all to sample?" Helena's open-eyed gaze circled the faces at the table, ending with Hakan's. "If you sailed in the next few days, you may get the last of the summer harvest. Erik, at least, could taste the fresh fruit."

"Boys always get to go a-viking," Aud groaned.

"As it should be," Mardred stated. "No daughter of mine is going adventuring."

"Father." Erik's eyes filled with excitement. "Can we take your new ship out to sea?"

"The vessel sits ready to sail, save a few carvings to complete. 'Twould be good for father and son," Halsten said before popping a morsel in his mouth.

"But Frankia? Why Frankia?" Mardred's brows pressed together. "So far away. Why not a small journey to Birka?"

"Because," Helena spoke loudly over the table. "Lord Hakan returns me to Frankia. He gave his word before his last voyage. Right, Sven?"

Hakan gripped the arms of his great chair. Something elusive slipped from his grasp right then, but he couldn't name it. What filled the void was pain, bone-jarring pain, as though falling from a tree. The tumble was as bad as the landing. Her bold words spread a pall of quiet across the longhouse. Sven froze where he sat.

Helena prodded. "Was there not a vow made?" She tipped her head at Sven. "One you witnessed sitting very near that same spot?"

Sven scratched his hairy cheek. "A vow?"

Hakan noted Sven's hooded glance at him. His friend would lie for him in an instant. This matter meant nothing to him. Helena set the earthen pitcher on the table with a thud, facing him at the far end of the table. Red drops of mead spilled on her arm and dripped slowly. She could be a fierce Valkyrie, so fine and strong, the way she looked in her Norse finery. But she served him as a thrall. Lamplight caught the wide silver ring wrapped around her upper arm, the mark that said she belonged to him. She dared him to honor his word.

"What?" Mardred gasped. "You *want* to return to Frankia?"

Helena's reply was cut short by Aud and Erik's excited banter about the merits of girls staying home and boys traveling far.

"'Tis not fair," wailed Aud.

"Aud, no man will want to marry you if you cannot learn the proper way to run his farmstead." Katla meant to comfort, but instead inflamed the spirited, younger girl. A lively discussion followed that invited comments from everyone—even thralls who had served the family for years.

Helena slipped outside the longhouse and Hakan followed. Outside, a small table held less decorous implements and dishes for the feast. She wiped a cooking rag on her arm, cleaning the red liquid streak. Hakan covered her arm where his ring curled around her smooth, oiled skin.

"Are you holding me to my word?" His voice was low and quiet amidst the noise spilling from inside. "Do you want to return to Frankia?"

She licked her lips. Her unbound hair was dark silk, framing her gentle features. Her face pinched, as if he asked the wrong question and she hoped for something else. The moods and minds of women were ever a mystery to him.

"Do you honor me, Hakan?" Her voice was velvet smooth and quiet.

"You know I do." He tried to read her, but she turned her face and stared at the distant river. Her profile, so fine and proud, could grace a kingdom's coin.

Beyond, the Norse skies splashed with dancing green and purple lights, artistry only found in these northern skies. She stared in the distance but said nothing. He shook her arm, vexed at losing control.

"Tell me what to say and I'll say it." His voice rose in frustration. "Tell me what to do and I'll do it."

She faced him again as laughter reached a high point in the longhouse. None of that joy could be found here; both were miserable. Her lips parted and Hakan yearned to touch the small space between her lips, to test the softness there.

"What maid wants to *ask* a man if he wants to marry her?"

Those words doused coldness on his senses.

"Is that what this is about?" His hand dropped to his side, and distance wedged between them from the subtle loss of contact. "You know I'll never marry again. But care for you better than I ever did for Astrid? I already do."

Her slender shoulders dropped a fraction. Helena's skin glistened with muted shine from fragrant oil, an enticement to touch. He willed control to wait and listen, but the discipline won him no favors.

"I want to be amongst my own people." Her voice hitched but no tears fell. "I honored you and brought Erik here. Now I need you to honor your vow."

This maid, to whom he gave much, all that he had, didn't want him. Hakan, impassive and distant, crossed his arms against the agony her words wrought. An unseen shield encircled him, heavy and stalwart like the wooden implements that graced his longhouse walls: nicks and marks failed to stop those tools of battle. Though pained, he uttered the words she wanted.

"We sail tomorrow."

17

Svea's shores drifted farther from sight. Hakan stood in stern, silent agony. No one grasped the depths of his pain at setting sail to return Helena to her homeland. Steering the rudder, he contemplated the good-byes made from the riverside shoreline of his sister's farmstead. Children jumped about as Mardred dispatched provisions, glancing from Hakan and Helena with worrisome furrows lining her forehead.

For once, his meddling sister had said nothing.

Even Sven was speechless. In truth, Sven dumbfounded Hakan once again. Hakan's second-in-command declined another voyage in little more than a score of days, when he'd always done a restless dance to be at sea. Truly, Hakan's world had turned upside down.

Staring at the western horizon, the still sun at his back, Hakan shook his head. His best friend and most trusted man in battle stayed back for mysterious reasons and...

...she looks west, far away from me. Is she at peace with never seeing me again?

"And the two women who gave me Erik want nothing to do with me," he said, thinking aloud.

Nearby, Erik leaned over the side of the ship, studying the waves. With the wind at their backs, Hakan's sleek new ship, smaller and faster than his Dragon Lady war vessel, would deliver them to the shores of Frankia in less than a sennight. If he pushed.

Aye, he'd push, and get her there. He'd be done with her.

'Tis a miserable lesson, treating a maid well, only to be kicked in the gut. Why didn't I learn from Astrid?

But Helena was nothing like Astrid. At least with Astrid, 'twas clear what she wanted. With Helena, he had no idea.

He remembered the evening of the Glima.

Did I not offer all I have? My protection? A good life? What more could she want?

Hakan groused under breath.

"Did you say something?" Erik's curious blue eyes looked up at him.

"Nothing."

This didn't deter the boy from settling in close to his father. Erik squirmed his boyish mass against Hakan's frame and smiled as hearty winds whipped at his hair. Looking down at his son, Hakan's hard heart softened. All that he ever wanted was close beside him. Had he not stood at the rudders of his other ship and said as much? Aye, the inner workings of women he'd leave to men more adept than he. He had Erik. This was reason enough to be glad.

...

Perched on a chest beside a small tent, the wind made a curtain of hair to cover Helena's face. She turned, sensing Hakan's eyes piercing her back. He was a sight to behold, commanding the ship. This time he wore a red cape that whipped around his shoulders. Though she couldn't see the direction of his gaze, she felt it. His helmet's iron eye rings and nose guard hid most of his face. Watching him smile at Erik and put a gentle arm around his son stung her. How she missed being close to him. The smell of his skin. The tickle of his face hair when he kissed her. She turned her back to Hakan and the sun.

"Emund," Hakan shouted over the wind. "Take the rudder."

From the corner of her eye, she watched him open the hatch. He emerged again with a lined, heavy woolen cape. She remembered that cape: 'twas mink-trimmed. He intended to trade the luxurious mantle, a beautiful piece made by Mardred. Helena faced the western sun, hanging in the sky less and less as summer waned. Her hair whipped again across her face as footsteps sounded behind her.

"Wear this." Hakan thrust the beautiful cape at her.

Turning to the shield of fur-lined wool, Helena's fingers touched, but didn't take, his offering.

"My lord, this cape...Mardred made it for you to trade . . ."

"Take it. I'll not have you die on my ship of exposure," he said, his voice rough to her ears. "'Tis no concern of yours how I care for my sister and her goods."

Helena flinched at the barb. "I'll take it, if you'll sit with me awhile. And please, take off your helmet. I can't see you."

Hakan draped the cloak over her shoulders, and she wrapped herself in the warmth. Hakan surprised her by removing his helmet and resting it under his arm. He sat on the chest beside her, so close their shoulders nearly touched.

Hakan cleared his throat. "With this strong wind, we should reach your homeland soon."

"Good." She folded the edges of her cloak a little tighter. Her fingers played with the shiny mink. "My parents will be so happy at my homecoming. I'm sure they, and—" she hesitated, "—and my betrothed will be overjoyed to know I live."

Hakan winced at the mention of her betrothed. "'Tis for the best."

She peeked at him from the corner of her eye. Hakan's head tilted back as he surveyed the clouds.

"Storm clouds come from the north, bringing frigid winds." Standing up, he returned the helmet to his head. "You sleep below tonight."

"But the tent? I thought I'd sleep again on deck...as before."

His mouth pulled in a grim line at her mention of that voyage, aye, the one she had showered accusations of his failed care for her.

"The hold." 'Twas a command, not a request.

"As you say, my lord." She squinted at the roiling clouds.

"Don't call me that. You're a freewoman now."

His sharp tone made her jump.

"It suited you once to call me by name," he said, soft-voiced and taunting.

"Very well...*Hakan*. I sleep below tonight."

She clasped her hands tightly in her lap, her back straighter than the ship's mast. Aye, the conversation ended. The chieftain's sharp footfalls sounded above the wind on the new wooden deck.

Oarsmen cast quick, knowing glances between her and their chieftain. Storms troubled them both on and around the ship. Helena sat unbending. Stubborn to be sure, she would not turn around to look at him again.

When the sun shined overlong in her face and her back began to ache from rigidness, Helena leaned against another chest and rubbed the small of her back. Her next companion planted himself on the chest and leaned close to her.

"Helena, what's wrong?" The wind stirred Erik's hair around his eyes.

"Wrong? Nothing," she said. "Why do you ask?"

"You and my father are not happy with each other. Is it because you return to Frankia?" He kicked the bottom of a barrel and slumped beside her. "I should've never said I wanted to go on a voyage."

"Why?" Helena stroked his wind-mussed hair.

"Because," he said, staring at the deck. "If I had never suggested this voyage, we'd still be in Svea and you and Father would be happy."

"I see." She hugged him close. "Erik, I've wanted to return home ever since I was first taken."

His dark blue eyes squinted at the west horizon, but his young shoulders drooped. How to explain this to a child? Especially as she was one barely experienced in the ways of the world herself? But she had grown to love his family and what she had learned in Svea. Helena would do nothing to harm his view of them, most certainly his father.

"Erik," Helena said, her gaze studying the uneven planks at her feet. "Your family...your Aunt Mardred, your cousins, your father, were all very kind to me. I'll never forget them. Your father saved me from the cruel Danes."

"He did?" His head popped up.

Helena would paint Hakan as the hero, for 'twas true.

"Aye." She nodded and her voice turned with relish to the story. "He walked into the Dane's camp, and I knew he was the one to save me. Everyone stopped to greet him out of respect."

"They did?" Erik swung around on their perch to steal a glance at his father. "He looks fierce, doesn't he? And *Solace* is the biggest sword."

Grey waves churned the sea. The ship slid through choppy water, nothing like the first voyage. A carved dragonhead, less elaborate than others Helena had seen, curled out from the ship where she and Erik sat.

"But think how much you missed your father when he went on his long voyages. 'Tis how much my own family misses me."

He nodded as a picture of understanding must have dawned behind his eyes. "They must miss you very much."

"Though I made new friends in Svea, my family needs me. And I need them."

"But why does my father seem so—" Erik's brows furrowed in the same way as Hakan's. "—so mad? He's not happy about taking you back."

Helena's fingertips rubbed the etched scar on her jaw as she considered that.

"You'll have to ask him. But, Erik, you're not to blame for this voyage. I want to go home, and your father is honor bound to take me."

"How did you get that scar?" His cheeks went red as he asked the question. "Aunt Mardred says I shouldn't ask such questions, like when I asked about Uncle Halsten's limp and how he lost his hand. But he told me, and he wasn't mad."

"Nor am I." Helena pulled him close, loving the kind-hearted boy. "I had a pouch around my neck with a piece of jewelry in it. A pendant. When the Danes raided my village, I stopped one of them from stealing it. The Dane tried to cut the leather thong from my neck and his knife cut me instead." Her hand rubbed the spot on her neck where she used to play with the pendant's chain. "'Twas a gift from my betrothed."

Erik swayed away from her, his eyes squinting. "Your betrothed must have been very important to you that you wanted to keep his gift."

"Aye, he was."

"Do you like my father? As much as you liked your betrothed?"

His direct questions caught her unawares, as did her honest answer. "Aye. Mayhap more."

"Yet, you go back to Frankia."

Honest questions flowed into honest answers, but the exchange left Helena hollow and sad. She had gained what she wanted, hadn't she? Freedom to return home. Helena slanted a look back across the ship, where Hakan guided the rudder. His red cape billowed and swirled about him, and if 'twere possible, the chieftain was more remote and distant.

Turning again to face west, she said, "And so I go back to Frankia. 'Tis for the best."

His mouth dipped in a frown. But the conversation ended when he was called to help. The chance to work the vessel like the other Norsemen gave Helena reprieve from vexing questions.

Erik trotted off to Emund. He wrestled with the sail's ropes, as four men worked to harness the great white and red striped square mass. The sail reminded her of happy summer days, wiling away the time with Hakan under the tree.

Bracing wind, a warning of changing seas, brought hard shivers. Her teeth began to chatter as icy winds cut exposed skin. The sky darkened with forceful clouds tumbling one after another. Helena finger-combed wind-gnarled hair, braiding it over her shoulder. By the time she tied off the end with a leather thong from her bootstraps, the sun had set low in the sky.

The heavens above and the waters below churned and roiled shades of grey. Helena removed herself to the small three-sided tent, huddling between heavy sacks of oat and barley. She would make this her bed for the night despite Hakan's command to sleep below. The hold was too dark and small to her liking. Resting her head on a sack of grain, she dozed.

In her sleep, warmth surrounded her. She burrowed closer to the heat, the comfort. Helena woke with a start. Her cheek brushed a scratchy pelt. She blinked, turning half-upright on her hip. Hakan knelt beside her.

"I told you to sleep below deck." His voice boomed over noise that shook the vessel.

His hair was gathered at his nape by a leather thong, but wet strands fell about his face. Hakan crouched close to her. Drowsy and unthinking, Helena reached out to brush his hair back, her fingers brushing his cheeks. The natural tenderness took them both by surprise, an easiness of previous days.

Loud noises pounded overhead. Wood creaked all around her as men shouted. She glanced around her; he'd taken her below deck. Hakan's calloused hands clasped hers and brought it to his lips. Her fingers were icy but he rubbed them, the intimacy sweet. The hold's dark confines and his lips brushing her skin stirred a different kind of warmth.

Hakan tucked her hand back in the fur's fold. "We're in a storm." The timbre of his voice was low and soothing. "We've taken refuge in an inlet, but I need you here."

"A storm?"

"Aye. It tests the ship's strength," he said. "I need to be on deck."

But he didn't rush to attend the vessel. Instead, crouched on his knees beside her, his fingers grazed her cheek.

"Erik?" she asked, her voice rising. "Where's Erik?"

"Shhhhh." He pointed at a large chest.

Helena pressed an elbow to the floor and checked around Hakan. Curled inside the hudfat, the boy slept.

"I suppose a father can be trusted with the well-being of his son."

"I can be trusted with the well-being of others, but I'm glad you care for Erik." His tired smile faded. Lines at the corners of his eyes showed the strain.

The ship lurched under the crash of a powerful wave and they gripped each other. Helena squeezed her eyes shut. The vessel rocked with greater force, then calmed once more.

"Hakan." She pulled away, making space between them. "I don't want this unhappiness between us."

He unfolded a hudfat and stretched the length of it across her. Helena accepted his care, watching him. 'Twas too dark to fully read his face.

"The unhappiness," he said, nodding. "You want to go home to Frankia, and I want you to stay in Svea." His voice was thick to her ears as he folded a side of the heavy fur underneath her with the utmost care. "We can't have it both ways, can we?"

When she was about to speak, Hakan placed a finger over her lips and the tang of salt seeped into her mouth.

"You were taken by force." His voice roughened to a hoarse whisper. "Why wouldn't you want to return home?"

He said generous, thoughtful words. Why did her heart sink from the hearing? "Something was taken from you...your freedom." The tip of his finger traced a feathery line from her lips to her jaw. "And I give it back."

Darkness hid their faces, a gentle mask for both.

"I need to see to the ship. Stay here and you'll be safe." Hakan rocked back from his knees and set his hand on the hold's trapdoor. "This storm bodes an early winter."

Once he was gone, her heart ached. She lay in the cluttered hold, cold and empty of joy.

18

"Look," Erik said, waving and pointing. "'Tis land."

Helena itched to be on land. The whole ship shared the yearning to stand on solid soil. Storms and strong waves had worn the travelers to the bone. They found safe harbor in one inlet after another, journeying at a snail's pace. Some men whispered that the seas schemed to push them back from whence they came. Helena gave their murmurings scarce thought.

Hakan gave her scant attention after that first night in the hold. His duties came first to ensure a safe journey. Helena eyed Hakan when she was allowed on deck. The closer they came to her homeland, the more distant he became.

She and Erik made a game of counting: eight turns of the glass for one watch, five turns of the glass for rowing duty. But the time of counting was done. Frankish shores stretched ahead.

"Helena, you have many orange and red trees. I've never seen the like of it in Svea."

She smiled at Erik's enthusiasm at the wondrous new world in front of him. Gone was the curiosity of things between his father and his father's former thrall.

Another vessel, Norse in design, listed in the harbor, but the port of Cherbourg, a sleepy village, looked smaller than she remembered. Seaside buildings bore the same dull gray as when she last saw them, awakening to life as a slave. Now the dense forest, once dark and forbidding, sang with color.

"Beautiful. Isn't it?" Shades of yellow, orange, brown, and red heralded their arrival like bright banners.

"Welcome home, Helena," she whispered to herself. A gentle breeze kissed her face.

No sign of the Danes touched the sleepy village now. No tents dotted the field. No ale-addled warriors walked the earthen lanes. Only images of that harsh time stamped her mind. Around her, the men tossed a stone anchor into shallow water and prepared to go ashore.

"Is this your home, Helena?" Erik squinted at her and then at the village.

She brushed the back of his unruly hair, laughing softly at how he found the port wanting. Though the day was cloudy, the sun's light made thick clouds silver rimmed.

"Nay, Aubergon is inland...one, two days' travel."

"As big as Uppsala?"

"Nay," she said, grinning at the curious boy. "Aubergon is small...a place for travelers to find rest on their way to other places."

"Are there any towns bigger than this in Frankia?"

"There is Paris. 'Tis where the king lives." Bending over, she kissed the crown of his head. "He's called 'Louis the Fat.' I hear he's quite round.

He grinned at that. "Have you never seen him?"

"Nay."

"Then, until you came to Svea, you never ventured anywhere before, did you?"

Their mirth over the fat king faded.

Erik's child-like view opened her eyes. She'd gained much from this Norse summer: seeing people, places, and a way of life that otherwise would have remained a mystery. How many summers had she tended her family's flock and dreamed of adventure? The bag she clutched in her hands, a smaller hudfat, contained all things Norse, relics of her travels. A few tunics, an elk bone comb, and the silver armband that had once marked her as Hakan's thrall filled the bag. All were Norse. Not a single item bespoke her Frankish birth. Her hand grazed the empty, pouchless space between her breasts.

Even my pendant's gone.

Erik tugged her sleeve and pointed at a giant of a man who stood on the shoreline facing their ship. "That looks like Jedvard."

"Who is Jedvard?

"He watched over me this summer." Erik shaded his eyes as he stared ashore.

Hakan approached and stood beside them, watching the shore.

"Father, why is Jedvard here?"

"I don't know." Hakan squinted at the solitary, giant Norseman who waited on the shore. "Let's go ashore and find out."

Emund brought a simple fisherman's boat to bring Helena and Erik ashore. Hakan and Emund pushed the tiny vessel through churning blue-grey waters. When they passed the break, the white-haired giant waded in to help. The small boat scraped the shore and Erik jumped up to greet the largest man Helena had ever seen.

"Jedvard, what are you doing here?" Erik asked as the Norseman hoisted him high and set him on the ground.

"I bear tidings." His voice sounded like thunder and he failed to smile.

Emund helped Helena reach dry land, and the massive-framed Jedvard watched her as she shook her skirts. His flaxen hair thinned atop his head, but what he had was pulled in a tight thong at his neck. Over-thick jaws framed the bottom of his face.

"Hakan. We must speak."

Hakan pulled *Solace* from the boat and slid the sword across his back. Tension writ across his frame upon seeing the odd giant. He pointed to a stone and wood building.

"At the tavern."

...

"Something of great import made you sail faster than me through stormy seas." Hakan rolled the horn of ale in his hands.

Nearby, Emund attempted to show Erik the finer points of Heftnaftl as both sat by the inn's fire. The blaze did little to warm the damp air. Helena huddled beside him in the shadows, wrapping her new mantle tighter, but he was sure 'twas as much from cold as the fright Jedvard gave.

"The Frankish woman. She cannot be here." Jedvard spoke the booming words in a low voice.

"I say, she stays." Hakan leaned his forearms on the table.

The giant's eyes, sunken from age and thick bones, beaded small. He gauged Hakan with those colorless eyes, but the old warrior didn't move a muscle except to speak.

"Olof sent me."

"Why?"

"He's no longer king of Svea. He lives at your ringed fort. On Gotland." Jedvard's large hand pulled out a small leather bag meant for coins, but his palm rested atop the bag. "Gorm claims the throne."

Helena gasped at the news. Hakan's fist pounded the table enough to startle Erik and Emund. His warriors paused midst conversation, some with horns mid-way to their mouths, all looking to him across the smoky room, but he did not give the signal.

"What do you mean?"

"Svea burns. Gorm and Anund Jakob...both claim to the throne." Jedvard's flat tone delivered this news. 'Twas the same as if he said it rained outside. "Much blood will spill in Uppsala."

How could he have missed the signs of rebellion?

"What happened?' Hakan asked. "Jakob is not yet fifteen winters."

"But has a man's beard and stands near tall as you." Jedvard stayed unmoving, but something flickered in his ghost-like eyes. "Sven is his second."

Jedvard's words swung a hammer's blow. That betrayal, the most unexpected, stung worse than Astrid's faithlessness. Good friends, the kind you trust to watch your back, were rare. In the space of one summer, Hakan had gained much and lost much. Erik's nearness warmed his soul. 'Twas right to have the boy with him. But without Helena, his future looked bleak and empty. Now this. Sven over-throwing the king, the man who had cared for Hakan like a father? The shock numbed him. His mind took over where emotions were unwelcome.

"The voyages he didn't take...disappearing for a time," Hakan said, piecing aloud recent events.

"Sven and Jakob keep Norse gods. Olof would not." Jedvard spoke, frugal with words and movement.

"And Gorm?"

The narrowing of the old man's fathomless eyes was his only show of emotion. "He spills blood to gain power and revenge."

"What else do you need to tell me, Jedvard?" Hakan's patience thinned with the old warrior's sparse way with words. "And when do we put Olof back on Svea's throne?"

"Olof finishes his days on Gotland under your protection, if you will it. Jakob Anund agreed to let his father live—"

"What?" Hakan's fist curled on the table. "Let me at the whelp. He'll sing a different tune."

"Olof wants this." Jedvard's hand stirred atop the bag. "His message, 'tis why I'm here."

Like a great, hulking ox, Jedvard opened the bag and another trefoil brooch clattered to the table. This brooch paired with the one Olof brought the night he admitted Gorm had killed his mother and father. Hakan didn't touch the brooch. Old visions tumbled from the past...his mother pinning the matching pair on her shoulders...the day his father gifted her with the humble jewelry...her joy at the receiving.

Bitterness edged his voice. "Olof has another secret?"

Jedvard's square head tilted. "He bade me tell you, but I'm no skald."

Helena's hand rested on Hakan's forearm. He glanced down at her face, as white as his must be.

"Then tell it."

"Long ago, young Olof, not yet a king, went to Jutland's court. He met a thrall seeking freedom. Her woman's ways snared him." The skin around Jedvard's deep-set eyes tightened. "Olof lay with her. He was newly married, but Estrid bared no living sons. This Jutland woman caused trouble in the Dane's court, and for Olof."

"Who was she?" Hakan asked.

"Borgunna, mother of Gorm."

"But, Olof's not Gorm's father—"

Jedvard shook his head. "When Olof became king, she came to Uppsala as a freewoman with Gorm. She aimed to replace the barren queen. He denied her. She tried to poison Olof—"

"Wait." Hakan held up a hand. "Gorm's mother tried to *poison* Olof?"

"Aye."

History wrote itself in small wrinkles across Jedvard's skin. These faint, crisscrossed patterns showed his age as greater than Olof's. Helena inched closer. Hakan welcomed her warmth pressing his body as both listened to the story of old intrigue.

"What happened to her? Gorm's mother?"

"Your father killed her."

A mere child could've knocked Hakan over with one finger. His mouth tried to form questions about this latest truth—or so Jedvard said 'twas truth. Hakan's mind numbed to the image the old Norseman painted. Jedvard was a warrior who thought little for tender care when delivering hard news…not when facts worked best.

"Olof gathered the few warriors he trusted. The woman's fate was decided, and your father drew the short straw. He took Borgunna to the far north. Left her where the Saarmi roam the ice." Jedvard's bone-heavy brow moved. "The Saarmi took her, or she died on the ice."

The way Jedvard spoke, Hakan was certain no Saarmi nomad saved the woman; someone waited to be sure she died on the ice. His father. The burden of such news weighed heavy on him. The cost of that single act was paid out today with Gorm's vengeance. Hakan almost understood the enemy he despised. Truly, he might've done the same.

"Fair punishment for a woman who tries to kill a king." The giant gave his pronouncement with a single nod.

Hakan's hand scrubbed his face. If he could wipe away the betrayal and lies, he'd start anew. Jedvard passed the brooch to Hakan and unfolded himself from the table.

"Gorm took a boy's revenge when he burned your farm, killed your mother and father." Jedvard towered over the table. "He vows to wipe out the seed of the man who killed his mother. Finish your task with the Frankish woman. You are needed elsewhere." He stared at Hakan. "I'll keep Erik safe."

Hakan stared at the table's uneven planks, warped from time. Helena's hand, clean of dyes and smooth from no thrall's labor, rested atop the wood. Hakan rose from the bench and let the bones of the story form in his mind. Much needed filling in today's sparse tale. Allegiances had shifted rapidly in the span of this short voyage. Many would soon demand to know the lay of his loyalty. Aye, the lay of his sword.

Helena looked up at him, and her deep blue gaze healed him, silent and tender. Mayhap 'twas best that she returned to a man who kept no warrior's ways. Yet, the pang of such a thought gouged him.

Jedvard moved and his cloak stirred open. His black-trousered legs carried an arsenal: two axes, a hammer, and three knives were strapped to his form.

Jedvard folded his arms beneath his dark cape. "When you're done, we travel to Gotland."

'Twas assumed he'd honor Olof, for all knew he dearly loved the old king. Yet, painful understanding slipped into place, a kind of hard-won wisdom born of disappointment.

"All these years, Olof taught me a good Norse chieftain never dallies with thralls." Hakan tipped his head back and spoke the words through a bitter laugh. "He always said, 'Causes too much trouble.'"

...

"This means good-bye, doesn't it? For Helena, I mean," Erik said.

Helena's throat dried. A knot lodged there like a rock, rendering her speechless. Jedvard stood behind Erik, nursing a Norse hammer in his arms the way mothers carried babes. A cloud passed over Erik's face as he glanced at Helena and then his father.

"So we must bid each other 'good-bye,' Erik." Need made Helena find her voice, but she couldn't stop the ache.

"I'll miss you." Erik buried his face in the folds of her mantle.

"And I shall miss you, very much." Her fingers combed his unruly locks. "'Tis been a pleasure coming to know a future chieftain of Svea."

He pulled away, pleased with her words.

"Three days," Hakan said to Jedvard and Emund.

He lifted Helena onto the horse, bidding her to sit astride. Then, he tied her hudfat to the saddle and swung onto the saddle of the other horse. He set the familiar iron helmet on his head, and then he said words that chilled her.

"If I'm not back in three days, come look for me." Those were the last words he would utter for the remainder of the day.

...

Unaccustomed to riding, Helena held both reins and mane in a tight vise grip. Tense and sore, she hurt in awkward places. The horses moved from smooth gallops to bone-jarring trots in Hakan's drive to get her home. He acted unbothered by either motion, sitting as one with his steed. She wanted to tease him that Agnar would be jealous, but his forbidding manner was cool and distant.

They were back to the business of her going home: like goods to be delivered, a task to be crossed off a list, a bothersome woman to be rid of.

She didn't want to trouble him with the need to stop. His life churned with new woes. How could she add more? Helena tried to ignore the discomfort—until her body screamed for mercy.

"Hakan, stop." Helena slumped in the saddle, blurting the words to his stalwart back.

"Stop?" Hakan reined his horse and circled around. "Why?"

"Please," she gasped. "I need a rest." Pointing at the faint lather on her horse's neck, she finished, "My horse and I need rest."

He eyed the sun's whitish glow behind stirring clouds. "A short stop, or we won't make your village by sundown."

Sliding off the horse, Helena hobbled to a large rock jutting from the ground. At her feet, limp and dying grass showed dull color. Helena pulled her mantle close about her, warding off a chill breeze. With summer lost, the earth prepared for winter's sleep.

Hakan eyed the far road, every inch a Norse warrior. His iron helmet ringed his eyes, and a round shield banded his left forearm. *Solace* hung across his back, the hilt angled over his left shoulder. A long knife, sheathed in leather, hugged one boot. All he needed was to swing his Norse hammer and bellow a battle cry. Aye, with or without the hammer, he'd rattle her humble village when they arrived. Yet, Hakan surveyed the dense forest that bracketed the road, and his arm muscles flexed visibly to her.

"There's nothing to fear, Hakan."

Then it struck her that he must have discomfort being in a foreign land. His ice-blue eyes flashed within the rings as he watched her shake dust from her hem.

"What? You've nothing to say?" She sighed. "We're close to Aubergon, you know. There are few wolves here. I vow, the most ferocious one stands in front of me."

Danes, Norse...all were from the northlands in the eyes of her people. To their fright-frozen minds, Hakan was another of the dreaded Norse, sweeping over the land like a plague and leaving little in the wake. But summer had yielded a different crop for her: not all Norse were vicious raiders out for death and plunder.

Hakan braced one foot on a rock. "And now the Norse wolf brings you safely home."

His nose guard pointed like an arrow to his mouth—a once smiling pair of lips that now made a straight, impassive line.

"Aye," she said.

Their gazes connected for a moment, but Hakan went back to silently scanning the trees. That he held himself distant nettled her.

"It must be very tiring to scare the wits out of innocent folk," she goaded. "Do you practice that?"

Hakan gave her the barest glance before he measured the sun's place in the sky. "Does the tartness of your tongue mean you've had enough rest?"

Helena pressed. "All this wariness and watching, and you say little. Don't you want to talk about the rebellion in Svea? About your father? The king?"

He stood up, and his gruff tone commanded obedience. "We go."

Hakan helped her mount her horse, and then he jumped into his saddle with the same force in which he began the journey. Riding a few paces ahead, Helena watched Hakan's broad shoulders. Tears stung her eyes. She ached for him, the befuddling news of Sven's betrayal, his kingdom in turmoil. 'Twas as if the more turmoil he faced, the more closed and controlled he became. Helena couldn't make a rock speak, but even more she hated how she could not lay claim to him.

The horses took them into familiar territory, places she had herded her sheep and goats. But instead of the joy of coming home, Helena wanted to curl up against the strong back of the Norseman before her. The farther they travelled, the more bereft she became, like wood afloat on a river, listless and lost.

With the sun's setting, she burrowed into her mantle and watched Hakan in his sleeveless leather jerkin. His arm rings, dusty from their travels, wrapped high around his arms. Blue trousers hugged his legs down to his cross-gartered boots. She would miss the sight of him. Nay, she would miss the easy companionship, the evenings in his longhouse.

Hakan held up his shield-covered arm when he crested a hill. She stopped beside him and drank in the serene village before them.

"Aubergon?" he asked.

"Aubergon."

Thick trees crescented one side of the tiny village. Patchwork fields claimed small spaces of earth, and nestled amongst humble homes sat one modest stone tower lit by rush torches. Smoke curled in lazy ribbons from simple chimneys, announcing eventide for all. One sentinel slumped against the tower's wall, rubbing his hands against the night's encroaching cold.

"Shall we?" He waved her ahead.

Helena spied the copse of trees on the village edge where her home sat. "My home is just past those oak trees." She pointed.

She imagined her family's faces, nudging the horse to a gallop. Exhilarated, Helena forgot about stiff, pained limbs, and horse and rider moved toward her home with great haste. They sped around a gnarled oak tree to find her home.

But, 'twas gone.

She jerked on the reins. Her horse reared, tossing her from his back. Slamming to the earth was no more painful than the sight that greeted her. Home was a few charred posts in the ground.

19

"Helena!" Hakan sprang from his horse and dropped to his knees beside her.

"What happened?" She cried as sharp stones bit her tender flesh.

"Are you hurt?" he asked, running his hands over her limbs.

The ground spun quickly though she gripped it on her hands and knees.

"Nay, I'm...I'm...."

Hakan crouched in the dirt beside her, holding her close. A sob jerked her body, working its way up her throat. Darkening skies made deeper inspection difficult. She pushed Hakan away and dusted dried leaves and dirt from her hands, circling what used to be her home. Where was her family? Hakan, still fully armed, was the gentle voice that pulled her from the fog.

"Mayhap they're in the tower."

The tower. Helena gulped a calming breath.

In the distance, Agnes, the tanner's wife, poked her head outside her door. The good wife shooed the few chickens that clucked and pecked at the dirt into a small outbuilding.

Agnes ambled back to her simple two-room home and opened the door.

"Agnes," Helena yelled, waving her arm overhead.

The woman scurried behind the door and used it as a shield. "Who goes there?"

Helena cupped her mouth and yelled, "'Tis me, Helena."

Agnes shrieked and covered her mouth with both hands. Helena grabbed her skirts and ran to her old neighbor. Hakan's solid footfalls sounded a few paces behind her.

"Agnes, my mother and father. Are they in the tower?"

Agnes cast a suspicious look at Hakan, but she stepped from the door.

"Helena, we'd given you up for dead...or worse. 'Tis glad I am you're safe." The older woman's hands fretted, but her gaze flicked to Hakan. "And who be this Nor'man?"

Hakan had removed his helmet, making him look less fearsome, though his weaponry was at the ready.

"He is Lord Hakan, a chieftain of Svea, escorting me home, but what—"

Her question was cut short by the thunder of hooves. Four men-at-arms rode into the tanner's yard, bearing torches. Hakan hefted his shield, covering his frame. His free hand flexed, as if ready to grab *Solace*.

One rider nudged his horse forward, and, puffing out his thin chest, demanded, "State your name and business."

"Sir Arval?" Helena squinted at the leader of the ragged group.

"Oh, Arval," Agnes cried. "'Tis Helena, old Simon the Apothecary's daughter. Drop your airs, man."

Arval was the oldest and most seasoned knight of those who defended Aubergon, but at best they were a small, tattered group, never surpassing six in number. Aubergon was too small and too poor a keep to warrant better men. The men's stained clothes sported uneven patchwork. The best-garbed man featured no less than three holes in his russet-colored leggings.

"Aye," he said, shifting in his saddle with self-importance. "I see Helena, but what of the Nor'man?"

Hakan moved to stand beside Helena. "I am Hakan of Svea, Helena's protector."

"A chieftain, no less, Arval, so you'd better mind," Agnes piped up, nodding her head in emphasis.

"A chieftain, you say?" The old, wiry Arval looked nervous, scanning the darkness around him. "Where's your warriors?"

"I came alone."

Mouths gaped. The youngest knight, his tunic a mottled design of stains, fidgeted in his creaking saddle as though the call of nature needed answering. His head swiveled right and left as he checked the area. Another man shook like a leaf.

Sir Arval scratched his jaw. "Then, come to the keep and speak to Lord Guerin."

"*Lord Guerin*," gasped Helena. "What happened to his mother and father."

Sir Arval's beady eyes flicked a glance her way. "At the keep, milord will explain all."

"And my mother, my father, my brother? They are there?"

Spitting out the side of his mouth, Arval ignored her and spoke to Hakan. "You there. Nor'man. Walk ahead."

The youngest guard mumbled something to Sir Arval.

"Death finds all men," Sir Arval grumbled. "Tonight it might find you."

Not accepting the rude treatment, Helena moved to Hakan's side.

"I walk with him." Helena slipped her arm through Hakan's while two of the men grabbed their horses. Yet, she understood the source of their unease. Hakan dwarfed the men. He could easily defeat these four unseasoned warriors.

"Suit yourself." Arval spat sideways once more. His long, lanky hair swung wide as he whirled his horse to the tower.

Now she understood why Hakan had come alone. If he had come with a dozen men as armed and able as him, terror would've spread amongst her people. Each man-at-arms was half Hakan's size, and none appeared well-trained in the art of battle. Slanting a look at Hakan, she appreciated his wisdom. Alone, he was intimidating. With his ship of warriors, he'd be formidable. Yet, he had undertaken this journey to see her home. Her heart swelled with warmth as they trudged the path in darkness toward the circular tower.

Once there, Arval pounded on the great oak door, demanding entry. Dry rot ate at a bottom corner of the massive door. Had Aubergon always been this way? Or, had she never noticed until fate had plucked her up and planted her elsewhere? The once impressive tower showed its age and lackluster care. A few stray weeds sprouted from the round wall, truly a haphazard pile of rocks, that made the building.

Hakan stood beside her and placed a warm hand at her back. The guards holding the flickering torches shuffled nervously. This Norseman was as foreign in this place as a fine warhorse among nags. Arval glared at Hakan once more and pounded anew.

Leather hinges bent and the door cracked a sliver. Night shadows, coupled with dim light behind the door, shrouded the opener's identity. Arval blocked the slim column of light while hissing whispers were exchanged.

"Helena?" A voice called from within.

She recognized that voice.

"Guerin?"

"Helena." Though opened fully, the portal emitted only a bit of light.

Stepping from the door, Guerin came into the full light of the torches. He gave her a warm smile. Dark-haired and even-featured, Guerin was boyishly handsome. His tunic sleeves flopped as he gripped her shoulders in welcome.

"'Tis truly you," he said, his youthful face cracking with a wider smile. "Come. We dare not stay out in the cold." He gave Hakan a quick, wide-eyed once over. "And you as well,

Nor'man. Any friend and protector of Helena is welcome at my table."

Despite Guerin's warm welcome, two men flanked Hakan while two fell in behind him, but he moved undaunted.

She sidled a look at Guerin. Of the same height, he looked young, yet old. His hair and clothes were unkempt, so unlike him, but 'twas tiredness and dark-circled eyes that changed his visage. He carried himself not erect and joyful as she remembered in times past: there was no sureness about him. Had it always been that way? He appeared to her a boy wearing a man's clothes.

The hall, always so grand in her mind, appeared dingy. Helena could not help but make comparisons to Hakan's longhouse. Why was the air so smoky in here? The haze fairly burned her eyes. And the floor. Rushes, limp and stained, covered the stone floor. Remnants of small bones from meals past crunched underfoot. A few mangy hounds lent their rank odor to the space. And what was that other smell? Guerin? She followed close behind him to realize 'twas the stench of his unwashed body.

The Norse summer had changed her. She looked with disdain at her surroundings. Old smoke, lazy from no escape hole, swirled overhead. And oh, how she appreciated the daily sauna most Norsemen enjoyed. Odors sweated from their bodies were then cleaned by cool river waters. Guerin could learn a thing or two from Hakan.

Settling into a large chair by the fire, Guerin bade them sit.

"Helena." Guerin took a deep breath and shook his head. "We all believed you dead."

Hakan stood behind her, his arms folded in his impassive way.

"Very much alive," she said with too much brightness. Something in all this made her uneasy.

Guerin canted his head and tapped his cheek while examining hers. "What happened?"

"Oh." One hand covered the marred cheek. "The Danes. After my capture."

Helena let her gaze wander over the room again. Pallets stretched in disorderly lines against the circular walls.

"Where does my family sleep?"

"Not...here," he said with odd hesitation. Tight lines etched his face, and he blinked overmuch. "But where are my manners?" He clapped his hands twice and called out, "Food and drink for our guests."

"Did I hear correctly? You are now 'Lord Guerin'? What happened to your older brother, Jean? And your father?"

"All dead." Guerin rubbed his red-rimmed eyes. "Summer was most difficult."

"I can see that. My home has burned to the ground, and my parents are nowhere to be found. If they are not here at the keep, where are they?"

Guerin's shoulders slumped under his baggy tunic. "Your mother, your father...they sleep...in the church yard." He shut his eyes a moment. "I'm sorry."

A vise seemed to cinch her chest. No limbs worked in agreement with her brain. Numbness seeped into her. Helena wanted to cry, to scream, to flee, but her body wouldn't move. Behind her, a large, warm hand touched her, a comforting hand on her shoulder. Hakan. She leaned against him, feeling him at her back. Tears blurred her vision, turning Guerin into a watery form.

"My brother?" she whispered.

"Gone to Paris to join the king's guard."

A young boy and one very old man, a pair she didn't recognize, in peasant's russet wool came from behind a large, half-formed wall with trays of simple fare. They poured watery ale into rough wooden cups. Guerin drained his cup, nodding for more, all the while studying Hakan. Helena noticed how his youthful stare flickered over the comforting arm Hakan placed around her shoulders. But she needed to know what happened.

"Tell me of that day...I remember so little." Her eyes burned as more fat drops spilled.

"The Danes...they burned much...half the village. They took mostly livestock." Guerin sounded solemn and defeated. "And you."

"But my mother and father?"

"Homes in the southwest part of the village burned." His eyes drooped with genuine sorrow. "Your mother and father died in the fire."

Both hands covered her mouth, stifling a sob. Guerin set his hands together as in prayer.

"We did nothing that night, but my father and brother promised to go with a band of men to the Duke of Normandy. But they never returned."

"The Danes?" she asked.

"Nay. Ambushed." Shaking his head in disbelief, he said, "Roving marauders." He jerked his head toward Sir Arval. "Only Arval made it back, half-dead, to tell the tale."

Arval grunted in his cup of ale at a bench farther away, his face twisting at the ugly memory. Hakan squeezed her shoulder with another reassuring touch. He was solid at her back, warm and strong.

"Why didn't you search for Helena?" Hakan asked, speaking with bold authority.

"I..." Hands fluttering, the young lord faltered. "I stayed behind to man the keep. There was no one here to protect what remained. Besides, with my father as lord here and brother as heir, 'twas their responsibility to go."

Two of the men-at-arms snorted in the hazy background. They served a poor, weakling lord. Guerin winced as he sank lower in his chair.

"We petitioned the king for help." Guerin offered this explanation while batting his hand in the air. "But 'twas useless. The king was unconcerned about the tribulations of a lesser noble, much less the disappearance of a single—"

He stopped short, his eyes spreading wide.

"—an apothecary's daughter." Helena supplied the rest.

"I'm sorry, Helena."

"Without your father, even my own mother died mid-summer from a fever."

"And my brother, Philippe?"

Guerin's mouth twisted in a rueful expression. "He hitched a ride on the next cart passing through, taking himself off to Paris."

"But he has no such training."

"There was little I could do to stop him." Lacing his fingers together, Guerin angled forward. "And, 'twas around that time some travelers came by way of Cherbourg, telling us of a dark-haired Frankish maid, her face marked by one of her captors." Guerin self-consciously touched his jaw. "And purchased by a Norseman. A Norseman bound for Svea, they said."

There was a note of condemnation in those final words as Guerin dared a harsh look at Hakan.

"Now the Norseman brings her home," Hakan countered smoothly. "To marry her betrothed."

"Aye." Guerin slumped back in his chair, running nervous hands through his hair.

Quiet descended on the room. Helena dried her tears with the corner of her mantle, sniffling. A young servant boy placed a new log on the fire that popped and crackled into the silence.

"Guerin?" A sleepy woman called out as she came down the narrow wooden stairs.

The upper portion of the small keep could not have housed more than two rooms. Who was this woman? Bluish veins traced her snow-white skin. Long black hair hung below her waist. From the round, ripening belly, there could be no mistake: she was great with child.

"Guerin? I waited for you, but fell asleep." She blinked as her gaze traveled from the large Norseman to the boyish lord.

Guerin rose, stiff and awkward, to stand by her side.

"Aye," he said, placing a hand on her shoulders. Guerin cleared his throat. "Marie, this is—" He extended a hand toward Hakan and stopped. "I've not learned your name, Nor'man."

"Hakan. Of Svea."

"Ah, this is Hakan, a chieftain from Svea."

Guerin hesitated in the silent keep. All eyes peered with great interest at Helena's tear-stained face. She scanned the room, uncertain as to why she bore the weight of their stares.

"And this is Helena, daughter of Aubergon's now-departed apothecary. Hakan has returned Helena to us." The sleepy-eyed woman blinked and set a protective hand on her belly.

"And, Helena," Guerin coughed into his hand while the other hand gripped the woman's shoulder, "this is my wife, Lady Marie of Paris."

20

Lady Marie gawked slack-jawed at Helena and then at Guerin and back to Helena. Hakan tightened his grip on her shoulder, but Helena absorbed this news like cloth soaking up color. She glanced at Hakan and read the anger flashing in his eyes: he wanted to wipe the filthy floor with Aubergon's lord. Helena touched his hand, pulling strength from him and giving assurance.

Sir Arval stood up. "Come on, men, we needs attend the watch." Benches scraped and feet shuffled as the men-at-arms escaped the unfolding scene.

"Guerin, I need to sit down." Lady Marie's hand fluttered over her stomach and Guerin helped her to the bench.

"Giles, some wine. Quickly," Guerin said, snapping his fingers at a servant.

Lady Marie gulped the ruby liquid from a wooden cup like a lusty, lowborn woman.

"More." Lady Marie held the vessel out for more but her eyes never left Hakan and Helena. She swallowed much wine before setting down the cup.

"Guerin told me you were taken by Danes." Marie's breath heaved as she stared at Helena. "Forgive me, but I thought you dead." The Lady's watchfulness shifted to Hakan and her neat brows twitched. "But, I see a Nor'man has returned you safely to Aubergon. A most unusual arrangement." Glancing at the scar on Helena's cheek, she winced and added without malice, "Methinks you've suffered many trials."

"Aye, there've been hardships, but 'twas a fair summer in many ways. Bittersweet, I think."

"Bittersweet." Marie nodded her agreement, rubbing her bulging belly. "Hard losses and sweet surprises."

"When does the child come?" Helena asked, the peaceful promise of a child warming her bruised heart.

"She comes by All Soul's Day, to be sure."

"She?"

"Aye. I'm certain I bear a girl." Marie beamed a proud smile. "And 'tis glad I am to have someone trained in the apothecary arts back in Aubergon."

Helena canted her head, and her brain counted the months leading to that feast.

"But, if you bear a child by All Soul's Day—"

Marie interrupted. "She was conceived while Guerin studied in Paris...just before the Danes attacked in early spring."

Helena's former betrothed squirmed, but anger failed to raise its sharp head in Helena's breast. Oddly, sadness of his betrayal mingled with...relief? Guerin blushed as he fiddled with a chipped fragment atop the trestle table. His wife patted his hand.

"'Tis done, Guerin." Lady Marie shook her head and clucked her tongue. "The truth is out." Turning to Helena, she confided, "We grew to care for each other when he came to study with my family tutor after Michaelmas."

Her eyes fairly twinkled as she said, "My father hoped we'd marry. He was desperate to find me a husband. He bemoans allowing me an education, but once I started learning, I couldn't stop."

Helena leaned fully against Hakan's legs behind her, and his hands gently rubbed her shoulders. The Lord and Lady of Aubergon engaged in their own dance of comfort amidst the awkwardness. The new lady of Aubergon was strong, intelligent, and capable but not beautiful. Her nose was overlong and large in the center of her face. Her lips made a wide, narrow line, but never mind such things. Her eyes sparkled full of life. She was strong where Guerin was weak, both well-suited for each other in ways that mattered.

Helena couldn't help but compare Hakan and Guerin. Had she not done this from time to time all summer? Hakan was strong and capable, content to learn from the world by experience. A man of honor, he kept his word to return her home despite the cost of this voyage.

Guerin, on the other hand, couldn't be counted on to honor a betrothal for a single winter. True, he was learned, but his experience came through tutors. He'd never venture far. If Aubergon ever grew to significance, 'twould be through the capable hands of the lady next to him. The odd dance between men and women, attraction that burned bright, was ever a mystery.

Helena cast a sidelong look at Hakan. He stood proud, silent. The chieftain never valued wealth, yet gained riches. Nor did he flaunt such things. He counted his treasures in his son, his friends, and his family. Such a strong face framed by thick blonde hair. He honored a thrall's wants over his own. Helena wished she had never said "nay" to him and the attraction that once threaded between them. Now, turmoil in Hakan's homeland demanded his attention, and she'd be nothing more than a memory. At the notion, her stomach clenched, filling with heaviness.

As though sensing her turmoil, Hakan asked, "Tired?"

Tears wet her eyes again. Agony at having to say good-bye to Hakan began to set.

"Of course you're tired." Lady Marie's hands fluttered to her chest. "But Guerin, where can we put our guests?"

"I—"

"Oh dear," Lady Marie interrupted. "We cannot put you in the room upstairs." She made a face of disgust. "Fleas. The bedding was thick with them. We burned it all just this morn."

"Don't worry about me, lady. My vessel awaits. The sooner I return, the better," Hakan said.

"Nay!" Helena's yell echoed in the high tower.

Lady Marie's assessing glance slid from Hakan to Helena and back again.

"'Tis late, and you told Emund three days..." Helena began.

Lady Marie clasped her hands in artful supplication, addressing Hakan. "You must stay. We put a new roof on the barn. The loft is clean and dry. And we'll honor you with a feast on the morrow...our thanks for bringing Helena home safe." Sounding very practical, she added, "At the very least, your horse must rest."

"'Tis decided." Guerin rose as if the matter was done. "Come."

Helena clasped Hakan's arm, not wanting to let go. Had she been a prideful fool? She stayed by his side as they walked to the barn. Insects droned their night chorus, so peaceful in the simple village. Within Helena, a song of heartbreak hummed: after tonight, she'd never see him again.

...

Helena tossed and turned, plumping hay beneath the blanket over which she lay. Nothing would satisfy. All felt wrong and ill-shaped. This makeshift bed didn't work. Her dress failed to fit.

The hideously patched pea green dress she wore was a loan from Lady Marie, since Helena's Norse tunic was filthy from the journey. But this Frankish dress...'twas all wrong, with seams that scratched her waist, side lacing cinched tight, and a too-small bodice. She tugged hard on the neckline, but stitches ripped loudly in the darkness.

"What've I done?" she mumbled, close to tears.

Her hands fumbled with the irksome side lacing, but the knot shrunk under her fingers. She groaned at the struggle, yanking all the harder on the tie that bound her.

A rustle of sweet-smelling hay and Hakan stirred. "Helena?"

"Sorry I woke you. This dress...I, I can't undo the knot," she wailed between gasps.

"Shhh," he soothed her. "I wasn't asleep."

Hakan's broad-shouldered form, a shadow in darkness, scooted near, and wetness, so like tiny spurs, pricked her eyes at his gentle demeanor. Helena swiped her face with the back of her sleeve.

"I don't want to cry anymore," she said, sniffling.

His smile crooked with mischief. "I agree. 'Tis an ugly dress. You can burn it come morning."

A small giggle unfurled, and Helena rested her head on his shoulder, sighing blissful contentment at his easy humor. He smelled clean, having earlier washed himself at a rain barrel. Hakan stroked the back of her head, a tender calming touch. More than stillness, 'twas trust and pleasure that blossomed within her at his closeness. She could stay this way all night. "You make me happy," she whispered.

Silence hung between them, the kind that held a wealth of words unsaid, yet neither ventured to fill the void. Hakan's arms gripped her tight before he loosened his hold.

"I tried." Strain etched his voice, and he moved a fraction from her. "Let me loosen this knot."

That narrow space could be a chasm, and the emptiness, the pang of loss, made her want to weep anew. What could she do? Hakan bent his head to the task. His large fingers moved over her side, grazing her dress-covered ribs.

"Lay down in the moonlight. I can't see the knot."

Helena reclined on the blanket. Overhead, clouds had cleared a path for the moon, and that orb's light filtered through cracks. When she looked up, Hakan's eyes glowed white-blue in pearled light. She lay vulnerable to this warrior. Threads of trust and longing entwined them as he loosened her dress, and she was struck with Hakan's concern for her comfort.

"You are most honorable among men," she said.

His ice-blue gaze flicked to her face and his fingers slowed their movement against her side.

"My thanks." A gruff note of surprise rang in his voice.

"'Tis true. Many have betrayed you, yet you hold to what is right. You have more honor than my former betrothed," she snorted. "If I measure his honor by the size of Lady Marie's belly."

Hakan shifted on the hay, resting an arm on one upraised knee. "Rail against the wrongness tonight, but tomorrow look to what comes next."

"Next," she whispered. "I lose you."

"Helena..." His voice trailed.

Agony squeezed her chest, making breath sparse. She turned her face into the blanket and heard iron's high-pitched song. He set his palm on her ribs and angled Helena on her side.

"I must cut the tie...the knot's too tight." His voice was thick. "Don't move."

The blade's tip nudged the lacing, then one gentle rocking motion and another and the tie snapped. She was free. The dress slackened, and Hakan's hand slipped into the slim opening, parting the garment at her side.

Her breath hitched when his thumb brushed her naked ribs. Such tantalizing friction teased her.

"Did I cut you?" His head dipped to check her skin.

"Nay. But, you've cut me free. Again." She rolled onto her back, feeling the warm invasion of his hand still on her, and managed a wobbly smile.

Awareness, thick and hazy, shrouded them when their gazes collided. Her attempt at conversation was lost. Labored breath moved in and out of her chest, and 'twas clear in that moment why women tossed well-laid plans to the four winds. A good man, the right man, muddled a woman's mind and made her want to bare body and soul. Make him handsome and strong, and temptation stripped away clear thinking, and gladly so.

Helena lay beneath him, open and wanting, but Hakan looked away and sheathed his knife, withdrawing his touch. That slight move away from her wilted her spirit.

She grasped his arm, intent on keeping their connection. "Stay, Hakan. I belong with you."

"You don't belong to me," he said, rough-voiced. "You're in the land of the Franks. A freewoman."

"Such practical counsel." She tipped her head back and hay crunched beneath her. Helena stretched on the blanket with slight invitation. Hakan's head snapped to attention. 'Twas enough to give her knowledge of the turmoil just beneath his control.

He stared at her as if she were a feast to be devoured, entranced by the rise and fall of her breasts. Her thumb stroked the corded flesh of his forearm. Hakan stiffened when her fingers moved in lazy, exploring swirls over his arm.

"Freedom isn't found in a place, Hakan." Her lips parted. Aye, all of her opened to him. 'Twas a sensation that spread across her limbs and settled between her legs as she lay before this hardened warrior. "My freedom is with you. I belong *with* you."

A wolf sounded in the distance. Did that fierce creature of the forest seek a mate? Or did he howl at the moon, lost? Helena read a play of emotions in Hakan's ice-blue eyes, eyes that darkened in moonlight. Masculine hair grazed her palm, and her seeking hand moved higher past the crook of his elbow, a deliberate summons to be with her.

"Touch me."

He inhaled sharply. "Understand what you're saying?" he asked, his voice raspy and pained.

"I do," she said and nodded ever so slowly.

A smile curved his mouth. The plain soap he must've used wafted from him, a warm, clean scent. Hakan braced one hand on the hay and leaned over her. His other hand sought the side opening of her dress and slipped back inside. Calloused fingers skimmed her midsection with lazy, caressing circles.

"I'll not rush this," he said, moving his thigh flush to hers.

She nodded and licked her lips as pleasure laced her skin. He planted whispery kisses on her hairline and temple, indulgent kisses, slow kisses, tender little touches of his mouth to her face. Waves of gooseflesh spread down her legs. Breath fluttered ragged and halting between her lips. Her eyelids drooped, growing heavier with each unhurried rotation of his hand inside her dress. Hakan's strokes moved feather-light across her belly, inviting bliss everywhere he touched, even places he didn't.

How could touch make this strange kind of torment? Helena squirmed. She wanted, nay *needed*, him to massage the same skin growing hot from his attentions, yet her body cried for those tantalizing circles to explore her. His hand grazed her ribs, moving higher. Her breasts, full and wanting, throbbed with need, yearning for contact.

Did he grasp her craving? Her eyes opened wider. She met the satisfied half-smile of a man who reveled in the sweet torture he rendered. Fraction by fraction, Hakan's thumb circled high, barely grazing the underside of her breast, until his warm palm kneaded that flesh, heavy and curved.

"So soft," he murmured above her.

Whimpering loudly, she wiggled closer to him, aching for more intimacy. When his thumb grazed her nipple, a cry left her lips and heat bolted through her. Her body strung taut and stiff from the shot of intense pleasure. No man had ever touched there. Helena slid her hand along the curve of her hip, stroking with invitation: *touch me here.*

Her skirt inched up her leg and cool night air caressed her ankle, her leg, her knee. The cumbersome cloth bothered hot, sensitive skin. Helena wanted the barrier gone. She wanted Hakan...to feel his skin, his scars, the masculine hairs of his legs brushing hers. She needed him closer.

Suddenly, his hand withdrew from her dress.

She began to protest, but beside her Hakan removed his leather jerkin. His broad back, roped with muscles and sinew, flexed as he moved to untie one boot. Helena hitched up on an elbow and drew unhurried circles on the small of his back. Languid fingers skimmed the top of his buttocks, scratching tight flesh through his trousers. Her impish touch earned a wave of gooseflesh across his back and a sharp, hungry look from Hakan, who quickly shucked the other boot.

He lay down beside her, and she nestled in his warmth. Helena pressed the shell of her ear to his chest and found the steady beat that promised strength and honor and comfort.

"I love the smell of you. Sea air, leather, and your skin...all of you." She sewed soft kisses over his chest, inching toward the hollow at the base of his neck. "You'll never be free of me."

His arms tightened like manacles, squeezing her closer. "Never have I wanted to be free of you."

"I vexed you often for my freedom." She closed her eyes, relishing being in his arms. "Now I'm here, and I want to go back to Svea."

"You've suffered much, but in time..." His voice vibrated from his chest to her ear.

"I'm sad at the loss of my mother and father. . ." She pulled away and peered up at him. "But I couldn't bear the loss of you. I love you, Hakan. I would be with you...always."

Her voice quavered, thick with a tumble of emotions and desire, both pained and sweet. Tears burned her eyes, blurring his face. Helena's eyelids fluttered shut and Hakan brushed his lips, feather light, over her eyelids. His warm mouth moved a tender trail over one eyebrow and then the other.

"Come back with me...as my wife." The muffled words came low as his lips moved in her hair. "I've been to many lands, but you are my rarest find...worth more than a thousand of your red stones."

Elation spilled through her chest, mixing with the heady arousal of being in his arms. She pulled back and searched his face, needing to see him fully. Her lips parted but words failed her, so fogged was she by want and need and surprise. Her hard Norseman had shown a tender side, and in the doing befuddled her. The corner of his mouth hooked up.

"I've rendered you speechless." He kissed her forehead and lingered there, his warm breath touching her face. "Do you know why I was so ill-tempered on the ship?" he whispered between kisses. "On the journey to your village?"

She shook her head, pressing her lips to his whiskered jaw. "Why?"

His mouth moved across her wounded cheek, following the trail of her scar. "Because I saw what a fool I was to think I'd never want a wife again. Truth finally sunk into my stubborn head that you're nothing like Astrid...nothing like any woman I've ever known."

She pulled a hands breath from him, sliding her palms up the hardness of his chest. "None of that matters."

She wanted to comfort him. Helena shook her head, but Hakan's face pinched as the painful revelation flowed from him. He would have his say.

"I didn't think you wanted me." He shut his eyes at the admission.

"Oh, Hakan..." Her hand slid into his hair.

"You think me an honorable man? I was a fool not to marry you long ago. I should've married you the first time you made me laugh."

Joy sung through her. Helena grabbed him, pressing her fingers into solid ribs and muscled flesh. She twined one leg with his, rubbing brawn with languid strokes. Her skirt hitched higher from the sensual tangle, and wondrous, wanting heat spread low in her abdomen.

"And when was the first time I made you laugh, my lord?" she asked, huskiness edging her voice.

"In the streets of Uppsala. Telling me the goats understood Frankish." His strained chuckle rumbled near her cheek. "Letting you go made me realize how much I love you." He stroked her hair. "How much I need you. 'Twas a mistake to say I'd never love again."

"I love you, too," she whispered. "And now I *need* you."

Her questing hands tugged at the waist of his trousers, demonstrating what kind of need.

"Does this mean you'll marry me?" His voice worked to keep evenness under her questing hands.

She kissed his flat male nipple and then the other. "Yes."

"Will your holy man wed you—" He sucked in a sharp breath and tremors of pleasure shook his frame as her fingers skimmed low on his belly. "—to a Norseman?"

Helena laughed, a low, muted sound, liking this power she had over him.

"None will deny you." Her hands ran up the broad plains of his chest, and she slipped her fingers into his loosely tied hair. Helena pressed hot, open-mouthed kisses to the center of his chest, working her way higher. "But are you ready to bear witness here?"

"'Tis time I believe in something greater than me." His voice thinned, apparently weakening from her kisses.

He grabbed her questing hands, moving them to her sides.

"I promised not to rush," he said, and levered on his side, looming close and trapping one arm.

Mischief curled the corners of his mouth once more. Hakan tucked her other arm to her side and kissed her full on the lips. His subtle growth of whiskers scraped soft skin around her mouth, but the kiss, so deep and long, was welcome. The odd pleasure of his firm but tender restraint thrilled her to the core. A braid of heat, emotions, and want twirled within Helena, pooling betwixt her legs. Her

Norseman demanded belonging with that kiss, and her seeking lips answered him back.

Who laid claim to whom?

Helena opened to him, pliant and yielding. 'Twas a woman's power, softening under him, and his warrior's body jerked. His breath came all the more ragged. A lazy, triumphant smile curved her mouth at that little victory of pleasure. But Hakan battled back, and his arsenal was a single touch, her neckline the battleground. He hooked a finger in her neckline, and his dark eyes studied hers, watching as he dragged the fabric down inch by agonizing inch. The contact, the waiting, pained her.

A rush of excitement flamed when he dipped his head and nuzzled her neck, a slow feast of hot kisses. Helena stretched back her head, hoping, waiting.

"Please..." she said, her voice hoarse to her ears.

Hakan's mouth moved lower, invading new, exposed skin. His lips grazed her collarbone, keeping a slim fraction of space as he hovered over the high swell of her breast. That white flesh had never seen the sun, much less born the attentions of a man, and her skin singed from the heat. 'Twas leisured devotion the way he moved from one moonlit breast to the other, his whiskers tickling soft flesh. Her nipples hidden at the edge of the fabric tightened with yearning need. She writhed beneath him, and he let her arm go. Freed at last, she turned on her side and stretched herself like a fevered cat against the length of him.

"Oh," he groaned. Air hissed from Hakan when she scratched his ribs lightly.

Helena laid hot kisses on his neck, where sun-browned skin tasted of him. Her hand travelled lower to his trousers, and the woolen fabric felt so warm to her touch. Tremors shook his frame under her wandering fingers, and she rejoiced in the giving.

This way between a man and a woman moved her, so mystical and wondrous, yet hot and solid. Hakan gripped her hip under the onslaught of another shiver as she explored his skin, halting to trace a smooth scar or two. Years of swordplay and battle had wrought his frame to hardness. She would not be denied this measured discovery, finding the slopes and valleys of his torso.

"Vixen." Hakan's deep voice vibrated through his body to hers.

"You like this?" She breathed the question and glanced up at him, already knowing the answer.

His eyes, so piercing and intense, stared back. "'Tis the best kind of torment."

He kissed her, a reverent connection that led to more. Four of Hakan's fingers traced the length of her spine, a gradual trail that circled low on her back where her dress gathered. The touch, downy soft, sent sensual quivers across her back.

She curled into him, moaning. "Feels so good."

A sound of masculine contentment rumbled in his chest. Hakan's searching fingers moved over fabric and slipped into the cleft of her bottom, rubbing gently.

"Oh!" She yelped at the singular invasion.

He answered with a squeeze to one rounded globe, massaging the flesh through wool.

All thoughts and words melted from the spiraling heat, a heat that turned them into a whirlpool of fevered touch, a heat of give and take. Moonlight and darkness painted limbs twined into a tangle shaded black and white, so like the image of the elk creature and wolf beast that once circled Helena's arm in a fierce clash. But this...this was the sweetest battle.

21

Animals stirred below as mounts from the night watch were rubbed down and fed. The servant boy, Giles, moved around with the stealth of a donkey. He tip-toed, trying to be quiet, in deference to the guests sleeping in the loft, but the watchmen, ending their night's duty, snorted and coughed.

Grumbling loudly of their increased patrols, they groused about Sir Arval's fear that Nor'men would besiege them in the night. Two men carped about having to ride the perimeter of Aubergon, rather than guard the village from the warmth and comfort of the watchtower.

Hakan called out to the whining guards below. "Be glad you serve an easy master. You'd not last a sennight in my service."

The two men cast nervous glances at the loft, then slunk away, mumbling an odd mixture of curses and prayers. Hakan's gaze shifted to Helena, now stirring beside him, her dark blue eyes half-opened in protest.

"Twould appear our hosts have arisen," he whispered in Helena's ear.

"And by the sound of it, you endear yourself to them."
She yawned, curling close to him. "Let me sleep."

"Wake up, Helena, for today we wed."

Bolting upright, long stalks of hay clinging to her hair,
she looked bleary eyed and beautiful to him.

"Wed. Aye, that has a pleasant sound." She wrapped her
mantle close and gave Hakan a soft kiss. "There's much to do.
We must go to Father Renaud and explain the need for
haste."

"The only thing that needs our attention is your holy
man. The sooner he says his words over us, the better—"

She punched his shoulder and laughed. "If you want to
convince Father Renaud that we should wed today, you need
to make an effort to better understand what we'll do."

"*Solace*," Hakan said, pointing to his gleaming sword and
smiling at their morning banter, "is all I need to convince any
man of my will."

Helena chided him. "Some things need delicacy."

He set two fingers under her chin and kissed her again. "I
can be as delicate as you need me be. But I know a score of
warriors who won't think that so important. We need to
move with all haste. Otherwise Emund and my men will." He
punctuated his words with another slow, soft kiss.

"I forgot about the men," she said, softening to him. "I'll
see what can be done. We need to be on our way before mid-
day."

*I'll have to remember the effect of such a kiss in the
morning.*

He grinned, well-pleased with the first revelation of a
soon-to-be-husband. Helena's husband.

"Come, we've much to do." Helena lowered one foot and
then another on the loft's ladder.

Outside, ducks quacked and chickens pecked their jerky
rhythm, searching the ground. A woman bent over a well,
knotting her russet headscarf about her head.

"Good morn," Helena called to the woman. "'Tis a
beautiful morn, I think."

The woman picked up twin buckets at her feet. "Some might think so." She looked up at the same silver-gray sky. "Others not."

Pushing open the great hall's door, Helena and Hakan moved inside to the stirring of the hounds. Guerin sat in the lord's chair, mulling over a cup.

"I trust you both slept well?" he asked, stirring in his chair.

Sliding onto the bench, Helena burst with the news, but Hakan remained standing. He itched to be on his way.

"Hakan and I are to wed this day." Helena's red-lipped smile spread across her face.

Guerin's jaw dropped, and his eyes resembled bulging fish eyes.

"Guerin," she sighed. "You should close your mouth and congratulate us."

"I wish you well." He raised his cup in salute.

Hakan nodded his thanks, glad to soon leave this odorous wreck of a tower.

The boyish lord grinned, revealing even teeth. "Aye, congratulations. Today's feast will serve as a wedding feast." He rose from his chair. "I must awaken Marie. There's much to do—"

"We leave by mid-day," said Hakan. He set one boot on the bench and reached for a hunk of bread. "No later."

Guerin issued instructions to three astonished servants who scampered away. 'Twas plainly writ on their faces: How could a Frankish woman willingly marry a Nor'man?

...

The next hour flew with the clatter of copper pots and wooden buckets. Old rushes were swept away, and new ones were scattered with precious herbs to add a pleasant scent to stale air.

Hakan went hunting to contribute to the feast. Helena, wearing yet another borrowed dress, cooked in the kitchen. This dress swayed about her, loose and tent-like, save for the apron she wore that braced the garment to her. Helena kneaded dough, sprinkling oatcakes flavored with honey. Women she'd known all her life and some strangers who must have come from Lady Marie's Paris home worked alongside her.

"Helena," Lady Marie called from her seat at the worktable. "Are you ready to bathe?"

She held up flour-streaked arms and hands. "I am sorely in need of a cleaning."

"Come. There's a silk dress I have 'twould fit you nicely...better than my old green one." Lady Marie's eyes sparkled as though she understood the fate of that ugly dress.

"'Tis gracious of you," Helena said, her mouth opening a fraction from surprise. "I've never worn silk."

In the background, a large frame filled the kitchen door. Hakan, a bloodied mess from skinning a deer carcass, held his hunter's knife loosely as he ducked inside the feminine domain. He nodded greetings to the skittish women who bent their heads to tasks before them, and if they didn't have one, one was quickly found.

The chieftain leaned a shoulder against the wall and crossed one boot in front of the other. Mischief creased Hakan's face. Flushed from kitchen fires, Helena brushed away a lock of hair with the back of her hand.

"I just met your holy man," he called across the room. "He's convinced we should wed."

"Hakan." Helena's voice rose in warning as she rubbed clumps of damp flour from her hands.

He tipped his head at the carcass that hung in plain view from a tree. "Shall I carve the meat?"

Helena wiped her hands down the borrowed apron and marched across the kitchen, eyeing his knife. She tipped her head at the knife and poked a floury finger at his chest.

"Put that away and go clean yourself. You," she sniffed the air twice, "smell."

"I smell like a man." He grinned, warming to their play.

"And you're scaring the villagers."

"I'm...*befriending* them." His whiskered cheeks cracked with a smile, so easy was his mood.

"And I shudder to think how you convinced Father Renaud to wed us so quickly."

"He's a man." He said, shrugging one dirt-dusted shoulder. "'Twas simple reasoning."

"Hakan," she began to scold, but muffled her laugh in her apron.

"Shall I carve the flanks?"

"Let another do that. You. Need. To bathe."

The audience of kitchen matrons gasped. Apparently, they could no longer contain their feigned silence. Hakan tipped his head at Lady Marie, who was nearby.

"Lady, have you any mint?"

"Mint?" she asked, confusion wrinkling her brow.

"Aye, mint. For cleaning my teeth."

The room of women tittered and whispered into their hands at the revelation: a barbaric Nor'man would clean his teeth.

Lady Marie motioned for a serving woman. "Aeltha, the soap, linens, and...some mint leaves for our guest."

While the serving woman retrieved these items, Lady Marie canted her head at him. "Would you like to bathe in the tub? I had it prepared for Helena, but we can heat more water for her quickly enough."

"Nay, I found a barrel of water behind your barn last night."

Helena moved aside for the serving woman to pass the requested items to Hakan. She stood behind Helena, stretching and leaning to pass the articles to the barbarian. She scampered away, eyes bulging from the sight. He reeked of deer blood, but Hakan was undaunted, planting a loud kiss on Helena's mouth. They walked out the door, and barely were they gone when the kitchen exploded with voices.

"Did you see the size of him?"

"...all that blood..."

"And she told him he *smells*."

"Father Renaud must've sprouted grey hairs at the sight of that knife. I think I sprouted a few."

"...he requested mint? Imagine, a Nor'man who wants to smell good for his wife?"

"Imagine a *Frankish* man who wants to smell good for his wife?" An explosion of laughter followed.

"I can't recall the last time my Eudes bathed...'twas a holy day, I think."

The women prattled on and decided a wedding, even a Frankish woman to a Nor'man, was a good excuse for a bath.

From outside, Helena laughed softly. "See what havoc you've played? The men will beg you to leave, and not because of *Solace...*or that." She pointed to his knife, where blood thickened on sharp edges, and then she placed an oil flagon in his hand.

"I vow these men could use lessons in the use of a sauna *and* weaponry." Hakan clasped the flagon by his forearm. "What's this for?"

"Oil. To clean your bloodied tunic. You look as if you have battled a bear." She turned back to the door and blew a kiss over her shoulder.

Entering the kitchen, she went to the hook holding her hudfat and mantle.

Considering both thoughtfully, she called out, "Lady Marie, would you have someone tend to my mantle." She eyed the cloak's gorgeous fur trim. "And clean it? I'll decline your gracious offer of the silk. I've something else to wear."

...

"So you would wear this?" Agnes held the garment over a steaming cauldron, working wrinkles from linen. Her former neighbor, a woman who had known her since birth, had come to assist Helena in the absence of her mother.

"Aye, 'tis fitting. After today, I'm no longer a Frankish woman, but Norse." Helena splashed in the lavender-scented water. They spoke of the same light blue tunic she had worn at the mid-summer festival.

239

"Well," the older woman said as she nodded, "'tis a beautiful *heathen* garment. The stitching is most interesting." Agnes's fingers pulled at the draped neckline. "Where are the sleeves?"

"There are none." Helena let Agnes's shock abate before adding, "The top portion is held by a brooch at each shoulder. The Nor people like their jewelry."

Agnes mumbled something about the source of that fine jewelry and laid the tunic over a chair.

"Come. You're going to shrivel to nothing. The morn is half over and word is about you must be gone by mid-day." Agnes wrapped a drying cloth around Helena.

The older woman combed Helena's hair with the elk bone comb that she brought with her from Svea, alternating drying with cloth and combing.

A remark about the comb's intricate carvings set Helena to regaling Agnes with tales of Svea. She told her about the carvings found on the doorways of the simplest homes. Rubbing scented oil on her skin, she told Agnes of the vanity of the Norse: bathing often after trips to those hot hives called saunas, the green glass smoothers for straightening wrinkles out of clothes, and, even gold and silver threads spun into their weft bands about their wrists.

Agnes clucked at the strange Norse, commenting on Hakan's habit of chewing mint leaves.

"Well, as to that." Helena stood up to have the tunic pulled over her head. "I enjoy the way he tastes."

Agnes gasped in surprise. "If your mother could hear such words."

The tunic was tied at the shoulders, and soft leather boots were strapped with cross-garters up her calves.

"What are these?" Digging at the bottom of the bag, Agnes pulled out the silver armband.

She cradled the ring in her hands, polishing the silver. "These marked me as Hakan's thrall."

"Imagine," Agnes breathed her awe, squinting at the artful carvings. "A slave wearing such jewelry. What'll you do with it?"

Helena turned the wide ring this way and that as Agnes draped her shoulders with the rich mantle. "I'm not sure."

Agnes stepped around and flung open the door. Radiant sunlight washed over Helena. The older Frankish woman set aged fingers on her cheeks as she studied Helena.

"Don't you look a fair sight. A heathen sight, but a fair one all the same." She tipped her cloth-covered head in deference. "Come. Your Nor'man awaits."

...

Hakan had polished clean every inch of his leather tunic, as well as the silver hilt of his sword and bone handle of his knife. Even his long, silver penannular clasp was polished to a sheen. But, ever wary, he wouldn't be defenseless in a foreign land: *Solace* slanted from the neck of his red wool mantle.

Hakan was pleased with the look of his bride as she approached. Standing on the stone steps of the church, raided generations past by other Norsemen, those steps bore witness to the wedding of one. A crowd of villagers gathered, gawkers to the spectacle.

'Twas no matter to Hakan as he kissed Helena when she took her place beside him.

"You look beautiful," he said quietly.

"I look like a Norsewoman." She brushed back the heavy mantle, displaying the Norse tunic and the polished arm ring.

He frowned.

"What's this?" His hand cupped her arm where the silver encircled her. "You're no thrall."

Her face turned at a proud angle. "I come to you willingly and wear this willingly...the same as I wear the Norse tunic. I'm a Norsewoman now. Your wife."

He bent to kiss her again, and a warm glow filled him at the knowledge that his people had become her people. Hakan's lips lingered on her cheeks and brushed her ear.

"Wear the ring, if it pleases you...wear it naked and willing beneath me."

Father Renaud coughed his displeasure at the unwonted show of affection during a solemn ceremony.

"My lord, 'tis not time for the sealing kiss...or such displays." He rocked up on his toes and coughed into his fist. "The vows first, if you please," he admonished. "Besides, you want to be on your way."

"Of course, holy man. Quickly, say your words." Hakan faced Helena, a loose grasp of her fingers in his. "In Frankish and your Latin."

When the priest bid them kneel on the bottom step, he launched into rapid Latin.

Helena whispered in Hakan's ear, "This is your doing?"

He glanced at the priest, whose face and hands lifted toward heaven, and whispered back, "What's my doing?"

"This fast ceremony in Latin and Frankish." Her whisper blew strands of his hair.

He liked the feel of her breath on his ear.

"I would know the vows I take." He squeezed her fingers, a gentle reminder that he'd never lose her. "And, I keep my promises."

Light glowed from Helena's dark blue eyes, which made the finest gift that day. She mouthed *thank you* as the holy man chanted his words from the upper step. 'Twas not the first time she did such a thing, nor, he vowed, would it be the last. The curling vine that had wrapped around Hakan's heart so long ago had finally tamed the restless wolf within. This time, he was well and truly wed.

Epilogue

"You are wed?" Emund shook his carrot-orange head in disbelief.

The other men stopped their leisurely pursuits in the tavern. Heftnaftl game pieces, gripped by meaty hands, hung in mid-air. Wooden ale cups jolted, sloshing their brew. A serving wench screeched, dumped from the lap of a stunned warrior who stood up too fast. The air churned with thick swirls of smoke. Only the fire crackled and popped in the jumble of rocks that made the hearth. The tavern looked small with the press of hulking Norsemen bent over tables.

"You are truly wed?" Erik peeked from behind Jedvard.

The giant Norseman moved so the boy could run to greet them. Erik's blue gaze went back and forth between his father and Helena.

"'Tis true," Hakan said.

"I am glad." Erik's face creased in a broad smile, revealing the gap of a newly lost tooth. He slid his hands into theirs, and stood as a link between them.

The men roared their approval. Cups were lifted once again. Astonished faces gave way to the joy on their chieftain's face and his Nordic-garbed bride. They settled at the table by the smooth, river-rock hearth, and Hakan called for mead and cider. Even Jedvard joined them at the table.

Erik showed them a Heftnaftl game piece he had begun to carve in their absence. He set the piece, the beginnings of a king, on the table and folded his hands.

"Jedvard says we won't go back to Svea. That we're going to Gotland." The boy tried hard to look older than his years.

Hakan held Helena's hand atop the table. His thumb stroked the back of her hand.

"I am not sure what or where we'll land, but I am certain of one thing," he said, smiling. "Our adventures have just begun."

Find out what happens next in the Norse Series saga

Survival's in his blood...
Rough-souled Brand has one task before he leaves Uppsala--protect the Frankish slave, Sestra. Her life's full of hardship...until she learns the location of a treasure. With war coming, stealing the enemy's riches will save lives, but only one man can defend her--the fierce Viking scout, Brandr.

The two have always traded taunts, now they must share trust. Passions flare as secrets unfold, leading one to make a daring sacrifice on their quest **_To Find a Viking Treasure_**.

Acknowledgments

Creativity requires lots of partners, doesn't it? My mom deserves a big "acknowledgment" hug, because she's my mom and we've been through much on this life road. I want to send a big thank you to author Janet Wellington, my first gentle reader and kind encourager years ago. My friend, Paula Steidl, has been the best cheerleader and beta reader on this journey. To my agent, Sarah E. Younger, thanks… Partnering with you has been the smartest writer's move I've ever made. Here's to many more "acknowledgment pages." Thank you to editor Erin Molta for making this process enjoyable and insightful (and for embracing Vikings…they're back!). Thank you to Entangled's PR experts, Jaime Arnold and Sarah Ellsworth, for your hard work.

And thank you Brian, Clay, and Chad, for believing in me and buying me nerdy history books. I love them and I love you guys!

May I pour lots of blessings back to each of you.

About the Author

Hi, I'm Gina Conkle, writer of Viking and Georgian romance. I grew up in southern California and despite all that sunshine, I love books over beaches and stone castles over sand castles. Now I live in Michigan with my favorite alpha male, Brian, and our two sons, where I'm known to occasionally garden and cook.

I hope you enjoyed a Viking romance escape in Hakan and Helena's story. Please leave a review and connect with me on social media. I love hearing from readers. It'd be great to hear from you.

~Gina

Need more guilty reads?
Follow me on BookBub for latest sales news
or
Join my Newsletter for exclusive free reads. I offer these to newsletter followers only...along with surprise giveaways!

Gina's Booklist

The Norse Series (in reading order)
Norse Jewel
To Find a Viking Treasure
Coming in 2017...
To Heal a Viking Heart
To Save a Viking Warrior
To Catch a Viking Hunter
To Love a Viking Chieftain

Midnight Meeting Series (in reading order)
Meet the Earl at Midnight
The Lady Meets Her Match
Coming in 2017...
The Lord Meets His Lady

Kissable Series
Kissables vol. 1: Hot & Modern
(Contemporary romance duology)
Coming in 2017...
Kissables vol. 2: How to Steal a Kilt
(Georgian/Highlander romance duology

83604721R00139

Made in the USA
Columbia, SC
11 December 2017